THE
MARK
TWAIN
MURDERS

EDITH SKOM

A BROWN BAG MYSTERY
FROM COUNCIL OAK BOOKS

T U L S A

Council Oak Books
Tulsa, Oklahoma 74120

First edition
Printed in the United States of America

LC 063116

ISBN 0-933031-17-3

Text Typography by Karen Slankard
Book and Cover Design by Carol Haralson

AUTHOR'S NOTE

ACKNOWLEDGMENTS

For technical advice on a variety of subjects, I would like to thank Leslie Bjorncrantz, Sue Clinton, David Reed, Harry Ross, Richard Rovner, Dante Scarpelli, Trudy Shoch, and Gerry Smyth. My thanks to Rick Rayle and Roslyn Schwartz for steady encouragement, to Harriet Skom Meyer and Jean Smith for encouragement and for expert editing. My thanks to Charles Yarnoff who saw me through. My thanks to Joe Skom, who read every chapter as soon as it was finished, and, he wants me to add, graciously accepted my rejections of all his suggestions — he was and is my best inspirer.

1

AT NIGHT, IF YOU STOOD BACK TO GET A BETTER LOOK, YOU could imagine that the new library was a gigantic, faintly menacing UFO. Against the dark sky, the concrete building, with its elongated sawtoothed contours, became a winged spacecraft, each research tower a signaling satellite, each late-burning study light a listening post. As the old chapel carillons sounded their hourly tune, the ivied Gothic halls retreated into the darkness, and the campus was transformed into a space age planet.

* * *

Beyond the library's revolving doors, five flights up, the illusion of a streamlined, wholly computerized world was shattered. South Tower, at the end of the quarter, looked like the aftermath of a literary orgy. Everywhere were the ghostly remains of Exam Week. Lifeless cans of Coke. Wrappers of departed candy bars. Books strewn over the floor like carcasses.

Gone were the library birds-in-passage. The undergrads, slouching over notebooks in every study cubicle, had left for Daytona Beach. The pre-laws, desperately memorizing LSAT prep books, had gone to be tested. Between quarters only the real possessors of the library remained, the vigilant librarians, the neatly suited old men who never stopped working on mysterious research projects, and the faculty — especially the faculty — catching the chance to put the finishing touches to articles they hoped to publish. The library regulars welcomed this quiet interval when they could start early and end late. Only an outsider would want to escape.

* * *

Deep in the South Tower, in study carrel 5710, an overflowing wastebasket, stacks of closely written index cards, and the fitful beat of a typewriter spelled student at work on late paper.

Marylou Peacock heard the carillons chime ten o'clock, thought only two hours till closing, and pounded the keys, fighting the Smith-Corona like the enemy. "Damn," she said suddenly, and grabbed the Correcto bottle. Drumming her fingers on the desk, she waited for the fluid to dry. "Shit," she said a moment later and again applied the Correcto brush. She leaned back and stretched her legs, all the while gazing balefully at the typewriter. She kicked off a sandal — so hard it ricocheted off the wall — then kicked off the other sandal, harder. The sight of her ragged toenails cheered her up. Tomorrow those nails would be filed and buffed. Tomorrow they would be covered with base coat and polished with Saturday Night Red. Cheering up more, she remembered that one good thing had happened today.

Tomorrow, of course, would be better. Tomorrow morning she would hand this paper in. Tomorrow afternoon she would be on the beach at Martha's Vineyard, starting the first layer of a tan. She would doze. Occasionally she would open her eyes and gaze at her beautifully pedicured nails.

Reluctantly, she turned to the typewriter and looked at the half-typed page, the dim print — oh God! The thing needed a new ribbon, and it took her at least a half hour to change a ribbon. This was too much. Marylou grabbed purse and keys and walked barefoot out the door.

The utter emptiness that greeted her made Marylou feel even more aggrieved. Every carrel door was closed, every seminar room deserted. She must be the only student left on campus.

She wasn't really alone, of course. A few study lights burned, and somewhere an electric typewriter clacked its beat against the buzz of the fluorescents. But between the spokes of shelves that made up the South Tower no one was in sight.

Another time, on another night, the deserted stacks might have frightened her and had her sensing a rapist behind every volumed shelf. But tonight, as she padded across the corridor, Marylou's thoughts were of nail polish, and a new bathing suit cut down to *there,* not of lecherous assailants. No more than she noticed the signs that she passed, TO COMPUTER BOOK TERMINAL, CAMPUS TELEPHONE FOR EMERGENCY USE ONLY, did she notice the bulky figure in a camouflage-print parka that walked out of the South Tower ahead of her.

She pushed the door marked WOMEN, stopped short and caught her breath. The room was pitch black. Her heart pounding, she fought the urge to run and looked behind her. The corridor was empty. Janitor's bucket and mop. Gurgling drinking fountain. Closed and silent elevators. Nothing else. No one. She turned around. Holding the door ajar, she looked doubtfully into the ladies' room, trying to penetrate the darkness. Suddenly she remembered. All over campus there had been an epidemic of signs. *Conserve Energy. Turn Lights Off When Not Needed.* Laughing at herself for the temporary shiver, she let the door close behind her and reached for the switch.

Light glared down on the row of sinks, the empty stalls, and the same old graffiti: "Isn't it just like the patriarchy? They give us a tampon machine and never refill it." Marylou moved past the resting room, went to a sink and pulled a comb out of her bag. Looking at herself in the mirror, she turned the ends up a bit, concentrating on the side over her left ear. She was still combing when she saw a taller, darker, camouflage-spotted figure reflected in the mirror. She wheeled around. "What are *you* —?" But Marylou never had time to finish the sentence. Her comb skidded across the brown tile; her T-shirted back smashed against the sink. Her body slid to the floor until her toenails rested against the metal wastebasket.

The comb was returned to the handbag and the ladies' room lights were turned off.

2

Morning. Vinetown.
Professor Elizabeth Austin's apartment.

Here's a how-de-do!
If I marry you.

Outside the open bay windows, the late June leaves seemed to flutter in time with the rollicking Gilbert and Sullivan rhythms.

When your time has come to perish
Then the maiden whom you cherish
Must be slaughtered, too!

Inside, the melody bounced off the ceiling and lost itself in the Bokhara rugs.

The apartment was a pleasant place, with the cheer and coziness that only money can buy. With its background of books, its mix of new and old, it had the look of a congenial library. An engraving of a middle-aged Charles Dickens stared out above a nineteenth century captain's desk. Exuberant Matisse dancers frolicked above an oak reading table. Dazzling sunlight poured over the rose-figured chintz that covered the chairs, the sofa, the deep cushions of the window seat.

"Must be slaughtered, too!" Beth Austin joined in with the chorus, and settled back in the cushions, her pencil poised over the crossword. She sat thinking, one foot tracing the orderly medallions of the rug, then abruptly lifted her head. Of course. If the theme was Opera and Tin Pan Alley, then *Die Walkurie* was "Sleepy Time Gal." Soon after, 141 across,

Rigoletto, became "Down by the Fireside," and Beth lounged back, gazing happily at the puzzle whose every square was filled.

She was getting rusty, she thought, and no wonder: her first crossword since the beginning of spring quarter. What with a raft of papers and exams to grade, today had been her first chance to relax. After breakfast, feeling gloriously truant, she had taken Gilbert and Sullivan out of retirement and eagerly opened last Sunday's *Times* to the crossword.

"I'm free," she sang, got up and went over to the desk. She looked at the Dickens engraving. "School's out! I'm free, Charles, free, do you hear?" On the table was a new book of crosswords. She looked at it, tempted to begin another. Then she reminded herself that she had also planned to use the summer to tackle her new book, starting with the notes on the desk. Next to them was a folder, neatly bound in transparent plastic.

She had nearly forgotten. She had promised Porter she would read a prizewinning student paper. Did Beth think the essay good enough for Midwestern's *English Bulletin?* She started the record over, then picked up the folder and sank into the window seat. *"Tom Sawyer,* an Oedipal Adventure," she read aloud. "Well, maybe," she said, raising her eyebrows at the subtitle — "The Case of the Phallic Fence."

She read slowly at first, then frowning, she paged ahead. "Damn," she muttered, and returning to the first page, quickly reread the essay. How could the committee have missed it? Couldn't they see this kid — she flipped back to the title page — this Marylou Peacock, never wrote this essay?

Only a few weeks ago, she remembered, the dean's office had warned that students guilty of academic dishonesty risked suspension. Though the warning was issued every quarter, stealing from other writers remained as popular as ever. Each quarter never failed to bring its new crop of plagiarists. The first copied paper had been a shock. But after several years and a covey of lifted papers on subjects ranging from Tennyson as scientist to Jane Eyre as feminist, Beth was no longer shocked, only amazed at the one unchanging characteristic in the copiers, the naive certainty that they would not be caught.

No, plagiarism no longer bowled her over, but it still made her angry, not just because it was wrong to steal ideas, but also because it was a terrible waste of her time. Should she bother now? She had notes to organize, puzzles to solve.

> My object all sublime
> I shall achieve in time —
> To make the punishment fit the crime.

Beth listened to the chorus, then walked to the desk and looked at Dickens. "Pilfering," she said musingly. "No different from picking a man's pocket. Nor would you approve," she said, giving a nod to John Stuart Mill as she walked past the etchings that lined the hallway.

In the bedroom she searched under a pile of double crostics, found her briefcase and thrust Marylou's paper inside. She would get it over with quickly and then the summer would be back on its normal track. Later she was to remember that thought and find it ironic.

* * *

Hub, Beth was thinking, that's where I'll start. She hurried down Vinetown's tree-lined streets, not taking her usual pleasure in the deep-porched Victorian houses, not wincing as she usually did at Midwestern's architectural smorgasbord. On she walked, past the gingerbread Gothic biology building, the Greco-Roman Hall of Science, toward the pride of Midwestern, the new library that Beth privately had named the 2001. The whine of a siren pierced her thoughts. Ahead of her, an ambulance sped down the sidewalk toward the library.

3

UP THE INCLINE AHEAD OF HER, BETH COULD SEE A CHAOTIC knot of machines and people. The ambulance had pulled up to the library steps. Parked next to it, on the sidewalk, were two bright blue Vinetown police cars, lights flashing. "Stand back! Give 'em room!" two policemen shouted superfluously. The crowd of early library people, briefcases and thermoses in hand, had already retreated to the grass. They were giving all their attention to the front of the building where the revolving doors had been folded back.

Separate from the crowd, a boy skated figure-eights around the concrete petunia-filled planters. "Hey!" Beth called out to him. "What's going on?"

"They aren't letting anyone in," he shouted back, making another swing around the planters. He screeched to a stop in front of her. "They found a stiff," he said breathlessly. "Somewhere in the library," and he rolled off.

Horrible. Someone must have had a heart attack. She hoped it wasn't the old man who worked mornings at the check-out counter. Well, she would find out soon enough. Meanwhile — she went up to a policeman who stood arms folded, staring at a girl in a tightfitting, faded "ERA ALL THE WAY" T-shirt. "Do you know how much longer the library will be closed?"

"Can't say, ma'am. Move back there!" He bellowed at a dignified gray-haired woman.

"But I need to get in," Beth persisted.

"Yeah, you and a million others. What have they got in there anyway — Fort Knox?" He turned and looked at Beth. "Now why don't you go home and put on your bikini and go get yourself a suntan on the beach?"

Droll Vinetown wit, thought Beth, and then she stiffened. Two white-uniformed men were guiding a stretcher through the doorway. She watched them carry the stretcher down the broad stone steps, then move in her direction. As they passed her, she saw a wrapped body, lying dreadfully still.

Suddenly all around her birds racketed into song. She put her hands to her ears and watched the attendants level the stretcher into the ambulance. A few seconds later the ambulance had navigated the walk and careened into the street. Sirens screaming, it took off in the direction of the hospital.

Around her people had gathered into excited little groups. She stood silent, apart. Unfair, she thought, to die on a golden summer day. Unfair to be on lonely display before a crowd.

Stop it. She was getting morbid. The library was out for the time. All right. She would begin somewhere else. Anything was better than standing here. Maybe she should find out if the essay awards could be delayed. She would talk with Porter.

Heavy steps sounded behind her. An overweight jogger, wearing headphones and oblivious to the excitement at the library, lumbered past her toward North campus. Beth followed him down the path.

4

AN IVIED GOTHIC OUTSIDE PROMISED AN INSIDE MELLOW WITH leather and oak, and furnishings that lent themselves to convivial talk among the ancient and honorable company of scholars. The English office, it seemed to Beth, had rebelled against the stately exterior of the building that housed it, with a setting guaranteed to promote misanthropy: dingy plaster walls, a dowdy percolator that brewed hot water, stiff clusters of "modernistic" vinyl furniture known in the trade as Borax.

Just inside, seated on a chair of pseudo-Scandinavian design, Noel Frazier, Gilchrist Professor of Literature, hummed a song to himself and stared pensively at a grade sheet. He looked elegant as usual and Beth thought again how remarkable it was that Noel could make whatever he wore — today a tieless shirt and jacket — seem exactly right, while men who imitated him looked either homespun or foppish.

"Yes, my dear," he looked up at her, "still deliberating. You know how I love to languish over trifles."

Despite his light tone, she knew Noel did agonize over grades and that he worried far more about students' reactions than his occasional dry wit suggested.

"Now this one," he said, tapping a name on the grade sheet, "— obviously trying to ingratiate himself — wants to write essays over the summer and send them to me for comment. I don't like to disappoint him, but anyone who can write that the Wesleyan movement was started by John Wesleyan would be better off spending the summer lifeguarding." He laughed. "Next we'll have D.H. Laurentian, and won't that reflect badly on us non-Ivy Leaguers?" He smiled and glanced meaningfully at the two men on the other side of the room.

Beth followed Noel's glance to the hideous decorator orange sofa where Professor Arthur Hewmann was declaiming to Assistant Professor Spencer Goldberg. Hewmann was wearing jeans, Harvard tie, and jacket, a combination meant to send a double message: here was a scholar who upheld Ivy League standards but could still "relate to" students. "I want you to feel free," he was saying, "to confide in me, even to show me the chapters that are giving you trouble."

Spence Goldberg, young, thin, alert brown eyes, nodded attentively and mumbled something about "not quite ready yet." He looked gloomy, Beth thought, but then for Spence, who walked gloomily, talked gloomily, and even, she had no doubt, brushed his teeth gloomily, gloom was a constant condition. Today he might be depressed about the book he was laboring over. Or it could be he was afraid that Hewmann, a power on the Tenure Committee, would suddenly notice and disapprove his tieless T-shirted condition.

"If you don't wish to show me the book," said Hewmann, "then I urge you to let me see any other work-in-progress. Sometimes the problem is simply that the writing lacks grace. Grace," he mused, "charm of expression. Musical prose (as an old Harvard professor of mine used to say) that sings, that —" he paused, looking upward to the paint-flaked ceiling for inspiration.

"— that just keeps rollin' along?" Noel offered loudly. "Like Ol' Man River?"

Hewmann brought his head down and glared at Noel, ready to give a sharp retort. Then he changed his mind. "Oh Beth," he said, turning on the smile that never reached his eyes, "that's a provocative little article of yours in *Literary Studies*. I want to discuss it with you."

"Yes, Arthur, soon," said Beth. And to herself she said, not soon — never. No one, except Noel, ever escaped unbludgeoned from a discussion with Arthur — who had now turned back to Spence.

"No but really, Goldberg," he said. "I don't understand your reluctance. You do have other work-in-progress?"

"Anything for me, Livy?" Spence called out, daringly interrupting Arthur and astonishing Beth.

At the far end of the room, Associate Professor T. Livingston Potter was peering into all the mail boxes. "They're always putting my letters in the wrong box," said Livy, as he said every day. "Nothing much, Goldberg. Just something from the *Boston Transcript*. Are you still writing crusading letters?"

Spence looked embarrassed and made some noncommittal reply which Livy ignored. "And how is Professor Austin today?" he said, the accent, slightly envious, on *professor.*

"Fine, Livy," and she made a move toward the inner office.

"Wait! Your carriage suggests something pressing — not life or death — but important. Am I right?" Livy asked, with the fervor of a neurologist studying reflexes. Livy was obsessed with body language. Ever since he had come upon a sentence in *Martin Chuzzlewitt* ("Jonas stuck one arm akimbo to show how at home he was") he had immersed himself in a study of nonverbal communication in Dickens, convinced it would win him the promotion he had been trying for years to attain.

"How's it going?" Beth asked.

"Well, very well," said Livy. "I got *you* right, didn't I?"

"Yes," she assured him patiently, because she really was fond of Livy, "you got me right," and again she moved away.

Livy looked crestfallen. "But I wanted to ask you about — " he stopped abruptly.

Dot Drennan, the departmental secretary, was standing in front of them. "Livingston Potter," she said, "you owe me exactly $14.23 for personal photocopying for April *and* May. And there's something funny about your March —"

Mumbling something about the bank and a broken machine, Livy quickly retreated in a way that he himself would have described as illustrative of anxiety.

Dot chuckled. "That did it. Come on," and she took Beth with her into the inner office. "Now don't let that little creep worry you," she said, without troubling to lower her voice. "He's always hanging around watching people. Hell, it's got so I'm afraid to make a move in front of him — hey! I've got a great book for you." She went to her desk and flourished a paperback of *Papillon*. "I'm reading it again — action all the way. Want to borrow it when I'm finished?"

Beth shook her head and gave Dot, with whom she got on very well, a warm smile. In a department devoted to the study of high literature, Dot was an oasis. Efficient, she did her work quickly with plenty of time left for reading, and she chose her own books, thank you. Ever since the day Dot had tried to read *Daisy Miller* because she thought it would be like *Princess Daisy,* she had hooted at the English reading lists. Dot knew what she liked — action and sex — and she bought her books where she bought her cigarettes. "Ever read *Sophie's Choice?*" she had once asked Beth. "Found it at Woolworth's. This Styron — ever hear of him? — he's got a good way of writing. Lots of words I don't know and some" (with a wink) "that I do know, darling. But don't read it. It'll make you sick."

Names didn't impress Dot and neither did the professorial titles that surrounded her. But she revered Porter DeMont, the department chairman. ("He's awfully smart, knows things you wouldn't believe, and he's read *all* the books in his office — not like some around here.")

Dot also admired Beth. "You're looking pretty sharp today, kiddo."

Beth thanked her and said, "I've got to take care of something, Dot. Is Porter in his office?"

"Yeah, he's there. What's your hurry?" said Dot, waving a paper in front of her. "Listen, about this course description — I wish to God Ida Garden would do her own typing — can you read this?"

Beth looked and read aloud: "'Female love appears in a context of violent domesticity.'"

"Female love appears *where?* That's not where it appears in my book, darling. For God's sake. That's just what you'd expect from that chesty, overdeveloped —"

"Buxom?" Beth suggested.

"Fat," said Dot. "Why doesn't she shut up and lose some weight and throw out those whatever you call 'em — caftans? You're the only one around here who dresses with some class."

"Dot, I've really got to see Porter. Is he busy?"

"Busy? Of course not. He's got some guy in there, though. Hey — he's kinda cute. You ought to —"

The door opened and Porter DeMont came out, an anxious look on his kind face. He was in the shirtsleeves he permitted himself in the summer, but his foulard tie was askew, a sign that DeMont, usually faultlessly groomed, was agitated.

"Uyuh — Miss Drennan, I —"

"Professor DeMont, Austin here wants to see you."

"Not now," he said, looking at the open door to his office. "I'm sorry, Beth, but —"

"It won't take a minute, Porter."

"I can't possibly," said the chairman. "Later perhaps" — he nervously rubbed the bald spot on his head — "it can wait, I assume?"

"Well, it is rather — pressing," said Beth, unconsciously echoing Livy. "Not life and death" — at that she caught a glint in the chairman's eye — "but important."

"What is it then?" he said impatiently, casting another look behind him.

"You know the essay you gave me to read? By Marylou Peacock? The one that —" she stopped at the look on Porter's face.

He stood motionless, staring at her. "Yes? What did you want to tell me about the essay?"

"It's plagiarized," she said, and the minute the words were out of her mouth she felt like a fool.

"So Nancy Drew is at it again!" Livy appeared in the doorway.

Porter wheeled, and gave him a withering look.

"Why don't you invite the lady to come in?" The voice came from the chairman's office.

"Invite her — ?" Porter answered the unknown voice. "Very well," he said, surprisingly docile. "Beth —"

"Professor DeMont," said Dot. "What did you want?"

"Uyuh —" Porter looked confused — "I don't recall — it doesn't matter. Beth, do come in now," and feeling like a schoolgirl called before the principal she followed him into his office.

In a chair opposite Porter's desk was a thin, very tall, sandy-haired man. His long legs stretched out on the tweed carpet, he sat relaxed, leafing through a book.

He stood as she came in and gave her a searching look. What was going on, she wondered, and simultaneously the thought flashed across her mind that Dot's kinda cute guy was indeed good-looking, if you liked fine-drawn, slightly quizzical features.

"Miss Austin," said Porter, "may I introduce —"

The man walked over and held out a hand. "Hello," he said, giving her a solid grip. "I'm Gil Bailey."

5

IT WOULD ALWAYS BE A MISTAKE, BETH WAS THINKING, TO assume that Porter DeMont's small stature and fastidious appearance indicated timidity. The chairman had a natural gift, when he decided to use it, for decisive action. He had taken charge quickly, motioning to Bailey to sit down and to Beth to take the other chair. Porter himself, tie straight now, sat erect behind his desk. The three of them, thought Beth, as they sat for the moment in silence, made a neat triangle, surveyed from above by an engraving of Dr. Johnson.

Porter glanced at Bailey. For an instant Beth imagined she saw an unspoken exchange between the two, as though this visitor (a Fellow in the Fine Arts, Porter had explained, here for the summer) was granting the chairman permission to proceed.

Porter cleared his throat. "Now Beth," he said, "as to the essay —?"

She started to answer, then looked at Bailey who had picked up the book again and was flipping the pages.

"It is perfectly — uyuh — proper," Porter said, answering her unspoken question, "for you to speak freely."

Proper — what did he mean by that? she wondered, and heard the chairman say, "Is it your conclusion then — uyuh — that the entire essay was plagiarized?"

She hesitated, then said slowly. "I'm not sure if it's word for word . . . I just read it this morning."

"Precisely *when* you read Miss Peacock's essay," Porter said dryly, "seems irrelevant. Was the entire essay plagiarized?" he repeated.

She gave a nod, started to speak — "What was the source?" Porter broke in.

Again, she hesitated. "I-I read it quickly," she said.

"Yes, yes, you read it quickly — but the source?" Porter insisted. He looked at her sternly, waiting. Both men were waiting, she noted, for Bailey had stopped flipping pages and had turned his eyes on her.

"I don't know the source," she admitted finally, and saw out of the corner of her eye that Bailey, looking skeptical, unimpressed, had returned to the book.

"— don't know the source! Then I do not understand." His tone said plainly that Porter's eighteenth century passion for accuracy was offended.

Could she have made a mistake, Beth thought confusedly. Porter's questioning, almost an interrogation, was making her doubt herself. Her mind raced back to the essay she had read a few hours ago. Mentally she reconsidered the pages, recalling certain allusions, striking turns of phrase — give-aways all. She lifted her head. "I don't have the source," she told Porter, "— yet," and went out on a limb defiantly: "I *am* sure that she plagiarized."

Porter looked away from her at Bailey. It was almost, she thought, as if the chairman was asking the visitor what to do next. Something was wrong, she realized suddenly, something that went way beyond plagiarism. "What is it, Porter?" she blurted out. "What's going on?"

He turned back to Beth. "Let me — uyuh — explain."

Bailey got up, walked casually to the door, and pushed it firmly shut.

The chairman waited for him to sit down. Then, speaking at a funeral pace, with the exaggerated deliberateness that sometimes drove his listeners wild, he said, "As you may know, during the break between quarters, the cleaning personnel, in their desire to complete their work early, are

somewhat — uyuh — overhasty in beginning their nightly —
uyuh — mopping." He paused, took a deep breath.

Cleaning personnel? Mopping? It was hard to believe that
Porter, so absorbed always in eighteenth-century books and
manuscripts, even knew that mops, or people who wielded
mops, existed. What was he getting at? She was at the point
of asking when Porter began to speak again.

"At seven o'clock this morning," he said slowly, "Marylou
Peacock was found on the fifth floor of the library, in the —
uyuh — ladies' room. Apparently she had been there since
last night. She was dead — uyuh —"

Dead. At once Beth's mind, prone to giant leaps, formed a
picture of a frightened girl, lacking all confidence in herself,
under pressure — family pressure? — to achieve. That was
it. She had plagiarized out of desperation. Then when she
found out she had won the prize, she must have been terrified. She must have . . . my God, she must have — "How
did she do it?" she said.

"Do it?" Porter looked puzzled. "I don't — oh, I see. She
did not — it was — uyuh — not suicide. Apparently Miss
Peacock slipped on the wet floor. Her neck — uyuh — was
broken."

Involuntarily, Beth's hand went to the back of her neck.
She felt dazed, sick to her stomach.

"About the essay," said Porter. "We will put aside any
question of publishing."

Beth nodded weakly.

"We will also," Porter said resolutely, "put aside the matter of plagiarism, which — I hesitate to say — seems, Beth,
to have become something of a mania with you."

A mania? That was unfair of Porter.

"We are far from certain," he went on, unmindful of Beth's resentment, "that it was plagiarized." Then, instead of addressing himself to her, Porter looked at Bailey, again as though seeking approval, and said, "I hardly think it necessary to cause Miss Peacock's family further anguish."

The other man nodded. "It's of no importance," he agreed, "though it's entirely possible" — he smiled at Beth — "that she did plagiarize."

What was this, Beth thought, ignoring Bailey's smile. Her mind was clear now, working at full speed. The chairman was always courteous to visitors, but this behavior went beyond the demands of civility. "Porter!" The chairman jumped, startled at her tone. "I've been as honest with you as I can be. I wish that you, both of you" — she stared at Bailey — "would be equally candid with me. Mr. Bailey, who are you?"

"Bailey" — Porter cast a glance at him — "is — uyuh —"

"I think," the other man cut in, "you should let me explain."

Looking relieved, Porter nodded, sat back and took his pipe from its stand.

Bailey closed the book hard — *The Great Oxford Debate,* she caught the title — and put it down on the desk. Then he turned to her and said quietly, almost casually, "I'm with the Federal Bureau of Investigation."

"The FBI!" Vague damning images of wiretapping and hidden cameras flocked to her mind. "What in the world" — she put as much venom in her voice as possible — "does the FBI have to do with this department — or Marylou Peacock?"

"I'm here," Bailey said calmly, "to investigate large-scale theft of valuable books from Midwestern's library."

"Large-scale theft?" She sat up straight. "How large could it be?"

"Large enough," he answered.

"And why the FBI?" She turned to the chairman — "Surely the Vinetown police can catch a book thief?"

But instead of responding, Porter gestured to Bailey and continued to fiddle with his pipe, knocking the old tobacco into the hollowed-out brass replica of London bridge that served as his ashtray.

"I'm afraid," said Bailey, "that literary first editions are beyond the training of the local police" — he smiled pleasantly, infuriatingly — "good as I'm sure they are."

"What makes an FBI agent any more qualified?"

"Beth!" Porter said sharply. "You are doing Mr. Bailey an injustice. He is a specialist — an expert in rare books. And valuable books are missing — from our library!"

"It seems clear," Bailey put in, "the thief does not suspect that anyone is aware of his activities."

Really, Beth thought, this is too much — "the thief does not suspect." He thinks he's Hercule Poirot. Any minute now he'll be saying, "Madame, the Library Thief overlooks the little gray cells of Agent Bailey." Aloud she said, "You still haven't explained the connection between the missing books and Marylou Peacock." Ignoring Porter's dramatic wince, she lit a cigarette, and waited, looking at Bailey.

"I don't know if there is a connection," he said finally, "but anything out of the ordinary at the library could be important — and a dead girl in the ladies' room is hardly ordinary."

"But" — she looked at Porter — "the girl simply had an accident."

"Maybe," said Bailey. "Maybe not. I'll wait for the medical examiner's report."

"I don't understand. What are you saying?"

"I'm saying, Miss Austin, that there is a good possibility she was murdered."

"Murdered? But why?" Again Beth felt sick. So Porter had been putting a gloss on the whole thing.

"It may be," said Bailey, "that Marylou Peacock had the bad luck to see something she wasn't meant to see."

"I fully expect," Porter broke in, "that the medical examiner will confirm the accidental nature of the tragedy."

But what, Beth thought, if Porter, always so precise in his thinking, was wrong for once and Bailey was right. Her mind took another leap. She imagined the library stacks at night, conjured a shadowy faceless figure, slipping a book inside his jacket. He looked up, saw someone — Marylou Peacock? — watching, and . . .

Porter's office, compared to the rest of the department, was usually a genial place. Now it seemed spooky, threatening, full of unspoken dangers, and she wanted to leave. She stumped out her cigarette in Porter's brass London Bridge. Porter turned it upside down into the wastebasket.

6

THE CAMPUS HAD RETURNED TO DROWSY SUMMER SERENITY. The body on the stretcher, Beth thought, gazing around her, might never have existed. In a grassy niche by the classics building a yawny semicircle of students reclined on the lawn, looking lazily at their instructor who was trying to stimulate discussion. In the distance, on the clover-covered meadow, a boy and girl were tossing a frisbee. Far ahead, in the courtyard of Moreberry Hall of Drama, a crew of undergrads could be seen, setting up platforms. Only an occasional roar of "TESTING, ONE, TWO, THREE" interrupted the tranquillity.

"*Is* it your mania?"

"Is what my mania?" said Beth, pretending not to know what he meant. She was provoked, with herself for allowing Bailey to maneuver himself into walking to the library with her, with Dot for her approving wink when they had left Porter's office together, with Livy for his knowing smile as they had walked out of the English office. Most of all, she was provoked with her new sidekick, Bailey.

"What DeMont said — uyuh - your - uyuh —" He broke off, laughing. "It's contagious!" And she had a hard time keeping back a smile. "I'll try again," he said, choking off his laughter. "I meant your preoccupation with plagiarism."

"I'm not obsessed with it," she said in a thin-lipped voice, "if that's what you mean, Mr. Bailey. When I see a student has passed someone else's work off as his own, I do take time to track down the source." God, she thought, I do sound priggish. Well, too bad. Refusing to meet his eyes, she looked up at a banner strung between the arch of elms: MIDWESTERN

THEATER UNDER THE STARS. *DOCTOR FAUSTUS.
THE IMPORTANCE OF BEING EARNEST.*

"But doesn't it take time to sniff out plagiarism? I thought English professors preferred to spend their odd hours writing articles on vexing linguistic questions."

Was he trying to get a rise out of her? "No," she said as calmly as she could, "it's not so hard to sniff out plagiarism."

"Really!" he said with mock astonishment. "How can you be sure it *is* plagiarism?"

"I'll tell you how!" she said, furious at him for picking up on Porter's misgivings. "When a student who has been writing like a robot — '*Little Dorrit*,'" she chanted, "'is a book by Charles Dickens. It is a book which contains valuable lessons' — suddenly writes — 'We may say of Dickens that at the time of *Little Dorrit* he was at a crisis of the will' or 'Dickens attempts to *épater le bourgeois*' — the plagiarism," Beth said dryly, "is rather obvious. If the sophistication isn't a giveaway," she went on, warming to her subject in spite of her resentment of Bailey, "the French idiom is. In Marylou Peacock's essay, for example —" She looked up, horrified. Careening toward her was a bicycle with a wolf-masked rider. She leaped to the side and would have fallen if Bailey hadn't caught her.

Just short of them the bicycle screeched to a stop, tumbling its rider to the ground. He rolled over, the wolf's head turned up at them. "Oh God, I'm *sorry!*" — out of the hideous foam-streaked mouth came a young and stagey voice. "Are you all right, Professor Austin?" The rider picked himself up and the mask was lifted to reveal a handsome, somewhat wild-eyed boy, looking at Beth with concern.

"I'm fine" — a second's hesitation — "Thorpe." The last time she had seen Thorpe he had been dressed in a tuxedo jacket and striped shorts.

"Sorry I wasn't watching. I'm late — for rehearsal," he said, staring at her curiously.

All at once she realized that Bailey's arm was still supporting her. She pulled herself away and proceeded to take a wholly false interest in Thorpe and his activities. "Oh," she said, heartily professorial, "you have a part in the August productions?"

"In *Faustus*" — Thorpe nodded proudly — "I'm Envy." He bent to examine a knife and a plastic bottle that dangled from the handlebars. "That's vinegar in the bottle and the rusty knife — you know — for the wound that festers. I'm in *Earnest,* too" — he put the wolf's head on — "I'm playing Bunbury."

"Bunbury?" said Beth. "But surely Bunbury is Algernon's imaginary friend in the country?"

"You mean it's not a real part? But they said —"

"Hey Thorpe" — a shout from the rehearsal area — "get moving." Thorpe was on his bicycle again, speeding toward the courtyard.

Bailey, looking amused, handed Beth her briefcase. Flustered, she took it without comment. She could still feel his arm around her back.

"One of your plagiarists?" he asked, grinning at her, but it was a pleasant smile, she decided, not a smirk.

They had moved away from the elms into the sunlight, and she noticed, for the first time, that he had a thin scar along one cheek. Line of duty? she wondered, and then realized he was still waiting for her answer. "Not at all," she said. "Thorpe is a dedicated theater major. Last quarter he handed a paper in late — an emergency tap-dancing lesson — but the writing, clearly, was his own."

"I take it," said Bailey, "that not only can you detect plagiarism instantly, you can also deduce that the copied essay is really the work, say, of a critical theorist, five feet eight inches tall, who walks with a limp, and teaches at Rutgers."

He was laughing at her now, and she wasn't sure she liked it. "I'm closer to Watson than Holmes, Mr. Bailey," she said brusquely.

He made no comment, and they continued toward the library. They had circled several small meandering groups, typical June threesomes, two feverishly enthusiastic parents with one surly prospective student, before he broke the silence. "The name," he said abruptly, "is Gil. Do you think we could dispense with the Mr. Bailey?"

She didn't answer immediately. There was a wonderful whiff of the lake in the air and, as they moved along, she caught a glimpse of sailboats on the water. Her mind was on her own behavior. I have been priggish, she was thinking, and unfair. He didn't ask to come to this campus. "All right," she said, " — Gil. And I'm Elizabeth — Beth — but you know that," speaking so quickly she surprised herself.

"Pretty name — Beth." He smiled at her again. The scar, she decided, made his face more interesting. "Tell me," he said, "how do you go about tracing a plagiarist's source?"

"You really want to know?"

"I really want to know."

"Well — first I check the major critics — Lionel Trilling, for instance." She waited for him to ask who Trilling was. He did not. "If I don't find the source among likely major writers," she continued, "I proceed to Cliff's Notes. Cliff's Notes failing, I move to the journals. As I said, Mr. — Gil, I'm a plodding Watson."

"You're being modest." She shook her head and he laughed and said, "I've always thought Watson was underrated. But why," he asked, "would a student copy instead of doing his own writing?"

"I haven't given it much thought," she said slowly. "I suppose for the same reason any writer — even a pro — would copy."

"And that is?"

She hesitated. "Fear."

"Of what?"

"Fear, I think — of being in over one's head, of not being good enough to make the grade."

"I see." He looked thoughtful. "But why do *you* do it?"

"Do what?"

"Work so hard to track down their sources?"

"Yes, well" — she had no intention of confiding her weakness for puzzles, and was that her only reason? "It's not that time-consuming," she said, and made a sudden decision. "One stop at Hub should be plenty for Marylou Peacock."

"You're not going to try to run down her plagiarism. I thought — didn't you say — you were going to work on your book?"

The anxiety in his voice made her look up — and away again quickly. There was a look in his eyes that made her feel something — she refused to identify the something — she knew she would not be feeling if she had been discussing plagiarism with someone else, Noel, say, or Spence. "The book can wait," she said firmly.

"But the plagiarism doesn't matter now. So why bother?"

"I — I'm honestly not sure why. I suppose because it's there. After all," she decided to turn the tables, "why do *you* pursue answers?"

"That's my job," he said, "tracking down answers."

"Ah, yes, your job. But how did all this get started?"

He hesitated a few seconds, as if deciding how much to tell her. Then he said, "A Boston bookseller reported receiving a book in the mail. It was easy enough to identify it as Mid-western's — it still had the library's stamp."

"That was all? No note? No request to sell it?"

"That was all — but it was enough to inspire an inventory. And then it came out that a significant number of books were missing from the stacks."

"But how much could they be worth? I thought really valuable books were kept in Special Collections."

Again he hesitated. "Certainly books of extraordinary value are in Special Collections. But there are other books, worth a great deal, still on the open shelves, freely available to anyone who walks in — and understands their value."

"You seem to think that your thief is a connoisseur, an expert — like you," she said with a touch of sarcasm. "Why are you so sure that he — or she — isn't a student?"

"Unlikely," he said. "Students usually go for textbooks, something a friend needs for a course. They sell the text cut-rate, for half what the friend would pay at the bookstore — for beer money."

"Isn't that all this amounts to — beer money?"

They had reached the meadow now, and he seemed engrossed in watching the frisbee players show off their dou-ble-spins and behind-the-back throws. "Last week," he said finally, "all twenty-four volumes of the Nonesuch Press Dickens were on the shelves. This week there are only twenty. The missing four aren't misfiled, and they aren't charged out. They've simply disappeared. Do you know how much a com-plete set of the Nonesuch is worth?" She shook her head. "Considerably more than beer money. And there are —" he cut himself off. "No," he said with certainty, "the thief isn't a student."

"All right," said Beth, "so you have a sophisticated thief."
She took a wild shot. "It's clear you think it's someone on the
faculty. Why rule *me* out?"

"I haven't ruled you out. It could be you," he said cheerfully.
"It could be anyone."

She gave him a wide-eyed look. "I suspect no one? I suspect
everyone?"

He grinned amiably. "I do sound like Inspector Clouseau,
don't I?"

"But you're not denying you think it's someone on the faculty! There are lots of departments at Midwestern. Why narrow down the investigation to English? That *is* what you're
doing?"

He studied her face a moment, and then said slowly, "The
Boston bookseller found a page of stationery inside the book —
from the Department of English."

"Isn't that rather flimsy evidence?" she asked. When he
made no reply, she said, "I take it that books are still disappearing. How is your thief getting them out? The library has checkers at every exit. They even have, what do you call them —
demagnetizing alarms? — at the exits. They just installed
them —" she broke off. "That was your doing, wasn't it?"

"Perhaps." He gave a noncommittal shrug.

"They've done all they can," she offered. "They can't possibly do anything else to stop your thief."

"I think they can."

"What, for instance?"

"Oh, many things. . . . For starters, they could have closed-
circuit television monitoring . . . guards to patrol the stacks at
night."

"Monitoring? Patrols? It sounds like a police state."

"I don't like it either," he said, "but I also don't like missing books. I wouldn't worry about it for now, however. Universities, you know, make changes slowly. Meanwhile," he looked grim, "the rewards are very attractive, attractive enough to make someone decide that Marylou Peacock's life is a small price to pay."

They were both quiet, thinking. Then, from the courtyard they heard a crackling sound from the microphone, followed by a booming amplified Faustus: "NOW HAST THOU ONE BARE HOUR TO LIVE." "Okay, okay," someone shouted. "We need more time to break it in. Take it over from the top of —"

"As I said," Bailey picked up the conversation, "it's my job."

"You seem to like your job — Gil."

"You seem to like yours, too — Beth."

"WAS THIS THE FACE THAT LAUNCHED A THOUSAND SHIPS," Faustus thundered. Beth could feel Bailey staring at her. She tried to think of something, anything, to say.

"Well, Beth" — a high officious voice — "exactly the person I'm looking for." A huge Virginia Woolf poster, lettered ASK A WOMAN'S ADVICE, appeared to be hurrying toward them. A second later Ida Garden's face emerged from behind the poster. She peered at Bailey a moment, then plunged excitedly into a description of the article she was writing about the subjugated female in the novels of Thomas Hardy. "Once and for all," said Ida, "I'm going to destroy Arthur Hewmann's theory of the man-eating vampire woman. All I need is something to catch attention at the start, some obvious male chauvinist group —" She broke off, looking speculatively at Gil. "What do you think, Beth — do you have any ideas?"

Beth hesitated, caught Gil's eye. "None at the moment," she said. "Ida, this is Gil Bailey — Visiting Fellow in the Fine Arts." He gave her an appreciative look.

"Are you sure?" said Ida, and at Beth's startled look, "That you have no ideas, I mean. This is so important." Then, struck by a sudden thought — "I think we should collaborate on this, Beth. It's your — your duty to work with me."

"Well, Ida, how enchanting you look today." It was Noel Frazier, just in time to prevent Ida from starting another speech.

"Oh Nooell!" Ida almost squealed her happiness. "I want to get your views on this."

"On what? . . . Thomas Hardy's women? A promising subject, if ever I heard one."

For a short time Noel stayed to chat amiably with Bailey and Beth, and then he took Ida off to lunch. Beth watched them walk past the library, Noel carrying the Virginia Woolf poster under one arm, his other arm linked through Ida's. She looked a strange figure, bulging out of her embroidered peasant dress, as she walked heavily down the path.

* * *

Inside the Library, partway up the steps, they paused. From where they were standing, they had a good view of the exit. A line had gathered behind a sign that proclaimed, "All Library Materials And The Borrower's I. D. Card Must Be Displayed To The Exit Attendant." Behind the counter, next to another sign warning that "All Cases, Bags, Purses, And Other Parcels Must Be Displayed For Inspection," the student-checker peered into backpacks and handbags.

Spence Goldberg reached the head of the line and lifted his briefcase to the counter. "Hi, Mr. Goldberg," said the student. "Sorry."

"No, don't be," said Spence, opening his briefcase.

Quickly the student examined the books, made sure they were charged out, and gave Spence a nod.

Spence jammed the books in the briefcase, moved through the turnstile, and trudged wearily down the steps, nodding briefly to Beth and Gil.

"See what I mean?" said Beth.

"What?"

"It works — look how carefully they're checking. How could anyone get books out?"

"That, Professor, is the question."

She nodded. "Well," she said, "I'm off to Hub."

"Be careful," he said.

"Of what?"

"I'm not sure — let's say of someone who would like Marylou Peacock forgotten as soon as possible."

"But who? Who cares? Who would care if I spend a few minutes on the paper?"

"Ida Garden might, for one. She followed us all the way through plagiarism and book theft before she picked up speed."

"Ida? If you knew her, you'd realize how funny —"

"Just the same, be careful."

"All right — but I'm still off to Hub. And you?" she asked.

"Oh, Periodicals, I think," he said vaguely.

She moved away a few steps.

"Beth?" She turned. "How about dinner tonight?" Before she could answer, he said, "I'll pick you up at eight."

7

OF ALL THE LIBRARY GALAXY, HUB'S STAR GLEAMED THE brightest. Chicago's Daley center had its Picasso. The glittering Water Tower complex had its glass-enclosed elevator. Midwestern had Hub.

Whereas the other library research towers were confined to one level, Hub's appointments — its circular velvet-covered sofas; its upholstered browsers' pit; its private study rooms; its CRT, the cathode ray terminal that could tell you instantly if the book you wanted was on the shelves — were distributed over three luxurious levels. So impressive was Hub that on certain great occasions the president of Midwestern himself could be seen showing off its wonders to potential benefactors. For less illustrious groups, the library provided student guides.

A group of entering students and their parents was visiting Hub now, and Beth stood a moment watching them. The students, scared and impressed, were trying to look bored. Their parents, bulgy and old-fashioned against Hub's ultramodern lines, were impressed too, and not afraid to show it. Eager to justify the thousands of dollars in checks they would write each year to Midwestern, they nodded approvingly at each marvel.

"Hub," the guide was saying, "is a library within the library." As she talked, a summer student, carefully balancing a tennis racket stacked with books and topped with a can of balls, edged past her, thrust out a hip and pushed the exit bar.

"Bong!" A chime echoed through the tower. At once the turnstile locked, throwing the boy against the bar, and scattering books, racket, and tennis balls into the tour group.

"Jesus Christ!" the student shouted — looked at the parents — "I mean oh my goodness. What happened?" A waggish younger brother crawled among the legs, retrieved the balls and began juggling them, until his mother made him stop clowning. Racket, books, and balls were returned to their owner, who stood at the exit, confused and embarrassed.

Marjorie Westwood, the Hub librarian, was at his side in an instant. "Jeez — what'd I do?" he asked. "Hub books," she said dryly, "do not circulate outside this tower."

There was a general chuckle from the tour group. "You mean," said a genial crewcut father, "that if they try to take books out of here you machine gun 'em?" "Or turn dogs on them?" suggested another wit.

"Great idea," Marge called after him. "So far we merely ask them to return the books."

"So that's how it's done," said Beth, watching Marge open a concealed panel next to the exit bar.

"That's how it's done," she said, pressing a button. A flashing red light changed to a steady green, the "Lock" sign switched from "On" to "Off," and the bar was released. They watched the student flee through the exit and tear around a corner.

"How's it going?" Beth asked, as she and Marge walked to the main desk.

"As usual," Marge said glumly.

"As usual? Too bad."

"We've got one guy threatening to sue because his three-ring notebook set off the alarm and he got a gate-bar in the groin — which he claims did him permanent damage. The CRT is saying that all fourteen copies of *Walden* are lost. And we've been warned to get rid of the obscene graffiti in the study rooms by Tuesday — they're bringing in a group of potential benefactors. Tours, always tours. Toujours tours — greetings Selby." Marge opened the desk gate for her assistant, a neatly dressed young man.

Beth said something about how hard it was to get anything done with so many interruptions.

"Tell me about it!" said Marge. "Between answering questions and leading people out — some old wacko couldn't find his way out of the lower level this morning — I never get finished. I complain and what does our head librarian tell me? 'You've got to keep a closer watch,' says Mr. Coleman Lenites. 'For what?' I ask him. 'For people with thermoses.' 'Why?' I ask him. 'Because I counted nine new coffee stains on the carpet!' Can you beat that? — Wait!" Marge called to her assistant. "It's just drinks and food they can't bring in, Selby. You can't keep someone out for chewing gum. The Enforcer," she told Beth.

Beth chuckled and moved away, passing the visitors. The whole group, even the students, appeared wide awake now, paying close attention to the guide, who stood one arm extended and pointing (like a flight attendant, Beth thought). "To my right," said the guide, "are the reference books, dictionaries, encyclopedias. To my left" — she extended the other arm — "is the catalog with a card for every book in Hub. This key private collection ensures the permanent availability of essential books, a convenience intended especially for undergraduates."

"Get that?" the crewcut father nudged his daughter. "A private collection for your convenience."

Yes indeed, Beth thought, as she went to the catalog, the Hub collection is a great convenience for undergraduates. She made up a few lines of her own tour speech: "The undergraduate who wishes to plagiarize is assured access to major sources. But — be fair — the professor who wishes to look up the undergraduate's source is assured the same convenience." Beth had made use of this convenience more often than she liked to remember.

True, she could spot plagiarism quickly, just as she had suggested to Gil Bailey. And sometimes she could find the source quickly — but only sometimes. Hoping this would be one of the times, she opened the TRE-TZ catalog drawer.

The card that read "Twain, Mark, pseud." advised that she see "Clemens, Samuel Langhorne." "Clemens, Samuel Langhorne, 1835-1910" revealed that she should head for the shelves marked 817.4C62. Beth circled Hub's upper level, took a few promising titles from the shelves, and sat down at a desk. Three books later she realized she had been way too optimistic. She pulled out more books and a few minutes later was balancing a dozen volumes down two carpeted flights.

Hub's glassed-in lower level was a popular spot. Here you could put your feet up and spread your books on a wide round table. Even now, early in the quarter, nearly every table was occupied. A few readers glanced up, then turned back to their books, as Beth walked around the circle, searching for an empty study. A peek through each windowed door told her that all the rooms were taken.

Over one study-room window someone had draped a camouflage-print parka, so you couldn't see inside. Covering the window was a popular ploy, a favorite of students who wanted to use a room for activities other than scholarly. Covering the window was also against the rules, but Beth was not going to argue about it. The privacy of a study denied her, she would settle for a table. Nearby, the table she liked best — just facing the plaza exit — she was pleased to see was empty.

Settled comfortably in a plush-covered chair, Beth looked out the wall-sized window at the passing parade. She saw Arthur Hewmann, neatly rolled umbrella under his arm, walk in the plaza entrance. Moments later Dot entered, probably on an errand for Porter, or maybe, Beth was amused, looking to see if the library had a copy of *Scruples*. She saw Thorpe, carrying his wolf's mask now, pull his bicycle into the stand and walk off hand in hand with a blond girl, sexy enough to be playing Helen of Troy. Then she got down to work.

She had brought Marylou's paper with her and she glanced over it once more. The main point of the essay was that the relation between Tom and Aunt Polly represented an unresolved Oedipal conflict within Mark Twain. Much was made of the Aunt Polly "kissing" passage in Chapter Nineteen. (*"Did* you kiss me Tom?" . . . "What did you kiss me for, Tom?" . . . "Kiss me again, Tom!") The idea was silly, puerile, pretentious, but one could say that of much of what was accepted for literary criticism. The phrasing, the wide-ranging references, reflected a sophistication beyond a junior in college. Putting the essay aside, she opened the first book.

An hour or so later she looked up, musing at what she had found. Beth's specialty was Victorian literature, and it had been a long time since she had looked at studies of Mark Twain. Some critics, she had discovered to her astonishment, saw the mood of *Tom Sawyer* as far from idyllic. Pointing to ghastly events, grave robbery, starvation, murder, they had unearthed dark adult emotions — jealousy, lust, vengefulness. She was interested in emotions all right, but she was hunting for a child's emotions and a passage that took in Freud, Oedipus, Tom, and Aunt Polly, and for this particular combination she looked in vain.

Within a few hours, she had added at least thirty books to the pile on the table. She had also filled out a hefty pile of note cards. But she still had no idea what writer Marylou Peacock had copied.

She went on checking indexes, searching between "Finn, Pap" and "Frog Story" for references to Freud, vaguely aware of people working at other tables, of muffled voices from the study rooms, of fierce blasts from the air conditioning, of a sneeze from one side of the circle, followed by a "God bless you" from the other side. Behind her, she heard someone go into the room with the camouflaged window, but she didn't bother to look around. Cursing the books that lacked an index, she skimmed them for Freudian references.

She learned from one critic that Freud had read and liked Mark Twain. She learned from another critic that Mark Twain had anticipated Freud. She learned from a penciled comment in the margin that the critic was full of shit. She learned that all sorts of Freudian neuroses had been found in Twain's writing. . . . After wading through a dozen emotional disorders without finding what she was looking for, she found herself humming, "Oh Doctor Freud, oh Doctor Freud, how I wish you had been otherwise employed."

It was getting late. The copying machines had ceased humming. The typewriters were quiet. Ignoring the groups that clattered out of the study rooms, she worked steadily, making notes of promising leads. Once she heard Marge tell Selby she was going for coffee. She hardly noticed. . . . She wasn't sure exactly when she sensed a different movement outside the window. Keeping her place in the book, she looked up.

It had started to rain and the passing parade on the plaza had halted. She looked around, then saw what had caught her attention. Immediately outside the window at the bike stand were two boys, about twelve and ten. While the younger boy kept a lookout, the older worked professionally with wire-cutters.

Beth ran to the window and pounded on it with a book. The boys glanced up and returned to their jobs. They knew she couldn't get at them. The older boy severed the second lock and they got on the bicycles.

Book in hand, Beth ran up the two flights to the exit. "Bong!" The chime went off and the bar locked. "Damn it! I forgot I had a book. Come here and let me out, Selby!"

"Well, I don't know." He looked around uncertainly.

"For God's sake, Selby" — she tossed the book at him — "they're stealing bikes on the plaza. Will you push that button *now!*" He shook his head and swearing under her breath, she opened the panel and pushed the button herself.

By the time she reached the exit, it was too late. She stood with the guard watching the boys coast gleefully away. "Yeah, sure," he said, when she asked the guard if he had called Security, "but they'll never make it. They can't find the library without a map."

A few minutes later Marge echoed the guard. "Security is the one group that *needs* a tour of this place," she told Beth. "I swear those meatballs still don't know where the front stairways are, let alone the back. They might as well put a Welcome Visiting Rapists sign on the ladies' room doors." She looked at Selby and lowered her voice. "Did you hear what happened last night on Five?"

"Yes," said Beth, "but I'm sure the whole thing was an accident."

"Who's feeding you that line?" said Marge. "I'm telling you women are sitting ducks in this building! I've warned them," she said, "we need twenty-four-hour guards, at least a panic button — but no one listens. Coleman Lenites doesn't care if we're all murdered in the toilets, as long as no one spills coffee on the carpet."

Downstairs the lower level had emptied out. The study rooms were dark, the tables clear. Only her table was full, the books she had collected scattered over the dark surface. But something was wrong.

Her notes! She'd had a whole pile of them. She looked under the table. She emptied her briefcase. She put everything back inside and emptied it again. She searched the copying room, the typing room. No sign of her index cards. She searched the studies, coming last to the one where the window had been covered. The door was closed, the window dark. When she turned on the light, she saw that the room was empty, a chair tipped over as if someone had left in a hurry.

Selby and Marge, it turned out, had been looking out the window, watching the goings-on in the plaza. Had they seen anyone? Yes, the two kids on the stolen bikes. Anyone *inside*, with her notes? No — but they wouldn't have noticed anyway. "Last week we had a leather jacket thief," said Marge, "but who wants note cards? Probably a fraternity gag."

On her way out of the library, she caught sight of Livy, leaning against the charge-out counter, studying the people who walked by. Oh no, she could not listen to another word about body language. She darted through a side door and found herself in the midst of another tour group. "At night," the guide was saying, apparently in answer to a question, "there's a trained student guard. He has an office in Stack Control, when he's not roaming the floor with his beeper."

Beth fell in with the group, and moved with them down a narrow corridor lined with small windowed rooms. The guide brought them to a halt. "This is the last stop on our Back of the Stacks tour, the heart of the library — Central Data Processing."

Beth stood on tiptoe, looking over heads through the window and had an instant impression of frenzied activity. Everything was in motion, whirring, spinning, printing. Glassy-eyed workers peered at video screens and punched keys. Oversized typewriters clicked away, long sheets, like ticker tapes, worming out of them, oozing down to the floor. She stared at an enormous machine, its red, green, and white lights blinking on and off, its colossal tape wheels rotating powerfully.

"The smaller machines, the printers and terminals," she heard the guide say, "are called peripherals, because they are peripheral to the main computer, the Central Processing Unit. The CPU directs the tape drives; it tells the other machines what to do." The group gazed at the gargantuan machine. Someone asked jokingly what would happen if you whacked it with a baseball bat. The guide looked startled, then annoyed. "It would kill the computer," she said coldly. "Oh, it's alive then," said the voice.

Someone else asked, "Why all the loose panels on the floor?" "The panels come up," explained the guide, "to make it easier to get to the wiring when new machines are installed." "All those wires," someone said. "Looks dangerous."

She did not wait for the guide's answer. Feeling sure it was safe now, Beth deserted the tour, found her way back to the main section of Level One — saw no sign of Livy — and walked out of the library into a pouring rain. Shielding herself with her briefcase, she crossed the meadow on the diagonal, on the theory that the shortest distance between two points was worth drenched feet.

8

IT WAS A LITTLE BEFORE SIX BY THE TIME BETH REACHED
home, wet through, tired, disgusted. As she pushed the
elevator button, she remembered that Bailey was picking her
up at eight. She did not want dinner out. All she wanted was a
bath. She pictured herself, resting in the warm water, thinking. She would mull over where she would start tomorrow —
or if she would start. She was almost ready to give up on
Mark Twain.

The red light on the phone machine was flashing. Beth
went over to it, pressed Rewind, and walked down the hall.
She threw her briefcase on the bed, undressed, and filled the
bath. In bra and briefs she walked back to the living room and
started the tape.

Her "electronic helpmate" appeared to have left the usual
collection of uninteresting messages. "Beep." Kroch's calling
to let her know the book she had ordered was in. "Beep." A
voice urged her to take a one-month special subscription to
the *Tribune*. "Beep." "Hi kiddo" — Dot telling her that
Porter had called a meeting for tomorrow afternoon. "Beep."
A whispered hiss. *"Sssnoop. I'm watching you. . . . Ssstop
sssnooping, or you die, too . . . like Marylou."*

Beth shuddered. Heart pounding, she rewound the tape
and stood listening to the messages, waiting for the last.
"Sssnoop," came the whisper. *"I'm watching you. . . ."*

Someone watching. Suddenly she ran across the room.
"Die, too . . . like Marylou," whispered the voice, as she
edged along the wall to the bay. She yanked the curtains over
the window. She looked around, saw her keys on the table.
Almost sobbing, she rushed to the door and turned the key in
the deadbolt lock. Then she went back to the machine.

There was something familiar about the whispered voice, some intonation, some rhythm, she thought, replaying the message again and again, trying to jog her memory. But the effort was futile and the words were making her feel queasy. *"Die, too . . . like Marylou . . . Die, too . . . like Marylou."* Her hand trembling, she pressed Erase and eradicated the whisper forever.

9

IT HAD BEEN A QUIET DRIVE INTO CHICAGO. AFTER AN INITIAL
clash of opinion, they had hardly talked. Gil had driven fast
along Michigan Boulevard, pulled off on a quiet side street,
and stopped the car outside an old townhouse that Beth
recognized.

She had dined at the Club LaCache before and remembered its owner, Victor Bilescu, well. She knew that Bilescu,
a Roumanian emigré entrepreneur, had directed the restora-
tion of the townhouse, down to the elaborate stonework
around each window and the marble mantel above each fireplace. Under his superintendence had emerged an elegant
club, behind whose unmarked front door were intimate din-
ing rooms, where silver gleamed, where shaded lamps cast a
soft glow on turn-of-the-century paneling, and where Victor
Bilescu cast a cold eye on the "vulgarities" he detested.

The city's most powerful restaurant critic had been refused
LaCache membership because Victor had spotted her taking
notes while she munched galantine of chicken. A famous
neurosurgeon had lost out because Victor had spied him
lighting a cigar between the oysters and the duckling. Chicago's mayor had been turned down because Victor had seen
him giving an off the fork "taste" to his companion. The effect
of these outrageously arrogant entrance policies was that
within a year Bilescu had rejected enough prominent Chicagoans to establish Club LaCache as the favored ren-
dezvous of the prominent Chicagoans he had permitted to
join.

Victor liked to station himself at the door, so that he could
assess members and their acolyte guests as they entered,
giving them the same keen scrutiny that presumably he had

given suspected informers when he served as a leader in the French resistance. He had been at the door tonight, his powerful frame packed into a dark three-piece suit, and he had greeted Gil Bailey enthusiastically. "Ah, Professor Austin," he had interrupted, when Gil started to introduce her. "I am enchanted to see you again," and looking her up and down with a connoisseur's appreciation, he had taken her hand and kissed it. Then with an autocratic wave of his hand, he had instructed the hovering maître d'.

How Gil Bailey merited the upstairs at LaCache — whether it was the FBI or Visiting Fellows in the Fine Arts that Victor particularly liked — Beth did not know and was not going to ask. She had no intention of showing even a passing interest in someone so eternally certain that only *he* was right. She had told him of her difficulty in tracing Marylou Peacock's source, and he had said, "Maybe she didn't plagiarize. Maybe she was smart." She had told him about the stolen notes, and he had passed over the theft as a prank. The threatening telephone message he had dismissed as "a crackpot making random calls."

"Random, hell!" said Beth, and slid along the velvet a little away from him. The maître d' had seated them at a corner banquette, a sequestered spot, marked out for flirtatious chitchat. "Someone is trying to scare me into giving up."

"A crank," Gil insisted. "He called you, and then he traveled down the phone book finding other machines to shoot the breeze with. By this time he's hissing threats to the 'K's. You'll never hear from your whisperer again. To absent friends," he said, and lifted his glass to her.

"You can't write it off that easily!" said Beth, and took an indignant sip of her drink. "What's happening is bizarre — stolen notes, threatening phone calls."

"One call," he corrected. "Answering machines," he said, in the same maddeningly reasonable tone, "invite jokers. You must have had crank messages before."

"Never," she lied.

"Let's say it wasn't a crank. It was a deliberate call to Professor Elizabeth Austin. Even the best professors" — he swept his arm toward her magnanimously — "have students who think they have good reason to be angry. One scintillating message on that machine — *voilà!* Former student has paid you back for the B that ought to have been an A."

"*Former* student? This person was talking about right now. He — she — (I know, I know, I shouldn't have erased it) — said I should stop snooping."

"(Correct. We now have techniques that go beyond the muddy footprint.) *Have* you snooped before?"

"Of course not!" She pulled out a cigarette. A tuxedoed waiter leaped with a lighter.

"But you did say you've looked up sources for other copied papers."

"That wasn't snooping! That was tracing plagiarism." He smiled and she saw that she had fallen into a trap.

"Couldn't there be someone who's still angry?" he seized the advantage. "Did you have a plagiarist last quarter?"

Instantly a student from spring quarter sprang to mind. Gil was watching her. He could tell she had thought of someone.

"Yes," she said, and quickly added, "but that boy wouldn't make threatening calls. He's not the type."

"There is no type."

Was there any convincing him, any point in explaining that the boy's personality was miles away from the adult authority of the whisper on the phone? "This was different —" she began.

The captain smiled at them benevolently. "Tonight," he said, (pronouncing the French names with a slight Chicago accent) "we have carré de agneau en crôute, paillarde de veau, suprême de turbot —"

"The turbot," said Gil. "And is it —"

She hardly listened. Agreeing indifferently to Gil's suggestions, she opened her cigarette case. Another waiter sprang with a lighter. Discreetly covering the cigarettes in the old ashtray, he placed another ashtray in front of her.

The captain left and Gil turned to her again. "You were saying this was different?"

"There's no point in talking about it. We're so far apart —"

The wine steward offered Gil a leatherbound book. He studied the list, asked if she had a preference.

She was tired. She was worried. She was hungry. Why was he bothering her with wines? "Blue Nun," she said loudly.

He looked up, gave her his cheerful grin. Then he ordered a 1970 Dom Perignon and, turning to her with a look that meant she had all his attention, he said, "*Now* you were about to tell me —"

"That there's no point in talking about the phone call any more, or Marylou Peacock's paper."

"But they are worth talking about," he said, "if you see a connection. What kind of connection?"

"I'm not sure," she said. "It's just that I have a feeling — call it a hunch —" Was there no end to the interruptions?

Gil tasted the champagne. Then while the steward filled their glasses, he tried to ask about her hunch, but she cut him off. In silence they sipped champagne and ate smoked salmon. Had she been foolish, she was thinking, magnifying the importance of one telephone call? No, damn it, she had

not. "Think about it," she said suddenly. "Why would someone want to steal my notes?"

"What was in your notes?"

"Leads to other sources, jottings about what I had found
out."

"What did you find out?"

So she told him. He listened carefully, asking an occasional
question, his eyes never leaving hers. "But there's nothing,"
she finished, "that points the way exactly."

"Of course you wouldn't want to drop the whole thing?" he
asked.

"Of course not."

"I know," he said, and he sounded as if he meant it.

She could tell he thought she was wasting her time, but he
seemed to understand that she needed to find out. One point
in his favor. And there was another: He had been tactful
enough not to remind her of her easy confidence earlier in the
day. "Let's forget plagiarism," she said. "What about your
mission? What's going on?"

"Theft is going on and it's getting more valuable."

"*More* valuable! Horrors! They haven't started heisting
the old yearbooks?"

"That would be serious," he agreed serenely. "No, luckily
it's not on the scale of the two million dollar robbery we
worked on last year."

"Two million! Where?"

"A library in London where an American professor was
doing 'research.' He brought home some souvenirs — three
suitcases of fifteenth- and sixteenth-century volumes."

"How did you catch him?"

"It wasn't just me. We worked with Scotland Yard, and
Interpol" — he chuckled — "and a New York bookseller."

"Something funny happened. Tell me!"

"We set it up for the bookseller to meet the thief at the New York University Club and pretend to buy some books. The bookseller was somewhat jittery — he wore a bulletproof vest to the meeting." Gil roared with laughter.

"Maybe," Beth suggested, laughing with him, "you can set up your Midwestern sting at the Club LaCache." She looked up and saw Victor watching her out of the corner of his eye, while he supervised a table. "But I can't see Victor in a bulletproof vest," she said, lowering her voice. "You still haven't told me. What's the latest on your Midwestern marauder?"

"The latest," said Gil, looking somber, "is a missing first edition of *The Moonstone* — by Wilkie Collins."

"Thanks," said Beth. "I know who wrote *The Moonstone,* the ancestor of modern detective stories."

"Sorry, Professor," giving her an apologetic smile that lit up his face. "I should have remembered you know the classics. Do you have any idea," he continued, "how much an 1860 edition of *The Moonstone* is worth? Especially," he said reverently, "if it's inscribed. Or a first American edition of *A Study in Scarlet,* which is also missing? Signed by Conan Doyle himself," he said sadly, and gazed thoughtfully at his champagne.

She waited a moment, watching him, then said, "Your thief seems to have a taste for mysteries."

Gil came back from his reverie. "I don't think it's taste. I think that our thief might be working from a shopping list, taking orders from clients. Oh well," he said lightly. "To one client a rare edition of Dickens" — he lifted his glass — "is like vintage champagne. To another —"

"Another client" — she forked an anchovy — "has saltier taste, for mysteries. Does your hypothetical shopping list call for Agatha Christie? You do know her work? 'It was five o'clock,'" Beth quoted, "'on a winter's morning in Syria.'"

He grinned and came back without a pause. *"Orient Express,* Chapter One." He gave her a challenging look and said, "'I have met people who enjoy a Channel crossing.'"

"The Big Four," Beth returned. She thought a moment. "'It was close on midnight when a man crossed the Place de la Concorde.'"

"Mystery of the Blue Train," he answered, "and that was much too easy. Here's a hard one — 'Who is there who has not felt a sudden startled pang at reliving an old experience or feeling an old emotion?'"

She was stumped and he had to tell her, *Curtain,* but she was less chagrined at missing the identification than at the aptness of the phrase. She *was* feeling an old emotion, and it was making her self-conscious. She was too aware of him, of his closeness to her on the banquette, of the intent gaze he was turning on her now.

Flustered she said, "The FBI requires a wider range of reading than I thought."

"Of course, and I think you've overlooked the importance of our work. We don't just protect library books." He sat up straight with an expression of bulldog courage. "If Prince Charles and Princess Diana decide to visit Midwestern, they can count on us."

He did have an engaging smile. He was, beyond doubt, the most attractive man in the room. But how could she, Beth, find an FBI agent attractive? Analyzing the question she decided that LaCache was working in Gil's favor. He was tall, yes, but next to the portly Victor he had seemed positively towering. Next to the counterfeit poise of the maître d', his self-assurance was bound to seem more genuine. For that matter, compared with the shallow talk of men at other tables (she had picked up phrases about strong portfolios, low handicaps) his conversation had to seem more sparkling. That was it — the contrasts.

"Isn't that one of your colleagues?" Gil's voice interrupted her thoughts.

Across the room was Arthur Hewmann, on his arm a distinguished, rather voluptuous woman, her hair done up in a chignon. As he waited to be seated, Arthur generously distributed his smile over the tables, as if he were a king and all the diners his loyal subjects. His eyes lit on them.

"Beth!" he called. "The very person I want to see. Stay there," he said. He escorted his companion to a table, gave loud instructions to the waiter, with asides in another language to the woman. "Dry, mind you," Arthur repeated, "the merest whisper of vermouth." Then he patted the woman's hair — she drew back — and he bowed and smiled his way toward Beth and Gil.

"A far cry from your yogurt," he said, eyeing Beth's raspberries and cream. "I know how slavishly you watch your weight. Not to worry." With a nod to Gil and a broad smile, he said, "But you, Beth, my dear, are not the only one called upon to entertain distinguished scholars. A sudden visit from a professor from Eötvös University in Budapest, and whom does Porter summon forth? Seems I'm the only one in the department — that's Harvard for you — who knows Hungarian. I agreed, but only on condition that the budget run to some decent cuisine and that Porter prevail upon Noel to use his LaCache membership." Arthur went on to explain that he had been here frequently as a guest and Noel had promised to sponsor him for membership. "For some reason," he finished, "I've never heard. Perhaps tonight I'll take it up with Victor."

At that moment Arthur looked up and saw Victor, leaning against the curved white mantel of the fireplace. He was frowning ominously — Victor hated table-hopping — and Arthur, usually oblivious to the impression he was making, looked shaken. "But I digress," he said hurriedly. "I wanted to alert you to expect a visit from a student. He was looking for you this afternoon and he seemed so distraught that I thought it only charitable to give him your carrel number. I made a memorandum of the name, something Gaelic" — and triumphantly pulling a pink department memo from his pocket — "McBride, that's it."

"Excuse me, sir." The waiter served their espresso, making clear with looks and gestures that Arthur was in the way.

"My professor will think I've deserted her," said Arthur. He smiled in the direction of his table, and waved coyly. *"Mindjárt jövök kedvesem,"* he called. The professor looked angry. "Just one word more, Beth. Do you know anything about this meeting Porter's called? I call it egregious interference. He knows I devote summers to my research."

Beth told him she had no idea.

"I had an idea it was something to do with the event at the library. You know about it, of course?"

"Yes, but I don't know a thing about the meeting."

Arthur looked at her closely. Then he straightened. "Well, I must be off to play the genial host."

"Is Hewmann from the East?" Gil asked.

"Don't let the accent mislead you," Beth answered. "Arthur grew up in Toledo, and attended Ohio State. But he makes the most of his graduate years at Harvard and, I might add, of several years of busing paprikash at a Hungarian restaurant in Boston."

"I take it that somewhere along the way Arthur acquired money?"

"He acquired a rather wealthy wife — whom he seems not to have invited tonight. I suppose Arthur does seem comfortable," she said, thinking of his house on the lake, of his much talked about wine cellar.

She looked across the room. Hewmann was gesturing boldly and smiling broadly. The professor sat upright, her face stony. She had placed a large brown leather handbag on the table between herself and Arthur.

Beth giggled. "The professor is keeping Arthur at a distance. Livy could write a whole chapter on that little scene."

"Why is that?" Gil looked interested.

So Beth told him about Livy's obsession. "Very hush-hush, remember. Livy frequently reminds me that there are more vicious idea-robbers in academia than there are in Hollywood. But he's told me in confidence that he's making such magnificent progress with Dickens that reading real life body language has become child's play. Claims he can tell from sixty feet whether or not a man and woman are married, even which anniversary they'll celebrate next. Now he's working on degrees of friendship at eighty feet."

"What would Livy say if he saw us now?" Gil asked idly.

Startled, Beth noticed they were on a perfect parallel. They sat leaning toward each other, their arms, as they held their cups, forming an arch. She had talked enough with Livy to know what the arch meant: they wanted privacy. Together, they were closing off a third person.

She put her cup down and sat up straight. "This study of Livy's," she said quickly, "if he ever finishes, just could get him his promotion. He's collected three volumes of notes."

"Speaking of volumes, how is Livy fixed for money?"

"You know, Mr. Bailey" — she was really annoyed — "you seem to define everyone by money."

"When you're a professor, the name of the game is publish," he answered lightheartedly. "When you're a G-man, it's money."

She looked at him sharply. "Livy talks to me about body language," she said, "not about his money worries, if he has any, which I doubt."

"Apparently your chivalrous rescuer of this morning has no money worries either."

"Rescuer — what do you mean?"

"Your knight-errant who took Miss Garden off your hands. Mr. Frazier."

"Oh, Noel. Noel is wonderful."

"Is he married?" Gil asked quickly.

"No — why?"

"I wondered if he makes it a practice to be as charming to all women as he was to Miss Garden."

"That's absurd. Noel saw I was in Ida's clutches — and he helped me out."

"I thought perhaps Frazier makes up with charm for what he lacks in academic achievement."

Beth was furious. "Noel doesn't need to charm anyone," she said. "He's already respected."

Gil still looked skeptical.

"You don't believe me. I tell you grad students come here especially to study with Noel. Noel's position is so lofty, so secure, that he — he —" she searched for an example "— he dares to brew coffee in his library carrel." In spite of herself, she laughed.

"An unusual status symbol," said Gil.

"Not at our library."

"Your faculty seem to have taken up permanent occupancy at the library. Everyone I've met was there Sunday night."

"Does that matter? Oh, I see. The night Marylou Peacock died. . . . Are you — do you still think — ?"

The waiter was at the table with two short-stemmed crystal goblets.

"But I didn't order brandy — yet," said Gil, accepting the glass.

"Mr. Bilescu's compliments, sir." The waiter looked toward the nearby doorway.

Victor stood there, beaming proudly. "Something special," he said to Gil. "I've been saving it for you."

Gil took a sip, saluted Victor, and Victor made a mock salute back.

"You seem to know him well," Beth remarked, watching Victor walk out of the room.

"I did him a favor once," he said shortly. "To answer your question — I don't think anything until I get the report from the medical examiner."

"Very well. But now it's my turn to ask something. What have you found out about Marylou Peacock?"

He looked wary. "What do you want to know?"

"What kind of a student is — was — she?"

"Oh, that —" Gil pulled a paper out of an inside pocket.

Beth looked at the heading. "Midwestern University, Vinetown Illinois, Office of the Registrar." Above it was the University seal, and motto, *Appono mihi veritatum,* "I serve myself with truth." Then she looked over the transcript. "Good grades," she commented, scanning a solid row of A's.

"I told you she was smart. Maybe she did write that paper herself."

"I see she never took a psych course."

"Neither did I."

"No? Maybe you should," she said absently, still looking at the transcript. "For someone who never even took Intro to Psych, Marylou certainly knew a lot about Freud."

"You're still infatuated with the plagiarism," he said, amusement in his voice.

Let him laugh, she said to herself.

"By the way," he said, as if he'd just thought of it, "did you notice anything unusual?"

"Where? In my apartment?"

"No, in Hub — when you were doing your detective work."

She thought of the tour group, of the boy with the tennis racket, of Marge's complaints, of Selby's officiousness.

"No," she said, "everything was exactly the way it usually is."

"Not everything. You've never had notes stolen before."

"That was unusual," she agreed, "but nothing else."

"Sure? Think again."

She pictured herself in Hub that morning, saw herself collecting books, walking down the stairs, looking through study room windows — the camouflaged window. She hesitated. "There *was*" — she was interrupted by the waiter.

"Mr. Bailey, you have a telephone call."

He was gone for only a minute, and when he came back his expression was grim.

"What is it?" she asked.

"That was the medical examiner. Marylou Peacock was murdered."

"How?" she said, keeping her voice steady only with effort.

"Karate blow to the neck," he said matter-of-factly. He signaled the waiter. "You're pale," he said, looking at her. "Would you like another brandy?"

She didn't answer. She was seeing a girl walk across a long stretch of gray carpet, push the ladies' room door. "The whisper," she said in a choking voice. "The whisper knew she was murdered."

"What are you talking about?" said Gil.

"My message, don't you remember? 'Die, too . . . like Marylou.' You only just told me she was murdered. How could anyone but the murderer have known that?"

"Good theorizing, professor, but it doesn't work. *I've* just had the confirmation. By the time you had your phone call, however, all of greater Chicago believed that Marylou Peacock was murdered. Didn't you watch the six o'clock news? Not only did Channel Two report what happened in a way that all but said homicide — police in suburban Vinetown refuse to comment on the question of murder — they added an editorial on safety in the libraries."

She kept replaying the scene, the empty corridor, the girl walking to the ladies' room. "Was it rape?"

"No," he answered. "By the way, didn't you start to tell me something about Hub?"

"It's not important." The camouflaged window, she decided, was not worth mentioning.

Then the waiter handed Gil a small tray, and stepped discreetly back. He looked the check over and reached for his wallet.

"How about splitting it?" Beth asked.

He stared at her, genuinely shocked.

"I hope you're not putting me on your expense account, Mr. Bailey. I don't want the FBI to pay for my dinner."

"I promise. No expense account."

"Then you really must let me."

He laughed. "Of course I won't let you."

"Well, then, Mr. Bailey," she said, echoing him, and not really expecting an answer, "where do you get *your* money? LaCache prices don't get along with an FBI income."

Unperturbed, he said, "The name is Gil, remember? As to where I get my money — that's a very rational question, professor" — he gave her his mock salute — "but you may find the answer clichéd. My father's sister married into cereals" — he named a famous company. "And I was Aunt Beatrice's favorite nephew. She had no children."

She wasn't sure if he was joking or not. "Did Aunt Beatrice know you were going to join the FBI?"

"She died before my fall from grace. But I think she would have approved."

"Just the same, I'd like to pay."

"You can get the next one," he said, standing. The waiter was ahead of him, pulling the table away from the banquette.

As they reached the door, Victor took his eyes off a plaid-jacketed man, who had just exhaled a cloud of cigar smoke, and turned to them. *"A bientôt,"* he said, kissing Beth's hand enthusiastically. "Keep her, Gilbert. She has humor, vivacity. Remember that, keep her. And remember, Gilbert" — giving him a powerful clap on the shoulder —" if there is *anything.*"

"I'll remember," said Gil, but he neglected to say what.

10

THE RAIN HAD STOPPED LONG SINCE. IT HAD TURNED INTO A
starry evening, a night when Chicago was at its best, when
the lights of the Outer Drive sparkled and the skyline was a
series of crystal sculptures. Slowly they drove along the
lakefront, past Lake Point Tower, the twin Mies towers. Gil
turned the radio to WFMT and strains of Rachmaninoff filled
the silence. Another romantic setting, Beth thought, if only
she and he, too, she was certain, had not been thinking about
Marylou Peacock.

The car rounded the big curve and the dazzling bend of
Lake Shore Drive came into full view. For this one enchanted
stretch, there still remained the extravagant relics of the
twenties boom, princely apartment buildings where door-
men under *porte-cochères* still handed ladies out of lim-
ousines, and a handful of mansions built for fortunes made in
steel or soybeans.

"Oh no," Beth murmured. They had drawn abreast of one
of her favorites and she saw scaffolding and the familiar
wrecker's insignia.

"What?" Gil asked, reaching out the window and just missing a heart-shaped "I Love Chicago" balloon that had bounced
against the car. She watched the balloon float across the
Drive, over the trees and into the scaffolding. "What is it?" he
asked again.

"They're tearing down the Cormackson mansion. This is
going to destroy Porter."

"Destroy the building anyway," said Gil, "but why
DeMont? He's small, but wiry. Your chairman can take a bit of
bad news."

"Porter is devastated when any of old Chicago comes down. It nearly killed him when they razed the Stock Exchange. He organized a Preserve the Ticker Committee. Had Dot typing letters day and night," said Beth, turning for a last look at the turrets and crenellated towers. The next time she came this way they would be gone.

"DeMont doesn't look like a crusader," said Gil, steering neatly around a jogger who had made a foolhardy sprint across the Drive.

"What do crusaders look like?"

"Oh," he said, "they're swashbuckling devils, who keep their eye on the big picture. DeMont seems more of a detail man. Think of his desk. No stray scraps of paper, books and pens lined up in military order."

Beth considered. "I don't see why being meticulous rules out being a crusader — when you believe strongly in something."

"What does DeMont believe in, other than preserving Windy City landmarks?"

Beth thought a moment before she answered.

"Literature," she said finally. "Porter believes in the study of literature, not women's literature, not black literature — literature. He's appalled by Johnny-come-lately courses, film, science fiction, pop culture." She giggled. "You should have heard him at the last department meeting. "'How will they learn rational thinking from a course on fantasy in — uyuh — Bruce Springsteen's greatest hits?'"

A jam of cars was entering the Drive from the Theater on the Lake, and Gil concentrated on threading through the traffic. They had passed Belmont Harbor before he spoke again, and then, sounding uncomfortable, he said, "Does your crusading Professor DeMont have —?"

"Yes," Beth interrupted indignantly, "Porter does have money. He'll be getting royalties forever from *The Age of Precision*. You won't have heard of it, but it's still used in all the basic eighteenth century courses. They've printed so many it can't possibly be a collector's item."

He chuckled. "No, Professor, I haven't heard of it. The subject of DeMont's bank account is hereby closed — for the time being."

They drove past the cemetery that separated Chicago from the North Shore suburbs and entered the outskirts of Vinetown where prairie-style houses mingled with Tudor mansions. The warm weather had brought people out. Beth looked out the window at the dignified couples walking their dogs under the elms.

Closer to campus the scene was livened by the festive sights and sounds of a summer night, when it was too late to study, and too early for mosquitoes. Fleets of bicycles paraded the streets. Barefoot beachgoers, carrying blankets and cassette players, boogied their way home. On one quiet block, a boy sat under a tree, piping "Greensleeves" on a recorder. As they reached fraternity row, they heard rock music bursting from the open windows of the Beta house and saw high up, perched on a gable, a boy munching a hamburger and drinking beer.

Next to the hamburger stand where they stopped for a red light, their ears were blasted by a roar like the clacking of a hundred broken lawn mowers. Trailing a cloud of noxious smoke, a rattletrap car pulled out of the drive and stopped next to them. The window was rolled down. "Beth, is that you?"

Through the smoke they could make out a face, wearing black-rimmed glasses. The figure took off the glasses, wiped them with a mustardy napkin, put them on again. "I thought it was you," said Spence Goldberg.

"Spence!" she said. "A late night?"

"Ah, mad naked summer night. Press close bare-bosom'd night," said Spence, nodding drunkenly to Gil. "A night to banish sorrows."

"You're mixing your poets," said Beth, laughing.

"As neatly as I mix my metaphors," he answered. "Sorry, I think I'm punchy."

"You're just leaving the library?" she asked.

He nodded. "Sat around all day, splitting hairs. My dead-line for the next chapter is Friday. Think I'll make it?"

"You'll make it," she said confidently.

"Thanks for that, Beth," and he drove off noisily, waving to two students lugging a trunk.

"Hi, Professor Goldberg," they chorused.

"Professor Goldberg," said Gil. "Beloved by students and library bookcheckers."

"Another suspect," said Beth. "Nobody but you would have thought of it."

"Exactly," he said, unruffled, "and why don't you tell me about him?"

"The sooner we get Spence off your list, the better. Where shall I start?"

"Anywhere."

"Well, let's see. Spence is the first one in his family to go to college."

"I'm interested in his present circumstances," Gil cut in.

"Take it easy on Spence," she said. "I like him."

They had reached the campus. The buildings were dark. Only at the library were lights still burning, for the benefit of late-working scholars. Gil turned a sharp corner around the new sculpture, a twist of steel tubing that represented the Lincoln-Douglas debates. "Is Goldberg married?" he asked.

"Yes," she said, surprised. "Has two children. Why?"

"It doesn't matter. You like him, you were saying."

"And I respect him. I hope he gets his tenure."

"How's he fixed for money?" said Gil.

"You saw his car. Spence is always broke — but he makes a joke of it. Says he's perpetually torn between the demands of his house and his Toyota. One week it's new storm windows, the next it's a new carburetor."

She looked over at Gil. Though he was keeping his eyes on a tandem bicycle ahead, he was looking too interested. Quickly she said, "It sounds as if Spence is desperate, but he wouldn't —. Is it so hard to believe that some people go to the library just to read the books, not to filch them?"

"So did the professor in London read books," said Gil.

* * *

Outside her building she thanked him and started to shake hands, but he kept her hand in his and motioned inside. "I'm coming up," he said.

"I don't remember inviting you."

Still holding her hand, he guided her to the elevator. "Just for a minute, Professor. Official business."

Inside her apartment, he whistled softly. "Wow," he said, "do you have an Aunt Beatrice, too?"

She laughed. "No, but I have a good broker." She took the raincoat he was carrying and put it in a chair near the door to indicate it was to be a short stay.

He was walking around the living room, taking in the comfortable chairs, the crowded bookshelves, the pictures.

He eyed the Matisse. "An original?" and when she nodded, he said, "How about giving me the name of your broker?" Then he went to the bookshelves and looked over the titles. "Have you read all these books, Professor?"

"Some of them twice," she answered.

"But," he asked, "have you read all of them once?" He moved to the desk and peered at the engraving of Dickens. "A hero of yours?" She nodded. "What's this?" he said, looking at a framed sheet below the engraving.

"Oh — just a page from *Nicholas Nickleby.*"

"'For instance,'" Gil read aloud, "'you take the uncompleted books of living authors, wet from the press, cut, hack, and carve them to your powers . . . all this without his permission and against his will; and then to crown the whole proceeding, publish in some mean pamphlet an unmeaning farrago of garbled extracts from his work, to which you put your name as author. . . . Now show me the distinction between such pilfering as this, and picking a man's pocket in the street.' So Dickens didn't like plagiarism either?"

"He hated it!" Beth called after him.

He had wandered into the hall. "Just what I would have expected," he said, studying the engravings that lined the walls. "Matthew Arnold. Carlyle. Mill. Do you have a favorite?"

"Well — Mill. Because he said, 'To question all things . . . to accept no doctrine either from ourselves or from other people without a rigid scrutiny —'"

"Sounds good," he said, dismissing Mill.

Annoyed she said, "Official business, I believe you told me."

"Right. Thought I'd just make sure you won't have to entertain any disgruntled former students tonight."

With that, he made a careful search of the apartment, not missing anything. He looked in the shower, under the bed, behind the clothes in the closet. "Nice wardrobe," he commented once. "Lots of shoes." He studied a pair of gold sandals with four-inch heels. "Aren't shoes supposed to mean something Freudian?"

"Any more insights," she said, taking the sandals from him, "and I'll think Marylou Peacock plagiarized from you."

She closed the closet door, but not before he observed, "Nice dress, the blue one. Wasn't Miss Garden wearing something similar this morning?"

"She was not," Beth said coldly. "Ida and I don't dress the same way at all."

"You seem to disapprove of your colleague."

"I don't disapprove of her," Beth said quickly, "only with the way she sees every setback as part of the war between men and women."

"For example?" He opened a corner cabinet, and a pile of crossword magazines spilled out on the floor. "You like puzzles?" he asked.

"Oh — sometimes. For example," she said, as they picked up the magazines, "Ida was assigned 8:00 A.M. classes for three straight quarters. A mix-up, that's all — and it was straightened out — but Ida says it was blatant sexism. Always sexism," said Beth. "Last week Ida told me that if scientists weren't so sexist penicillin would have been discovered twenty years earlier."

"I don't — oh, I see." Gil put the last magazine in and closed the cabinet. "She means a woman would have discovered penicillin."

"Exactly — and she's probably right. But Ida overdoes it — just a bit — when she says it's too bad penicillin made it possible for so many male chauvinists to survive."

"Lots of hostility there," he said. "Perhaps a stress reaction?"

"Still Freudian, I see. Me, I like simple explanations. Ida's furious because she wasn't promoted and that, too, she blames on sexism."

"*Is* that why?"

"Midwestern," Beth replied, "is no different from any other university. The place is a hotbed of sexism. However," she added, "Midwestern needs more token women. There's only one reason Ida wasn't promoted — she hasn't published enough."

Gil went over to the bay and pulled the curtains back. Beth walked over slowly and stood next to him, looking out the window. The street was quiet. Only a boy and girl strolling hand in hand under the trees. While they watched, the girl blew the seeds of a dandelion into the air. It must be the first dandelion of the summer, Beth thought.

Gil closed the curtains abruptly. "Does Miss Garden need money?" he asked.

"I haven't the faintest idea."

There was a silence. Beth felt vaguely depressed. The truth was someone was stealing books. She hated to think it might be someone she knew.

"I think you can rest easy tonight," Gil said. "I see you have no messages."

The machine. She couldn't believe she had forgotten to check for messages. But now she saw that the red light shone steady and unblinking.

"You know," she said, walking to the door with him, "all this searching — cloak and dagger stuff. I thought you weren't taking my phone call seriously." She handed him his coat.

"Are you going to the library tomorrow?" he asked.

"Yes. Why?"

"I'll pick you up. Nine all right?"

"I suppose so. But why?"

"If you're determined to keep on with your detective work, it might be a good idea to have company."

"I thought you weren't taking the phone call seriously," she repeated. "You've also given me the impression you think the plagiarism is trivial."

"Correct on both counts, Professor," he said, opening the door. "However, I also think that Marylou Peacock's murderer doesn't want anyone looking into her affairs, for any reason."

For a moment he stood in the doorway, looking at her. Very gently he brushed her hair off her cheek, tilted her face toward him, and kissed her. Then he walked out, closing the door behind him.

"Double-lock it," he said.

* * *

Before she fell asleep it occurred to her that he had made up the observation about the blue dress just to get her to talk about Ida.

11

"WHAT?" SAID ARTHUR HEWMANN. "YOU HAVEN'T READ *Conundrums in Marginalism?* My dear Goldberg, an egregious omission," and Arthur fell happily into one of his "Haven't you read?" inquisitions that always made Beth want to snap that she spent her leisure hours reading Barbara Cartland. Spence, however, listened with every appearance of interest as Hewmann talked, raising his voice so he could be heard.

Summer redecoration had begun, and a painter had taken over the English office. After shoving the furniture every which way, he had topped a stack of bound dissertations with his radio and turned it on full blast. Arthur, after demanding in three languages that the painter turn off the radio, to be answered each time with a blank look, had thrown up his hands. So "Garbageman" belted the room, while the painter placidly covered the walls with a new and hideous color. ("Artichoke Green, darling," Dot had told Beth. "And I don't know who picked it. Probably the Dean.")

Though the blare, combined with Arthur's high-pitched harangue, made it hard to concentrate, Beth refused to be annoyed. For one thing, it was Tuesday, and she had always agreed with Lewis Carroll that Tuesdays were good days. For another, she had spent the last few hours reading Mark Twain's letters, which gave her the pleasant feeling she always got when she grappled with an intellectual problem. Finally, there had been her morning walk to the library with Gil. She pondered the point that a walk she took every day could be charged with excitement, that almost anything — a pajama clad man fishing the morning newspaper out of the bushes — could be something to laugh about.

"What's funny?" asked Noel, who had just come in. He was wearing tennis clothes, and carrying a racket.

She shook her head and he didn't pursue it. Instead, he bent to read the title of her book. Raising an eyebrow at Mark Twain, he sank down next to her on the sofa, opened his briefcase, and began correcting proofs of his latest article.

And Noel makes six, Beth thought. A full hour before the meeting and except for Porter all the faculty had arrived. On the far side of the room, where the painter had not yet encroached, Ida fed the copying machine page after page. Closer, next to the mail boxes, Livy, frowning in concentration, paced a few steps, murmured "Intimate distance," paced a few more steps and murmured "Social distance."

Dot charged in, puffing on a cigarette. "For you, Potter," she said, holding a large book out to Livy. "Opened it by mistake." She looked at the title. *"Body Movements in Public?* Is it anything like *Love Is A Grapple?* Talk about body movements!"

Looking as if he'd like to grapple Dot into silence, Livy said desperately, "Please, I'm not ready to make my research public." He began mumbling incoherently about "idea robbers" and "thought pirates," and might have gone on indefinitely had Ida not left the copying machine and confronted him.

"You, Potter," she said bitterly, "can afford to spend all your time on research. You've got tenure — how you got it I'll never know — but if you don't start revving up your teaching, some day the Midwestern Department of English will have a lawsuit on its hands, all because of *you,*" and she jabbed a vicious finger into Livy's velvet vest.

"What are you talking about?" said Livy, retreating from Ida's jabs and almost falling into a can of paint.

"Don't you read the paper, or" — Ida looked meaningfully at *Body Movements* — "are you too wrapped up in your silly kinesics?" She watched scornfully as Livy jammed the book into a satchel labeled My Bag. "Don't worry. I'm not interested in your paltry ideas. I'm talking about today's headline — Sues For Right To Knowledge" — and Ida loudly recited the case of a pre-law student at the University of California, Beachside Branch, who was suing the English department for incompetent teaching.

By this time Ida had all their attention. Beth had closed Mark Twain. Noel had allowed the proof sheets to dangle over his knees. Dot stood in the doorway watching.

It was Arthur, however, who galloped into the conversation. "She's right, you know."

"Thank you," Ida said. "At last I'm right about something."

"These are litigious times in academia," said Arthur, ignoring the interruption. We should all —" and (with frequent citations of Harvard) Arthur went on to give Livy a lecture on quality teaching.

Livy, during Arthur's talk, had busied himself stuffing *Body Movements* under the other books. Now, as the speech ended, he buckled his satchel defiantly, got up, and, navigating around cans of paint, crossed the room to Arthur. "And what," asked Livy, pulling himself up so belligerently that his five foot stature seemed for a moment like six, "makes you think you are so pedagogically tiptop — *Professor Nembutal?*"

There was a shocked silence. The words "Professor Nembutal" seemed to hang over the room. For Livy, goaded first by Ida and then by Arthur, had broken a taboo and quoted a notorious comment from Arthur's student evaluations.

In the final class of each quarter, faculty were required to hand out forms that asked such questions as: Did the professor seem genuinely enthusiastic? Did the professor make the material interesting? How could the professor improve the course?

Once students understood they did not have to sign their names, they reached for the forms with the frenzied eagerness of the huddled masses yearning to breathe free. Here was the chance to pay back the prof for the humiliating comment, the slaughtered paper, the low grade. At the end of the year, their answers were compiled in a paperbound book, which the Dean had titled *Guide To Your Professors*. He could not have foreseen it would be shortened to GYP.

Everyone on the faculty pretended not to read GYP. Everyone did read it, but — except for devilishly apt comments, like Arthur's Professor Nembutal, which somehow worked its way all over campus — no one, it was understood, ever talked about it. For the faculty were far more thin-skinned than they claimed. Good evaluations could not help the untenured gain the great prize, tenure; but poor evaluations humiliated tenured and untenured alike. Even one unflattering comment was felt keenly as a loss of face in front of one's colleagues.

It was no wonder that Arthur looked angry enough to get out of his chair and take a swing at Livy. And Livy — Livy looked as if he hoped Arthur would try.

"Last quarter," Beth said quickly, wondering why she felt it was up to her to keep the peace, "someone suggested I find a way to make class more interesting. If it was that music major who couldn't stay awake for more than two minutes — " "A narcoleptic perhaps?" Noel asked sympathetically.

" — I'd like to ask her how would she know if discussion was interesting. She treated the class like a motel."

"You shouldn't have supplied daily clean towels," said Spence.

"There are times, " said Noel, "when I'd like to write my comments about them. For instance, I'd like to tell the kid who said I should be more open to students' ideas that it's hard to be receptive to someone who thinks the Magna Carta first appeared in the *Norton Anthology.*"

"And I, " said Livy, diverted now from Arthur, "have a few things I'd like to tell Midwestern's star fullback who said the books were boring."

Someone asked how Livy knew it was the fullback, and he answered triumphantly, "Compared handwriting."

Nothing was said about Liyy's detection method. They were too taken up with his subject. Unintentionally, he had unleashed a torrent of feeling.

"I spent so much time listening to his theories about *Hamlet"* — Spence was talking indignantly about a former student — "I almost invited the kid to move in with us. And do you know what he said? 'Prof should be more available outside class'!"

"Come what may, Goldberg," said Arthur, "we must all be prepared to meet our students' needs."

Arthur had no right to be so condescending, Beth thought. Out of fifty comments on his courses, twenty-five were likely to be denunciations. "You know Spence's students love him," Beth said protectively. "What about the one who wrote that you should stay as sweet as you are?" she said. Too late she remembered that now Spence would know she read his evaluations.

Far from minding, Spence seemed pleased. "What about you?" he answered. "'Prof has a fascinating personality.'"

"It's the personal comments I hate," said Ida. "'Don't talk with your hands' — if they put pockets in women's clothes, then I'd have some place to put my hands."

Relax, Ida was told, they had all been dealt worse.

"Do you know," Arthur said rather enviously, "that someone once wrote that Porter's exams are like pulling out toenails?"

At that they looked around — but the door to the chairman's office was closed.

"I don't know that that's such a bad comment — the exam one I mean," said Noel. "Students respect Porter."

"And you, too, Noel," said Spence generously. "'Frazier's lectures, '" he quoted, "'are the best in four years.'"

"Some day," said Noel, with a grateful glance at Spence, "good teaching will be mandatory for tenure."

"And some day," said Ida, "the coach of the Chicago Bears will be a woman. Where's the incentive? It's publishing that gets tenure."

"It's strange," Spence said suddenly. "No other line of work has tenure. My father has sold shoes for twenty years, and if he doesn't keep up his sales, he could still get fired. It doesn't make sense to guarantee a job, but we still demand that guarantee. It can't be for the money — we could get better pay selling shoes. We need it for our egos. We want it so much, so desperately —" he gazed at the books that littered the room as though, if he stared long enough, they would supply him with some complex psychological theory he was trying to form. "I think," he said finally, "that someone would kill for tenure."

The strength of Spence's feeling and perhaps the truth of his remarks rendered everyone speechless for at least a minute.

Then Livy said, "Speaking of murder, Beth — how are you coming with Marylou Peacock's plagiarized paper?"

"*She* plagiarized!" said Ida. "And you're using a free summer to find the source? But then —"

Ida left the sentence unfinished, but Beth knew what she would have said — you have tenure.

"I know how you feel," said Spence. "People steal ideas all over the place — even recipes."

"Recipes?" said Arthur, giving Spence a strange look.

"Yeah," said Spence, looking embarrassed, "haven't you heard of recipe plagiarism?" He turned back to Beth. "But the girl is dead," he said. "Why risk hurting her family?"

He was right about that, Beth thought, feeling confused.

"Why bother anyway?" said Ida. "Everyone plagiarizes — not just students. It's just that everyone doesn't get caught. Take *Home Town Girls*" — Ida named a best seller — "*Pride and Prejudice* all over again, with some kinky sex."

Arthur pointed out pedantically that plagiarism was not borrowing a story line, that it was out and out copying of an author's original idea.

"Okay," said Ida, "but I still say everyone steals and always has, and that includes the biggies — Shakespeare, Coleridge. I can see following up when the source is obvious."

"Yes," said Noel, "like the one who copied the introduction from my last book."

"But," Ida continued, "when it's not obvious, why waste your time? I know what you do, Beth. Seven, eight hours in the library — maybe more. And what's the result when you do track it down? A bunch of silly excuses."

"You said it," said Livy. "Talk about chutzpah — 'The quotation marks on my typewriter were broken.'"

"Beth," Ida persisted, "don't you think you're getting to be like what's-his-name in *Les Miserables?*"

"Inspector Javert," said Noel.

"That's it — Inspector Javert. You're making a big deal out of the equivalent of a loaf of bread. Ideas are a dime a dozen."

"That's just it," said Beth. "Ideas are *not* a dime a dozen." And suddenly she no longer felt confused, for Ida, whether she knew it or not, had pinpointed the problem. "You act as if all they're stealing is a piece of paper," she said to Ida. "You'd be more indignant," she added, "if someone stole your first edition of *The Feminine Mystique.*"

"You're damn right I would — or my first edition of *Room of One's Own!*"

"But what plagiarists steal is more valuable than all your first editions. They're stealing someone's hours of pain. They're stealing" — she searched for words — "the synapses from the brain, the blood from the heart, the —"

"Stop her, someone," said Livy, "before she reaches the viscera."

"So that's why you're on this plagiarism kick?" said Spence.

"Yes," she said curtly, "that's why."

"You have a right to spend your time as you see fit, Beth," said Noel. "But are you sure it was plagiarism? Maybe the girl was just taking up an idea that was in the air anyway."

"Yes, I'm sure," said Beth, disappointed in Noel for doubting her, disappointed in all of them. "This was plagiarism," she said angrily.

"Uyuh — plagiarism. An interesting topic."

And in came Porter, dapper in navy suit and red and navy striped tie, immune apparently to the ninety-nine percent humidity. Behind him was Gil, wearing the suit jacket he had carried that morning.

"I recall a lawsuit," said Porter, "written up in Alexander Lindey's *Plagiarism and Originality*. Was it 1947? No — 1948. Fascinating business. The — uyuh — 'Hubba Hubba' case, a matter of song titles. The plaintiff — uyuh — 'Hubba Hubba' charged plagiarism against the defendant — 'Dig You Later: A Hubba Hubba Hubba.'"

"What happened?" someone asked.

"'Hubba Hubba,' of course lost. I recall the ruling," and to the astonishment of no one, except perhaps Gil, Porter quoted, "'Should the suspicion arise that the defendant's use of these strange words is the product of copying, it is immediately dissipated by the fact that five distinct hubba hubba songs were copyrighted before either of the songs in issue.' The judge who presided" — Porter paused — "was Rifkind. Yes," Porter nodded, "that is correct — Rifkind. A good man."

Having satisfied himself that he had delivered this information accurately, the chairman walked over and spoke quietly to the painter. Without a word, the painter put down his roller, turned off the radio, and ambled out of the room with a sidelong look in Arthur's direction.

"Now," said Porter, "to the business at hand. Some of you have already met Mr. Bailey as a Visiting Fellow. It is my duty to explain that Mr. Bailey is not precisely here to — uyuh — pursue the Fine Arts, that he is — uyuh" — Porter had an inspiration — "he is here to preserve them. Mr. Bailey is a Special Agent of the FBI, with Squad Two of the Chicago

Field Office, and he was called in originally to assist — uyuh — in the recovery of stolen books."

12

THE NEWS THAT AN FBI AGENT HAD BEEN CALLED IN TO ASSIST with the recovery of stolen books was received by the faculty with as much enthusiasm as an announcement that Torquemada had been summoned to instruct them on how to get along with students. Beth could almost feel the marshaling of fury. She had expected protest. She had not expected Spence, usually so amicable, to lead off the attack. Never had she seen him so red-faced.

"The FBI!" he said, in a voice like thunder, "invading our campus!"

Porter, who had taken a chair next to Gil, tried to say that Bailey should be given a chance to speak, but Spence, if he heard him, took no notice. He had removed his glasses, and now he waved them in the air wildly and began taunting Gil like a prosecuting attorney. "What steps have you taken so far?" he shouted. "Questioned our neighbors? Interrogated the janitor about our relatives?" He stopped abruptly, took a handkerchief out of his pocket, and started polishing his glasses furiously.

"No, no, Spence — Agent Bailey could be useful," said Arthur. "He could help Beth apply FBI methods to her plagiarist hunt. Right, Beth?"

Just like Arthur, she thought, always the liberal when it doesn't cost him anything.

"Hire a known plagiarist," Arthur continued, when Beth did not respond, "— I believe, Mr. Bailey, you call such endeavors undercover operations — to bait the hook for the other ones."

Several voices were raised following suit. Someone sarcastically quoted J. Edgar Hoover — "'The FBI is as close to you as the nearest telephone.'"

"Maybe closer," Spence said darkly. "Have you tapped our telephones yet, Bailey?" He put his glasses on and stared at Gil. Beth would never have believed Spence could look so terrifying.

They weren't giving him a chance, Beth thought, forgetting her own stabs at Gil the day before. She looked around the room, searching for something, anything other than Gil, to fix her eyes on. Automatically she started reading the jumble of notices on the office door.

Then she caught a movement from Gil's direction.

But before he could speak — "No, Bailey. Allow me," said Porter, as if it were a point of pride for him to restore order to a gathering that had erupted out of his control. "Quiet, please" — in a voice that would brook no defiance. *"Silence.* You are forgetting," he said sternly, "that Mr. Bailey is here on a mission that affects us as scholars and teachers."

"How as teachers?" asked Noel.

"Teachers and scholars require books," Porter replied, with an uncharacteristic lack of hesitation. "You must understand," he said, "that Midwestern's books are being, as it were, usurped — by dastardly interlopers. I myself saw the first straw in the wind when I opened *Hours In A Library* and found "Dr. Johnson" razored out. When I reported the incident I was told that such vandalism is not at all unusual. Horrifying enough, but next —" and he went on to tell them about the missing books, omitting only the connection with the English department. "Books," Porter said, in a tone that someone else might have used for speaking of Rembrandts, "are being stolen and sold, treated," he said contemptuously, "as over-the-counter merchandise — by thieves with no interest whatever in their contents. This arrogant trafficking in knowledge must be stopped! In a word," he looked at each of them, his expression grim, "we need Bailey to preserve scholarship."

"Scholarship indeed," said Arthur, who despite Porter's eloquence clearly intended to have his say. "Your point is well taken," giving the chairman a nod of respect, "but" — he paused significantly — "what does the FBI know about scholarship?" Leaning forward so that his Phi Beta Kappa key dangled prominently, Arthur turned to Gil. "What *are* your qualifications, Bailey? To work among books requires the knowledge of the academic who mingles readily with books, a knowledge" — he fingered the Phi Beta Kappa key — "beyond fingerprints and hooligans."

If Gil had been struggling to keep his temper all this time, he hadn't shown it — though at Arthur's "academic" Beth thought she caught a flicker of resentment that disappeared so quickly she could not be sure.

"Not to say you have no skills" — Arthur expanded on his theme — "but the skills your work demands are, shall we say, non-academic?" and he drew back his handsome head, extended his arms, took aim and fired an imaginary machine gun.

"Come on, Arthur —"

"Come off it —"

Spence, looking somewhat ashamed, and Noel spoke together, but Gil cut them off.

"You seem, Mr. Hewmann," he said lightly, "to have been watching reruns of old movies. You also seem to misunderstand my work. Squad Two doesn't deal in bank robberies. We're responsible for thefts of other negotiable securities."

"Is that what you call books?" said Arthur.

"Stolen books, yes, and any other stolen property worth more than $5,000, from truckloads of coal" — Arthur snorted — "to million dollar Cezannes — fine art, fine furniture, fine china."

"Fine china" — Arthur had been lying in wait. "Ah, now I understand. Let me congratulate you, Bailey. It must be your own Squad Two that foiled the dastards who made off with the München Restaurant Hummel collection. Owing to the tireless efforts of Squad Two, customers can once again nibble their schwartzbrot and gaze at insipid Hansels and Gretels in museum quality porcelain. That, according to the papers, was your latest triumph, and if I am not mistaken you traveled all the way to an oasis on the Kennedy Expressway to retrieve these *objets d'art.*"

"Thanks," said Gil, "but you're wrong. Our latest triumph was the recovery of a Tiffany floor lamp, and for that I traveled all the way to Oshkosh."

"Indeed." Arthur floundered a moment, muttering "all the way to Oshkosh," and said, finally, with mock admiration, "Then it *is* more than china figurines. No doubt you are also an expert on diamond Kiwanis pins."

"I can't tell a diamond from a zircon," Gil said without regret.

"More to the point," said Arthur, "what can you tell? Can you verify a fine painting? How would you begin to tell a real Picasso from a forgery?"

"To begin," Gil said, with a touch of sarcasm, "I'd look to see if the paint is dry — or if the stretcher has been cut within the last six months."

Noel, proof sheets between his knees, applauded loudly. "Bravo, Mr. Bailey. Come on, Arthur, admit defeat."

Grudgingly, Hewmann said, "I suppose they do give you some elementary training. But," he probed further, "are you trained in discerning a valuable book? How, for example, would you distinguish a true edition of *Sonnets from the Portuguese* — by Elizabeth Barrett Browning," he added kindly, "from a fake?" It was clear that Arthur was sure he had him there, and he looked around the room for appreciation.

"Do you mean fake," Gil asked, entirely unmoved, "or do you mean forgery?"

"I mean fake, of course," Arthur snapped.

"I rather thought — since you mention the Browning — that you meant forgery. I assume you're referring to T. J. Wise and the 'Reading *Sonnets*' scandal. Wise's edition of course was a forgery, and the paper — chemical wood with a trace of rag — was the giveaway. The typeface, too, of course: the broken-back *f;* the kernless *j.*"

"Bravo, bravissimo!" Noel called out. He rolled up his proof sheets in a businesslike way. "Now, Arthur," he asked, with the assurance of a first-rate leader of discussion groups, "can you develop the point? What precisely is a kernless *j?*"

"Or," said Livy, "a broken-back *f?*"

"Can you explain," said Noel, "the difference between a fake and a forgery?"

"Yes, yes," Hewmann said irritably. "I said fake. I meant forgery."

"Certainly you must have meant forgery, Mr. Hewmann," said Gil. "You are, I understand, a bibliophile?"

"I confess —" Arthur began.

"You confess?" said Livy. "I thought so!"

"— to a tyro's interest in rare books," said Arthur, glaring at Livy.

"Then perhaps," said Gil, "you can confirm my recollection about misprints in the first edition of *The Moonstone?*"

Beth knew Gil was watching Hewmann's reaction, but Arthur only looked, or pretended to look, puzzled. "Ah, *The Moonstone*," he said. "Collins's best of course, in point of suspense. Now it is very interesting that *The Woman in White*, not nearly so good a book, brings a higher price than —"

"You seem expert in so many fields, Mr. Bailey." Ida, who had remained silent all this time, headed into the conversation. "Had I known when we were introduced yesterday —" she glowered at Beth "— I would have asked about your own field. Can you explain why the FBI doesn't have more women agents?"

Ida's expression could only be described as deliberately grave. Beth remembered her praise of a recent study that concluded that women smile too much, and that men interpret a smile as a sign of submission.

Gil, however, did smile — politely. "Do you want to be an agent, Professor Garden?"

"What possible difference could that make?" Ida said, her face stony.

"As it happens," said Gil, "the FBI needs more women special agents."

"Are you trying to tell me that the FBI would hire me?"

"I am. I should think you have a good chance of being hired. Let me jot down a name —" Gil reached for a pen in his shirt pocket.

"No, no — don't bother," said Ida. "But if things don't change around here, I just might talk to you —"

"Any time at all."

It is no affair of mine, Beth thought, if Ida can switch so easily from literature to the FBI, nor is it my affair if Gil is interested in helping Ida who after all is not unattractive.

"I had a student who wanted to be an FBI agent," said Noel, "and he asked me for advice. I wish — what should I have told him?"

"To graduate from college," said Gil, "and —"

"He did graduate," said Noel.

" — and do something else for at least three years. Then walk into any of the fifty-nine field offices and apply. The FBI doesn't want raw twenty-two-year-olds. Professor Garden, for example, would have the experience, the maturity —"

Ida smiled — and caught herself.

Before anyone could comment, Dot reappeared in the doorway. "When's your birthday, Bailey?"

For once, Gil appeared flabbergasted. "Not for a while, Miss Drennan — November 10."

"I knew it," said Dot. "You're a Scorpio — like me — only I'm on the cusp. You're a true Scorpio. You know what that means?"

Gil said that he did not.

"Domineering. Successful. Sexy. You know what the *Tribune* said about us today? 'Windfalls, popularity, and achievement make you magnetic.' And I got a dividend on my Ameritech in today's mail!"

Everyone began to laugh. "Bailey," said Noel, "you may now consider yourself accepted."

"Frazier is quite right, Bailey," said Arthur. "You have so to speak been ratified, by reason of approval from our nominal head — our resident bwana — our permanent Grand Sachem. Miss Drennan is quite a fixture around here. She — " Arthur's voice wavered and he came to a halt. During his fanciful lecture, Dot had been looking at him with a scorn that had finally registered.

Giving Hewmann a look of disdain, Dot picked up a pile of manila envelopes and headed for the door. "I'm going to take these to the post office now, Professor DeMont — unless you need me for something."

Porter assured her that he did not, and Dot thrust her bag over her shoulder and started out of the room. "Oh," she turned and looked at Gil. "Let me know if you ever want any typing done, Bailey." The door slammed.

"You mentioned a first edition of *The Moonstone*," said Spence. He seemed calmer now, Beth thought, more himself. "How did Midwestern lay hands on anything that valuable?"

Gil told him that it was not at all unusual for alumni to bequeath collections that included valuable books.

"Well, if that's the case," Spence said, "we *should* start protecting our books, but" — with a hostile glance at Gil — "we can do that without the FBI. Porter said 'originally,' Mr. Bailey," Spence went on. "He said you were called in originally on book theft."

Gil said that was correct.

"That implies some change," Spence persisted. "What are you here for now?"

"I'm still investigating the thefts," Gil answered. "I am also," he said quietly, "investigating the murder of Marylou Peacock."

"I thought so!" said Hewmann. "The ladies' room skullduggery. Oh come, come, Spence, we can hardly be surprised considering the three-inch headlines this morning. On the other hand, Bailey, don't you think you're overreaching yourself — with a government probe into what amounts to *Enquirer* material. The month of June. A pretty girl. Obviously a campus *crime passionel.* I would suggest you look to the boyfriend —"

"Quiet, Arthur," said Spence, with a vigor and a reckless indifference to Arthur's vote on the Tenure Committee that surprised Beth and silenced Hewmann. "Seriously, Bailey," Spence went on, "why the FBI? Surely the murder is the province of the Vinetown police." He took out his handkerchief and began polishing his immaculate glasses.

"You're quite right," Gil answered calmly. "Under typical circumstances this murder would be a local police matter, but these circumstances —" He explained that there was reason to assume a connection between the murder and the book theft, and that he had received a formal request for assistance from the Vinetown police. Then he stood, looked around casually, meeting Beth's eyes for a second. "Now — merely as a matter of form — I'll need to talk with each of you in private."

"Interrogation!" Livy rose out of his chair, tipping a paint can and spattering green drops on Noel's proof sheets and Arthur's Brooks Brothers loafers. "Do you think I'm a killer?"

"Keep calm, Livy," said Noel. He picked up the can of paint and carried it across the room. "Bailey isn't accusing any of us of anything. Isn't that true?"

Gil said that he merely wanted to find out if any of them had seen or heard anything Sunday night that might prove useful.

"On the contrary, Bailey." Arthur finished wiping his shoes with a scarf he had found in Dot's desk. "It is my clear understanding that we *are* suspects, and I would suggest that you have found your way to the wrong department." He pointed the paint-streaked scarf toward South campus. "Try

Psychology. I understand they're doing some interesting experiments."

"Yeah," said Ida, "with rat behavior. Arthur's a fool," she said to Beth.

"I heard that," said Hewmann.

"Enough," Porter said, in a voice so chilly that even Arthur didn't dare challenge him. "Allow Mr. Bailey to proceed."

During the excited discussion, Beth had been thinking her own thoughts about her colleagues. She had tried casting each of them for murder. Spence. Arthur. Ida. Noel. She looked at the chairman. Mustn't leave Porter out. In novels everyone is a suspect. He had taken out his pipe and was talking quietly with Gil. Impossible. She couldn't imagine Porter — or any of them. These were English faculty, teachers of the humanities, people, or so cliché had it, who took their emotions second-hand, from novels. A cliché, she mused, that the hostilities of the last hour had refuted. Her mind swayed back and forth. It was not possible that people she talked books with, ate with — . She thought about dinner with Ida last week. Would a killer order a broccoli omelet? Beth laughed aloud.

"For chrissake! What are you laughing about?" said Spence.

"Omelets," Beth said crazily.

"Professor Austin," said Gil, "I'd like to talk with you now."

13

Gil looked up briefly as Beth came in, and motioned to one of the chairs. She sat back, trying to appear more composed than she felt. It struck her that the chairman's office without the chairman had an entirely different feeling. A bewigged Samuel Johnson still looked down wisely from the wall. The ivy still invaded the window, open today against the tropical heat. But now Gil occupied Porter's desk and the atmosphere of tranquillity had been sent packing.

He had taken off his jacket and folded it neatly over Porter's eighteenth century globe, but even in shirtsleeves he conveyed a governmental authority that made Beth feel as if she were on trial. She looked around uneasily, almost expecting to hear a clerk announce that court was now in session. The telephone rang and she nearly jumped to attention.

Gil lifted the receiver. "Bailey," he said. "Yes, I know. Yes? I thought so. That much?" He whistled. "Thanks. No" — he glanced at Beth — "just beginning. I'll call in later." He put the receiver down, and scribbled a note.

Beth crossed her legs, felt the weight of the two Mark Twain volumes in her lap. She tried to tuck the books next to her on the chair, changed her mind, and put them on the floor.

Gil paid no attention. He closed one notebook and opened another. Then he put on a pair of glasses. They gave him a scholarly look that Beth, had she not been feeling so jittery, might have found attractive.

"I didn't know you wore glasses," she said absurdly.

Gil ignored the comment. His face was serious, contained, almost, she thought, as if he were trying to make up for any lapses from officialdom last night or this morning.

He glanced at his notes. "Your name," he said, looking up at her, "is Elizabeth Marie Austin, and you live at 2515 Greenleaf Avenue, Vinetown?"

He was playing it straight. Okay, so would she. "My full name," she answered, "is Elizabeth Marie Amelia Austin."

"I didn't know about the Amelia. Unusual to have four names," he said, unsmiling, and wrote something in the notebook.

Beth thought about telling him that her mother had not only believed that a woman could do anything — she also believed in hedging her bets. Therefore: Elizabeth I. Marie Curie. Amelia Earhart. "The Amelia belongs there, too," she said firmly, and to herself, she said, Amelia's *solo* flights were her greatest achievements.

"You are," Gil said, "a professor of English at Midwestern?"

"Associate Professor."

"Your previous employment?"

"Assistant Professor of English. Princeton University."

"For how long?"

She named the years.

"Before that," he said, "what was your previous employment?"

"How far back," Beth asked, her voice deliberately cold, "do you want me to go?"

"As far as you can."

"Before that, research assistant, Victorian journals project, Princeton, two years." She hesitated. "And before that," she went on, "ice cream vendor — two years."

He gave her a quizzical look. "That doesn't seem to fit the job pattern."

"Summers only, I should have said, when I was in college. The Ravinia Festival — music under the stars? Should you care to verify this, Mr. Bailey, the favorite ice cream two years running was Trilby mousse —" and suddenly she could taste the creamy marshmallow, see the trees illuminated against the dark sky, hear the music and feel herself falling in love. No man she then knew could compete with the buoyant Seiji Ozawa. Everything about him — his lithe frame, his mod haircut, his dancing black hair — tallied with his freeswinging podium style. It is always the whole picture, she thought. Every piece has to fit. Gil, for instance, would be wrong if he had a beard or wore a gold chain.

"What about you, Mr. Bailey?" she asked impulsively.

"What about me — what?" he said, surprised out of officialdom.

"What did *you* do in the summers? Good Humor man?" she suggested. "Chimney sweep?"

"Close," he said, breaking into a smile. "I was a book duster at the Gotham Book Mart."

"And after that —?"

"After that what?"

"What did you do before you began secret agenting?"

He took off his glasses. "Look, Professor," he said. "I'm asking the questions."

"I didn't know you wore glasses, Mr. Bailey," she said, smiling.

"And I," he said, meeting her eyes head-on, "didn't know your name was Amelia. And I don't — wear glasses, I mean. These" — returning them to his shirt pocket — "are clear. Useful," he said, with a look of mock reproof, "for when I'm questioning uncooperative subjects. And the name is Gil."

He loosened his tie and sat back in the chair, stretching his long legs.

"Now, Professor," he said cheerfully. "I want you to tell me how you spent Sunday night — from six o'clock on."

He sat quietly, waiting, humming under his breath. What was that tune?

"On Sunday night at six," Beth said finally, "I was eating dinner."

"Where and with whom?" he asked quickly.

Suppressing a desire to invent a cultivated man and an evening at Le Français, Beth answered, "Home and alone."

"And after dinner," Gil said, "you went out?"

"No."

"What did you do?"

Beth thought back to Sunday night, remembered that she had thought about calling Noel to ask if he wanted to see *The 39 Steps* at the film festival, changed her mind, finished three crosswords, started a fourth, then — "I watched television," she said, looking over Gil's head and out the window. A bicycle whizzed by.

"What did you watch?"

"If you must know," Beth said, looking past him at the neatly arranged books on Porter's shelves, "I watched *Now Voyager.*"

"That wasn't on Sunday night."

"How do you know?" Beth returned.

"I was watching television myself, Professor."

She looked out the window. The rider was getting off the bicycle. He looks like Thorpe McBride, Beth thought idly. Gil was waiting for an answer. "Nevertheless," she said, "I was watching *Now Voyager* — a tape," she said uncomfortably.

He looked at her closely. "What do you remember about the movie?"

Startled, Beth blurted out, "I remember that Bette Davis plucks her eyebrows and men fall in love with her."

Gil roared. "Funny — I remember that Paul Henried kept lighting two cigarettes at once."

Beth told him she saw why he remembered that.

"But," said Gil, "as Professor Hewmann would surely say, we digress. *Now Voyager* is a long movie. You must have been watching until nine-thirty."

It was at least eleven, Beth said to herself. He doesn't know about the crosswords.

"And then," said Gil, "no doubt you began to read some scholarly work?"

"And then," said Beth, "I watched a tape of *Lady In The Dark*" — and she thought about Ginger Rogers saying that she needed a man to lean on.

Gil gave it up. "When you are not watching tapes," he said, "I presume you spend a great deal of time in the library?"

She answered yes, sure that his amused look meant that he saw her as a hermit, either sitting in front of a television screen, or brooding over a book.

"Did you ever see Marylou Peacock there?"

"I never saw her anywhere," Beth answered. "I didn't know what she looked like until I saw her picture." Beth thought of the young and confident face, smiling the way newspaper faces always smile, in eerie contradiction to the headlines above them.

"Did any of your colleagues know her?"

Did they, Beth wondered. She must have had a class with one of them, but — "I have no idea," she said.

He nodded, made a note. "By the way, Professor" — very casually — "did you receive any telephone calls Sunday night?"

Beth thought a moment. "Yes," she said, "one."

Gil asked who and she told him that Spence had called at about ten o'clock.

She thought he would want to know what Spence had called about, but he only asked where he was calling from. and she said the library.

"How do you know?"

"He said so —" She hesitated. "I suppose *you* think it's significant that he was in the library?"

"All your eminent colleagues were in the library, Professor."

A silence. Gil sat still, absentmindedly toying with Porter's paraphernalia. He picked up London Bridge and put it down. He picked up a book and looked at it admiringly. He was humming again — what *was* that song?

"Hewmann," Gil said abruptly, "seems interested in rare books. I don't suppose any of your other colleagues are collectors?

Confused by the sudden change of subject, Beth faltered. "I don't think — of course —" She stopped.

"What —?"

"It doesn't mean anything — Ida Garden collects first editions of feminist literature. In a very amateur way," Beth added quickly. "You don't suspect Ida?"

He didn't answer.

"All of us," Beth said earnestly, "are interested in books. Doctors have stethoscopes. Lawyers" — she groped — "have documents. Academics," she finished, "have books. They're our equipment."

"And some shoplifters," Gil said unsympathetically, "have baby buggies with false bottoms." He paused. "How old are Goldberg's children?"

Was he trying to banter her into revealing something incriminating about Spence? She felt hemmed in. She liked fencing with Gil, but not when the subject was her colleagues.

"Exactly what are you getting at?" she asked.

"I'm saying," he answered, completely unmoved by her caustic tone, "that there's equipment and equipment. And someone among your elite professorhood —"

"They aren't all full professors —"

" — is equipped with far more than an amateur's knowledge of books. He — or she — is also well equipped" — Gil smiled grimly — "with a sophisticated rabbit punch."

"You don't really think that one of them" — Beth looked in the direction of the outer office — "committed murder as some kind of crazy cover-up for book theft?"

"What have I just been telling you, Professor?"

Beth noticed vaguely how dark it was outside, how still, not even a lake breeze to stir the ivy. The room had become oppressively hot, and she was finding it harder and harder to reason clearly.

Gil got up. "Okay," he said, walking over to her chair. "You can leave now, Professor."

"Is that all?" Beth asked, sounding, she hoped, carelessly indifferent. "Don't you want to check me for laundry marks? — or lipstick brands?"

"No, and I also don't want to see your old dental x-rays. Or the label on the very pretty outfit you are wearing. You're confusing victim with killer, Professor. We know who the victim is."

"Are you going to tell me anything about who you think — ?"

"I'm going to tell you nothing — except watch it. Whoever zapped that girl knew exactly where to aim, right here" — he touched the back of Beth's neck — "just below what the medical examiner calls the *foramen magnum.*"

"All right," said Beth, shivering, whether because of Gil's touch or Marylou Peacock was uncertain. "I understand."

"Good." Smiling, he tugged his tie into place. "I'm going to call Professor Garden in now," he said, "and then I'll talk with your other friends, but I see no reason why that should interfere with our plans."

"What plans?"

"For you to give me an after dinner brandy. It's going to be a long day, Professor."

"You forgot something," said Gil, as she started to leave. He retrieved Mark Twain from the floor, and keeping the books tucked under his arm, he covered her hand with his. "Where are you off to now?"

"Plagiarism hunting."

"Oh yes." He made as if to toss Mark Twain into the wastebasket. "Watch yourself, Professor," he repeated sternly. "You're treating this murder like a Chinese puzzle. I tell you, the killer doesn't like what you're doing."

Beth tried to look pleasantly nonchalant. But it suddenly struck her — what if he was right? Well, she answered herself, what if he was? She still had to know.

"*Mon ami,*" she said flippantly, taking the books from his grasp, "'if you wish you may wait to put salt on the little bird's tail, but for me I do not waste my time so.'"

"*The Big Four,*" said Gil. "And you are not Hercule Poirot, flexing your little gray cells. And I am not the bumbling Inspector Japp. This is the real thing, Professor. On second thought," he said, "wait for me at the library. I'll pick you up about six. We'll have dinner."

"How will you know where to find me?"

"I'll find you."

Preoccupied, hardly noticing as Gil led Ida in, Beth left the chairman's office. She glanced in the other room, saw that Noel, Spence, Livy, and Porter were still there. They sat silently, looking as if they were in a dentist's waiting room. She decided to leave by the other door.

She walked down the corridor, humming Gil's tune. Softly, she intoned the catchy rhythm, murmuring, "Once you vowed — *you'd* never fall again" — the words came back in a rush. "Stay well-zipped — *not* to be zapped again. Now you're tripped — *totally* trapped again." She chuckled, and wondered if Gil knew what he was humming. She passed the empty classrooms, her mind delightfully full of Gil, opened the door and went outside. There, leaning against a tree was Thorpe, talking with the painter.

"Professor Austin," he called. "I thought you'd leave this way, toward the library."

It was too much. Everyone, even her former students, was obsessed with her affinity for the library.

"I've been waiting for you," said Thorpe. "Oh — this is my friend Smitty."

Beth said hello and the painter grinned.

"Well, Thorpe?" she said.

"Smitty's been telling me (All right, Smitty, it's not your fault they left the window open) about what's going on in there." Thorpe gestured toward the English office. "That's sort of what I wanted to talk to you about."

"Well?" she asked again.

He looked around. "Not here. Let's walk a little further. *Ciao,* Smitty."

Beth followed his look and saw Dot heading down the path toward him. They walked to the journalism building and stopped at the rose garden. For a moment Thorpe was silent. Then, his voice wavering, he said, "Professor Austin, I —"

"Thorpe," she noticed how white-faced he was. "Aren't you feeling well?"

"I'm all right."

"What is it then?"

"I didn't know who else to tell," he burst out. "I didn't really know her that well — Marylou Peacock. But we live — lived — in the same dorm. The day before she was — murdered we were having dinner together. And she told me — she told me —"

"She told you what?"

"She said to me, 'I could die tomorrow and be a contented corpse, because I've done one thing in my life I'm satisfied with.'"

14

No frisbee players on the meadow, and no outdoor classes either. Mid-afternoon and it had turned so dark it was as if someone had switched off a light. Thunder clapped overhead and Beth, who had been strolling along the path, picked up speed.

She heard another rumble, but this, she could tell, was stage thunder, coming from the drama courtyard. The theater players had resumed rehearsal, and a booming Faustus could be heard, summoning Mephistopheles to rise and serve him. Thorpe must be there somewhere, thought Beth, looking at the milling crowd of angels and devils.

She wondered now if she should have asked Thorpe more questions. But he had been in such a hurry. And Beth was so certain: Marylou Peacock's "I've done one thing in my life that I'm satisfied with" could only mean that the girl was proud of a slick plagiarizing job.

What kind of a person was Marylou Peacock, and why was she under so much pressure to excel? Beth had no answers to these questions, but she firmly believed what she had told Gil yesterday. Students plagiarized because they were afraid — either they dreaded slipping from the bottom rung of the ladder, or they were scared stiff they could no longer hold on at the top. Marylou, surely, belonged in the second category. But why was she so afraid she could not keep up her high grades?

"*Go bear these tidings to the great Lucifer,*" bellowed Faustus, breaking into Beth's thoughts. "*Say he surrenders up to him his soul so he will spare him four and twenty years, letting him live in all voluptuousness.*"

Faustus knew what he was bargaining for. What had Mary-lou hoped to gain? Had she set her heart on winning the prize? Whatever she had wanted, Beth was sure that Mar-ylou's "If I died tomorrow, I'd be a contented corpse" had nothing to do with her murder. The choice of words was a spooky coincidence, but coincidence only, and she had no intention of mentioning the incident to Gil. All that had happened was that Thorpe had bumped into Marylou Peacock when she was feeling elated. The girl's bravado, her arrogant boasting about her plagiarized paper, could be of no possible interest to Gil.

Still thinking about Marylou, Beth drew abreast of the drama courtyard just as Mephistophilis stepped to the microphone. His booming demand to Faustus drummed into her ears — *"But now thou must bequeath it solemnly And write a deed of gift with thine own blood."*

Write. She could not escape the word today. Students wrote papers. Faculty wrote books and articles and prayed they would be published. Publish or perish. The saying was substantially true, and everyone knew it. What else was behind Livy's avid research but the desire for promotion? And Ida's exaggerated contempt for all academic writing obviously sprang from the knowledge that failure to publish had cost her her job.

"Lo, Mephistophilis," Faustus cried out eagerly. *"I cut mine arm, and with my proper blood Assure my soul to be great Lucifer's."*

Had there been much blood? No, of course not. Gil had said a sophisticated rabbit punch had killed the girl. But *why* had she been killed? Beth still had the uneasy feeling that there was some link between the plagiarized paper and the murder.

Absurd. She was being thoroughly absurd. Gil was on the track of the murderer. She was merely looking for the source of the plagiarism, and she knew what she had to do. Broaden the research. Read the next echelon of Mark Twain criticism, the books that were not in Hub. By the end of the afternoon, the answer would come to light, and then, Beth promised herself as she hurried along the path, she would forget plagiarism forever.

A moment later she stopped abruptly. She had reached the foot of the broad library steps. It was here that the ambulance had pulled up, here where they had carried the stretcher with the girl's body. The murdered body, Beth corrected herself, as she stared at the pavement.

Another clap of thunder cracked over the campus. A drop of rain splashed on Mark Twain's letters. Beth ran up the steps and pushed hard on the revolving door.

Inside, the sleek modern foyer gleamed with a harsh brightness. Recessed spotlights exposed the worry lines on the faces of people gripping umbrellas, grimly preparing to brave the storm. Another cluster of lights caught the bald spot on the book-checker's head, as he pushed books past the magnetized bar, sliding them around the metal sign: PACEMAKER WEARERS WHO WISH TO BYPASS ELEC-TRONIC SYSTEM PLEASE SHOW PACEMAKER I.D. TO ATTENDANT.

Down the steps, level one was brighter still, but it seemed much more cheerful. The whole block-length area, flooded in noonday fluorescent light, exuded a reassuring busy-ness. Far ahead, in the Periodicals Room, readers sprawled in lounge chairs. Closer, within the long rows of the main card catalog, scholars in swim trunks and shorts bent over draw-ers of index cards. At the near wall, a blue-jeaned student, wastebasket in hand, eyed the ceiling warily. Beth watched him stand back, take aim, and center the wastebasket to catch the steady drip, drip, drip of the rain.

"Rain — that's all we need. Hi, Beth." Marge joined her, and they stood for a moment, watching the student center another wastebasket. Beth commented that the library must have an endless supply, and then wished she hadn't said it.

"Why Midwestern hired a flat-roof California architect," Marge began, and Beth tried to look sympathetic as she listened to Marge rampage over familiar ground. A Chicago architect would have known that in this crazy climate you need a pitched roof to let the snow and rain run off. Any day now there would be a flood in rare books, a ceiling collapse in Hub, all because Midwestern hired architects out of hot tubs in Beverly Hills. "Wait!" said Marge. "They'll be sifting through our rubble like they studied Pompeii. Have you seen the Wall?" — referring to a section of level three that had been replastered a dozen times. "Someone created a picture!"

Beth asked of what, but Marge told her that she should see for herself, that there were some who thought the picture ought to be preserved. "Not your chairman. Professor DeMont says, 'Uyuh — expunge that rubbish — uyuh — obliterate it!'"

Marge chattered on, apparently to no purpose, but Beth had the feeling she really wanted to talk about something else. "You've heard?" Marge said finally. "It *was* murder. They say it wasn't a rape — I don't believe it." Her darting black eyes, under their cover of bright green shadow, looked terrified. "I'm telling you," she said, "something like this —"

She broke off to stare at a man carrying a book whose title, *Sexually Abused,* was clearly visible. "Something like this,"

Marge continued in a lower voice, "triggers all the kookamungas," and she burst out with a jumble of library horror stories, of vagrants living out of the photocopy room lockers, of men stripping naked in Anglo-Saxon literature. "Even the staff is turning weird," she said, gazing distractedly at a damp patch on the wall. "Lenites is stop-searching students outside the lounge — claims they're smuggling milk cartons into the stacks. Someone is feeding obscenities into the computer — I never saw words like that on a bathroom wall!"

"Speaking of computers," Beth said resolutely, taking advantage of Marge's pause for breath, "I'm about to use LUIS — for the first time."

"You mean you don't know LUIS?" Marge's panic vanished. "Come on, honey," she said, once more the efficient librarian, and, ignoring Beth's protests, she walked with her to the cluster of Library User Information Service terminals, the computer catalog system, better known as LUIS. "Time you learned, because some day, honey, we won't have a card catalog. That's right," nodding her head for emphasis, "it'll be phased out. For all I know they'll be phasing the books out, too."

Beth sat down at a computer terminal and read over the directions. Then she typed *S =,* the command for subject search, followed up with *Clemens, Samuel,* and pressed the ENTER key. The screen lit up.

LUIS SEARCH REQUEST. S = Clemens, Samuel
NO SUBJECT HEADINGS FOUND

"That's impossible," said Beth.

"Let me see," said Marge, who had left her temporarily to tell the student to get more wastebaskets. "No, honey," she said, looking at the screen, "what you want is 'Twain, Mark.'"

"But why? In the card catalog it's Clemens."

"Tell me about it! For the same reason it's 'Buonarotti' in the card catalog and 'Michelangelo' on LUIS . . . By the way, why Mark Twain? What are you working on?"

"A rafting trip down the Mississippi," Beth answered, without looking up. She wished Marge wouldn't bellow.

Marge gave Beth a curious look, and then, "Hey!" she called to the student. "Put one over there. No — not there — " She walked over to the student and grabbed the wastebasket. "See you later, Beth," she called over her shoulder.

Beth corrected to *Twain, Mark* and pressed ENTER. The small black screen filled up with green print.

LUIS SEARCH REQUEST: S = Twain, Mark
SUBJECT HEADING GUIDE 27 HEADINGS
FOUND 1-18 DISPLAYED

    1 MARK TWAIN (1835-1910)
    2 ANECDOTES
    3 BIBLIOGRAPHY
    4 BIOGRAPHY
    5 BIOGRAPHY — JUVENILE LITERATURE
    6 BIOGRAPHY — LAST YEARS AND DEATH
    7 BOOKS AND READING
    8 CHARACTERS
    9 CORRESPONDENCE

```
10 CRITICISM AND INTERPRETATION
11 HOMES AND HAUNTS
12 JUVENILE LITERATURE
13 LIBRARY — CATALOGUES
14 MANUSCRIPTS
15 PLOTS
16 POLITICAL AND SOCIAL VIEWS
17 PORTRAITS, ETC.
18 SOCIETIES, PERIODICALS


TYPE LINE NUMBER FOR TITLES
TYPE g FOR RETURN TO GUIDE
TYPE m FOR MORE SUBJECT HEADINGS
```

"And type *h* for help," said Spence. He and Noel were standing beside her.

"*More* Mark Twain?" said Noel quizzically. "What are you up to?"

"Whitewashing a fence," Beth answered.

Noel looked surprised and a little hurt at her sarcastic tone. Then his eyes flickered with sudden comprehension. "Of course," he said, "your plagiarist," and he looked at the list on the screen more closely. "I'd start with plots," he said. "How about *The Mysterious Stranger?* Fits right in with the strange doings in the English department. What do *you* think?" — turning from the screen to look at Beth — "Does Mr. Bailey really suspect one of us?"

There was a silence. Noel's sudden subject change had caught Beth off guard. Trying to sound indifferent, she asked if the questioning were over. "He's finished with Spence and me," said Noel, " — and Ida. You didn't see Ida? She was —"

"One of us *could* be," said Spence. Could be what, they asked. "The murderer, of course," he answered irritably. "Turns out we were all in the library Sunday night."

Beth, remembering Gil's "All your eminent colleagues were in the library," felt her face turn red as she asked Spence how he knew that. "We had plenty of time to compare notes," said Noel, "while Bailey was questioning you."

"The question remains, however," said a voice in rich Eastern accents, "why?" They wheeled around. There stood Arthur, looking very contented with himself in his neatly-belted Burberry. His loafers gleamed, all traces of paint removed. "Why," he asked, smiling, "would one of us want to kill her?" He shook out his smart Knirps umbrella, splashing them with water, and repeated, "Why?"

"Obviously, Arthur — for the money," said Noel. "You know how the value of collectibles has soared."

"Or at least," said Spence, "that's what Agent Bailey thinks." His intense intellectual face, as he pronounced Gil's name, expressed extreme distaste. "Perhaps Bailey knows that most college faculty don't have money for the little extras, like baseball mitts, and piano lessons. And car batteries," Spence went on excitedly, "and a new furnace, and —"

"Bailey seems competent enough," Arthur said loudly, with the complacency of a man whose wife footed the bills. "He quite won me over." They looked at him, astonished. "But I mustn't let you detain me," he said. "I have an appointment with an extraordinarily able student. Typically Midwest of course. Lacks the benefits of a good prep school." He consulted his watch. "Just time to get up to my study. Fortunately, Bailey questions efficiently. He spent much more time, my dear Beth" — he tapped her on the shoulder with the point of his Knirps — "with you. I *am* happy. You spend far too much time closeted up with books. At Harvard they have a saying — 'The fledgling mind expands as much in the Yard as in the lecture hall,'" and Arthur sailed off in high spirits.

"You can always tell a Harvard man," Noel sang softly.

" — but," Spence finished, "you cannot tell him much."

Beth could feel them looking at her. She had swiveled around and was staring furiously at the computer. Spence bent to look at the screen. "What *did* the girl write about, Beth? Don't tell me — *Huckleberry Finn*. The Cliff's Notes are superb."

"Was it *Jumping Frog?*" asked Noel. "Students love to discover Christ figures in *Jumping Frog*."

"By the way," Beth turned to look at them, hoping she sounded more composed than she felt, "what are you two jumping into?"

Noel said he was going to finish correcting proofs. Spence looked at him with open envy. Then he scowled at the leather satchel he was carrying, so jammed with manuscript pages it wouldn't close. "Publish before I perish," he said. "You don't get tenure on half a book."

Beth watched them walk toward the elevators, Noel tall, confident, towering over Spence by half a foot, Spence head down, looking depressed, as if his satchel were weighing him down. She turned back to the computer. "All the modern inconveniences" — a line from Mark Twain popped into her mind. If LUIS were really convenient, she could merely type in a few key words — *Aunt Polly, Tom, Whitewash, Oedipal guilt* — press ENTER, and have her answer. As it was — she typed 10 for Criticism and Interpretation and watched gloomily as the screen blanked out for a second and then crammed itself with print.

Mark Twain and Mussolini; Mark Twain and Richard M. Nixon; Mark Twain and the Russians; Beth ran her eyes over several screensful of "and" titles. She pressed *m* for more: *Mark Twain at your Fingertips; Mark Twain at Large; Mark Twain at Work.* Beth dimly remembered that Mark Twain had despised literary criticism. What would he have said about the hundreds of volumes he had inspired? She kept pressing *m. Mark Twain in Germany; Mark Twain in Three Moods; Mark Twain als literarische Persönlichkeit; The Revolt against Romanticism in American Literature as Evidenced in the Works of S. L. Clemens* — the titles were endless. Some could be ruled out easily; the others — She took out a notebook and groaned inwardly as she stared at the packed screen. It looked as if she might have taken on more than an afternoon's work.

* * *

Beth banged her briefcase on the rubber casing. The doors slid back and she stepped inside the elevator. Two boys, shouldering backpacks, stared at her and then resumed their discussion. "The key to success in calculus —" said the taller boy, pausing importantly. The elevator stopped and Beth got off, straining to hear the end of the sentence. " — is don't let it scare you." That, honey, as Marge would say, is the key to success in almost anything.

Level three was a repeat of levels four and five. To the left, a long corridor extended to the East and North towers. To the right, a shorter corridor led to the South tower. Far

ahead, outside the North tower, a boy and girl, legs inter-
twined, were lying on the floor, talking. Closer, where the
corridors met, another boy and girl sat on top of the book
charge-out terminal. As Beth passed the girl playfully hit the
boy, and he caught her hand and kissed her. Maybe, thought
Beth, Arthur was right about June and a *crime passionel*.

She turned toward the South tower, and there was the
Wall. She saw why Porter was angry. Paint splatters and
plaster dust covered the carpet. But she saw what Marge
meant, too. The crumbling wall had been transformed into a
mural that depicted Picassoesque nudes. Beth lingered a
moment, admiring the deft hand that had brushstroked plaster chips into majestic breasts and thighs. Then she walked
into the stacks.

California architect or not, Three South, the circular tower
that housed American literature, was a scholar's dream. Tall
windows around the perimeter overlooked a pleasant mix of
maples and oaks and Gothic spires. Nestled between the
windows were reading alcoves and typing rooms. The mass
of the tower was taken up with bookshelves, stretching out
from the center like the spokes of a wheel, forming a dizzy
radial pattern that made newcomers feel giddy.

Beth walked purposefully around the circle, noting that
today the usually crowded tower was empty. There were
signs that the staff had taken advantage of the break to repair
the ravages of exam week. She could smell wet wool — the
janitors had been shampooing Coke® and coffee stains out of
the carpet. She passed a tiered wagon packed with books —
scattered volumes had been retrieved and arranged in order
for reshelving. At the row marked 817.4 she stopped, gazing
at the books in dismay. A good eighteen shelves of Mark
Twain!

Well — Beth opened her briefcase — she had to begin somewhere. She consulted her list, took a book from the shelf, and stood motionless — holding the book suspended in air. Though she could not say why exactly, she suddenly had the definite sense that someone was watching her. Instantly one of Marge's horror stories crept into her mind. Marge had been in the stacks, reading. She had glanced through a gap in the shelves — "and there was some pervert showing off his — his — privates." Probably Marge's over-active imagination, and the only point of the story was that the radial shelf arrangement allowed someone to come very close without being seen. Still, Beth felt very shaky. Only the petty feeling that she would be acting like a fool kept her from making a run for it.

She took a deep breath and forced herself to think. Then she returned the book to the shelf and walked slowly and deliberately to the middle of the tower. There she stood, the entire wheel offering itself for her inspection.

What she saw should have been reassuring. In the center, where comfortable chairs surrounded a continuous circle of upholstered footstools, were two readers, a boy reviewing a stack of index cards, and a middle-aged man Beth had seen before, a newspaper columnist who often did his research at Midwestern. She could see only one other reader, actually a dozer, fast asleep in the reading alcove, head so far down Beth could not tell if it was a man or a woman. Not at all unusual and clearly nothing to be afraid of. Then why did she still feel so unsettled?

Resolutely, Beth turned and walked back to Mark Twain. Quickly, without bothering to consult her list, she pulled a book from the shelves and began to leaf through the pages.

Gradually her fear dissipated, and holding the book open, she sank down on the carpet, the better to read.

She pored over old photographs — Mark Twain in bed, reading, smoking a cigar, Mark Twain playing miniature golf with Woodrow Wilson. She read old headlines — Mark Twain Amuses Congressmen, Advocates Copyright in Perpetuity . . . Mark Twain Goes to Bermuda But Denies He Is Ill . . . Mark Twain Dead At 74. Beth studied the last photograph of Mark Twain, ill, being carried off the boat at New York. How very grim he looks, she thought. Then she told herself to stop going off on tangents.

She glanced through several books that included specific discussions of *Tom Sawyer,* but resisted the temptation to read them then and there. For what must have been another half hour she looked through more volumes, stockpiling all the best prospects. Finally, she got to her feet and began gathering books. Something yellow fluttered to the carpet — a Vinetown parking ticket. As she put it on the shelf, she heard a pinging noise that made her jump. She wheeled around. Only rain drumming into a wastebasket. She was alone. The columnist had left, and so had the boy, and she had not even noticed. Almost alone. The dozer was still fast asleep — the steady breathing sounded clearly across the silent tower. No reason at all to be nervous, but still — well, get out of here then and get on with it.

15

Nor, Beth thought distractedly as she circled Five South, had Marge's California architect done so badly with carrels. Beth ticked off the good points of the closed studies — plenty of room, plenty of shelves. She was approaching Spence's carrel. Maybe she would stop for a fast hello, just to get rid of the jitters.

But Spence's study was dark. Beth glanced through the window, and saw among the litter of books and manuscript pages, something new. Propped against the file cabinet was a drawing of DADY, a huge face, wearing enormous glasses, supported by a tiny polka-dotted body. Another time she might have laughed. Now the child's drawing seemed part of the menacing atmosphere.

It was almost a shock to see that her study was as usual. Books. Typewriter. Everything in place. Kicking the door shut behind her, she sighed with relief as she dropped the heavy books on the desk. She pushed a pile of papers out of the way and arranged the books in neat stacks. Methodically she lined up the scholar's equipment: felt-tip pens, index cards, legal-size note pad. Only then did she allow herself to plunge into the first book.

At the end of an hour, she had moved back a century to the summer of 1874, when Mark Twain had begun to write *Tom Sawyer*. She was inside Twain's study, a cozy place, snug as a pilot house, high on a hill above Elmira, New York. There, removed from all noise, Twain was writing steadily, fifty pages a day. Beth read on, oblivious to the rain beating against her window. One night in September, Twain's writing came to a sudden halt. Though he had written only half his novel, try as he might, he could not make *Tom Sawyer*

proceed. He felt worked out, vacant, devoid of ideas; his
"tank," he said, had "run dry". . . . Exactly what it feels like,
Beth thought, when you are sure you will never write another
line. Absently she looked up at the door — and froze.

Was that a movement — a face — disappearing rapidly
from the window? For a few seconds she sat perfectly still.
Then she got up, opened the door and looked around, alert
for a movement. Her eyes met only familiar objects, the red
exit sign, the candy bar wrappers that had been on the floor
for days. Gazing thoughtfully at the tall forbidding shelves,
she considered making a survey of the entire tower, then
changed her mind.

She went back inside the carrel, got her key and was out
again in a moment. She slid the key into the lock, turning it to
the left so her study could not be opened from the outside.
There. No more seeing things. She could return to Mark
Twain with a sense of security.

He had pigeonholed *Tom Sawyer.* Not until the following
summer did he allow himself to look at the manuscript again.
It was then Mark Twain made his great discovery: When the
tank runs dry, you only have to leave it alone, and it will fill up
again in time. Fascinating. Was he right? But it brought her no
closer to the source of Tom's Oedipal adventure. Beth tossed
the book on the reject pile and reached for Marylou's essay.

It was remarkable, she reflected again, that Marylou, who
had never taken a psych course, had chosen to copy a mass of
pseudo-psychology.

> *Tom Sawyer* [Beth read] centers around the
> most important conflict a small child faces in
> relation to his parents, the *Oedipus complex.*

> Tom's budding sexual impulses are directed upon
> Aunt Polly who symbolizes the mother. . . .

As the carillons tolled the afternoon away, Beth plodded
through the essay again. The rival for "Mother Polly's" favor
was Tom's symbolic father.

> Twain returns obsessively to the father figure,
> symbolized by Sid, who tells on Tom, the
> schoolmaster who flogs him, and — most
> striking — *the fence.* In the legendary fence
> episode, the phallic rivalry is quite unmistakable.

Here the essay quoted the "extraordinarily hostile" phallic
passage.

> [Tom] surveyed the fence and all gladness left
> him and a deep melancholy settled on his spirit.
> Thirty yards of board fence nine feet high.

Thirty yards, rather, the essay declared, of father's phallus,
which Tom renders impotent.

> "Say, Tom. Let *me* whitewash a little."
> "No — no — I reckon it wouldn't hardly do,
> Ben. You see Aunt Polly's awful particular about
> this fence. . . . I reckon there ain't one boy in a
> thousand, maybe two thousand that can do it the
> way it's got to be done."
> "No — is that so? Oh, come now — lemme
> just try."

Annihilation of the father, the essay asserted, through extraordinarily successful schoolboy manipulation. Extraor-

dinarily silly, thought Beth, flipping the dog-eared essay across the desk.

She picked up another book and started serious "parallel hunting," looking for repeats of key phrases from Marylou's essay. After some time, she sighed and thumped the book shut. As usual, plenty of jargon, some literary and some psychological, but rather than Oedipal conflict, she had found only another discussion of an aesthetic conflict within Mark Twain, a battle between the serious artist and the buffoon. As a writer, the critics seemed to agree, Mark Twain was a split personality. Strong words. They conjured up a Jekyll-Hyde. Beth lit what she promised herself would be her last cigarette and pondered the meaning of split personality. Did Marylou Peacock have a split personality? Does a plagiarist have a split personality?

What was it like to be a plagiarist? She tried to imagine someone deliberately choosing to copy, looking through likely books, deciding on a chapter, stealthily making notes. Or was it the other way around? Did a plagiarist first look over the books and then decide to copy? Oh, what did it matter? Get back to it, she told herself irritably, reaching for another book. Maybe this one would develop the phallic fence.

Four books later, Beth lit a cigarette and stared moodily at the growing stack of rejects, exasperated because all her efforts so far had come to nothing, vexed because she could not rid herself of the feeling that she was missing something, some familiar turn of phrase. Restlessly, she rose out of her chair and stretched, tall to the ceiling, wide to the bulletin board. The carillons began ringing their hourly tune and Beth, arms still outstretched, counted. One. Two. Three. Four. Five. Six chimes. She had no idea it was so late.

Wondering what had happened to Gil, she shoved the books aside and leaned over her desk to look out the window.

Rain pelted the campus, turning walks and pathways into little rivers. Flowing tributaries had formed around bicycle racks and lamp posts. Far below, a girl forlornly pulled a suitcase through an ankle deep puddle.

Beth sat back and looked wearily at the books she had yet to read. Temporarily at least, they no longer held out the promise of discovery. Like Mark Twain, she was worked out.

* * *

The cleaning crew were gathered around the vending machines, talking about Wimbledon. "The British, see," said a janitor, gesturing with mop and pail as though he was pouring out tea, "are a very proper people —" He stopped talking and stared at Beth. She put her coins in the machine, waited for the cup to fill, and fled. But there was no refuge in the lounge. At the last table sat Livy, gazing out the window at the scurrying figures on the plaza, pausing now and then to write a note. Still holding her coffee, Beth walked quickly to the elevator and pushed Five.

TO COMPUTER BOOK TERMINAL. CAMPUS TELE-PHONE FOR EMERGENCY USE ONLY. Absentmindedly, Beth registered the signs as she walked to the door marked Women. Her mind was on the books she would look at next. Perhaps she should also look over some journals, the *Twainian,* or *American Quarterly.* Absorbed in thought, she set her coffee on the narrow shelf, opened her briefcase and took out a small makeup bag. Something bright on the floor caught her eye. She picked it up — a brass button. Where had

she seen one like it? And as suddenly as she remembered —
on the uniform of a Vinetown policeman — she also remembered that she was standing in the room where Marylou
Peacock was murdered.

All at once everyday objects took on a hideous significance. The roller towel. Had Marylou been drying her
hands? The mirrors. Had she been combing her hair, looking
at her reflection? Or had she perhaps put on lipstick, blotted
it, and turned to throw the tissue in the green metal wastebasket, when —

Beth tried to picture a body on the brown tiles. Feet under
the sink? Head against the wall? She leaned against the sink,
feeling more and more disconcerted, acutely aware of every
sound.

A toilet flushed in the adjacent men's room. She could hear
water running. Gradually she realized that she was hearing a
noise that did not belong, something other than the gurgle of
plumbing. Behind her. A scuffling sound. Coming from the
resting room. For the second time that afternoon, Beth
fought the impulse to run. She listened closely, but the noise
was not repeated. Perhaps she had imagined it. Surely what
she had been feeling was the same jumpiness that had
afflicted her all afternoon. Nerves, that was all, and she
would prove it to herself.

Slowly Beth walked toward the small room just off the
narrow entry. "Is someone in there?" she called out. She
tried to sound commanding, but her voice came out in a timid
wail. Keeping her hand on the doorknob, she called out again,
"Is someone in there?" Silence. She pushed the door wide
open. Complete darkness. She fumbled along the wall. What
would she do if instead of a light switch she felt a hand? But
her fingers touched only the switch. She clicked it on — and

gasped with horror. On the sofa. A body. Head lolling on the pillow, legs dangling over the side.

She took another look and let out her breath in one long slightly hysterical sigh. What a fool she was. In the dim light, a stack of books at one end of the sofa had become a head, and a raincoat, sleeves falling over the other end, had become legs. A forgetful student had left her belongings behind, and Beth's overactive imagination had dreamed up a phantom body.

Nothing at all — and still she felt alarmed. Beth washed her hands and splashed her face with water. The mirror reflected a pale face and messed up hair. She really wanted to leave. *No.* What had that boy in the elevator said? Don't let it scare you. She took out her comb, and began running it through her hair. Think about something else. The coffee cup on the edge of the shelf. The briefcase, balanced precariously between two sinks, catching soap drips. She put the comb away and rummaged for her lipstick.

A faint creaking from behind her made Beth jump and spin around. Her heart raced. She knew that sound. The resting room door had creaked precisely the same way when she had opened it. The lipstick fell from her hand, striking the tile with a light clink that seemed as loud as a tolling bell.

The creaking stopped abruptly. There is someone in there, Beth thought. *The sofa.* I should have looked under the sofa. The creaking resumed and Beth knew, as surely as she knew that she could not move, that if she looked around the corner she would see the door slowly opening.

"Austin!" A sudden shout from outside. "Austin!" Again the shout followed by a bold pounding on the outside door. The pounding grew louder and a high voice called out imperiously, "All right, Austin. Come out! I know you're in there."

Beth grabbed her briefcase. Leaving her lipstick under the sink, she ran out of the room, noticing in flight that the resting room door was closed.

Coleman Lenites, in a gray shirt the color of the library regulations book, paced back and forth furiously. The instant she came out, he pounced on Beth. "You thought you could get away with it!" His whole body, from the tiny mustache to the little pot belly, quivered with outrage. "You are *not*," he squealed, "to bring coffee out of the lounge."

"What coffee?" she had just wits enough to ask.

"Hmpf! I should go inside and collect the evidence." He stood, uncertain, looking longingly at the door. "Is anyone in there?"

"Yes. I mean no." She hoped he would go in.

He looked at her suspiciously. "No, Austin, I'm not falling for that," and he began shouting — "This is the third time I've warned you!"

Beth walked toward her carrel, Lenites trailing her, rattling out regulations about consumption of hot foods and beverages. She hardly heard him. Of course it had all been her imagination. Look at the way her imagination had tricked her with the books and raincoat. Just the same, never before had she been relieved to see Coleman Lenites. "One more offense," he shouted as they reached her carrel, "and you lose your library privileges!"

When they were well out of sight, a figure in the resting room rolled up a camouflage jacket and tucked it away. The figure stepped to the door of the women's room, looked up and down the corridor, slipped out and walked briskly to the elevators.

16

"So," Gil was saying, "*Tom Sawyer* is a filthy book —"

"They banned it in Brooklyn," said Beth.

"They did? When?"

"In 1905," she said, and he chuckled.

"Would you mind lifting your trays?" Obediently, they lifted, and the aproned, bespectacled woman began to wipe their table. Beth turned away from the well-used rag and looked out the window.

Outside the Student Center and just up the beach, the observatory light winked steadily; ten miles further, the Chicago skyline carved itself in gleaming silhouette. So clear was the night, now that the rain had ended, she could probably see the twin antennae on the Hancock, if she had been interested in looking closely. She was still feeling shaken, still trying to decide if she should tell Gil what had happened in the ladies' room.

She debated with herself, gazing abstractedly at a passing jogger, watching him cross the breakwater and sprint toward the lake. She looked beyond him at the water, so calm tonight you wanted to go for a swim. Winter, and the ice floes that would crowd the gray January lake, seemed as remote and improbable as — ladies' room interlopers.

And suddenly, as she watched the wavelets wash against the rocks and listened to the buzz of law student talk in the next booth, Beth felt at ease, convinced that nothing, really, had happened. The feeling that she was being spied on had fueled her imagination so that the creaking door had made her dream up a melodrama. The only reality was the Coleman Lenites entrapment and that was the stuff of comedy. She thought about the way Coleman kept interrupting his tirade to pick up candy bar wrappers and started to laugh.

She caught Gil's eye. He looked as if he had been studying her for some time. "I was just thinking about Coleman Lenites —"

"I've met him," and they both laughed so hard the food jiggled on their trays.

The woman stopped wiping and looked up, first at Beth, then at Gil. "It's nice," she said, her face softening into a smile, "to see such a happy engaged couple."

Gil smiled back. "How did you know?"

"I can always tell. It's something in the eyes," she said, as she stuffed the rag into her pocket. "I wish you every happiness."

"Thank you," Gil called after her.

The woman turned and smiled intimately at Beth who put down her tray so quickly some Coke spilled out of the paper cup.

"You've decided then," Gil resumed, "that *Tom Sawyer* should be kept out of the hands of small children?"

Beth pretended to mull it over. "It might be safe, if they cleaned up the fence episode."

"Out with the whitewash," said Gil. He picked up his beer and traced a broad arc in the air. "Make a clean sweep." Then he said more seriously, "But you're not giving up?"

"Never!"

"A whole afternoon locked in that cramped study and you have the heart for more?"

"It's not so cramped."

"If you haven't had any success so far," he said, "why do you think you'll ever find out?"

"But I have found something out," Beth said with some spirit. She put her elbows on the table and leaned forward. "Not only did Marylou Peacock not copy from the basic critical works — she didn't copy from major works in the next echelon either. Don't you see?" she said, responding to his quizzical look. "It's like working a crossword. First you fill in the easy blanks. Then comes the challenge. That means expanding my research —" She stopped at his smile. "What are you thinking?"

"I think you are very pretty and that Aunt Beatrice would have liked you. Aunty Bea admired persistence." He looked at her fondly, holding her eyes until she had to look away. It was then that she saw Ida and Porter at the head of the next aisle.

They watched Porter, casting his eyes over the room, while Ida waited indifferently, staring at the nearby tables. At that moment she spotted them and waved eagerly. But Porter, rather to Beth's relief, took a firm hold on Ida's arm and gestured toward a booth in the far corner. Ida shrugged her shoulders, gave Gil an arch look, and followed Porter with quick, reluctant little steps. As they sailed past, her face was thrown into profile, and for a fleeting moment Beth thought of the Wicked Witch of the West. But the idea of the witch with Ida's full bust made her want to laugh. Quickly she looked down at the tray Ida was carrying.

Funny, Beth thought. One day Ida eats granola and tofu. Tonight a milk shake and pie. Exactly like Ida's swings of mood. While Porter — arranged geometrically on his tray were a pot of tea, a plate of toast, and a salad — consistent with his ascetic spirit.

"Isn't that a somewhat unusual combination?" Gil asked.

"Tomato and lettuce?"

"Very clever, Professor. I mean your chairman and Miss Garden."

"Porter is probably advising Ida," said Beth. "It's especially decent of him," she added, "to take time to help her when he's so pressured."

"Pressured?" Gil looked interested.

"Relax, Inspector. Pressured because he's working on a new edition of *The Age of Precision*. It *is* pressure," she said, when Gil looked doubtful, "citing new studies, bringing footnotes up to date. All that takes time, and every minute with Ida —"

"What's he helping her with?"

"Finding a job. You see, Ida was on what's called a tenure track. That's what it means to be an assistant professor."

"Ah," Gil said wearily, "the academic hierarchy. Instructor," he intoned, "assistant professor, associate professor, professor. At the top of the heap," he continued, "the full professor with an endowed chair. At the bottom, the terminal instructor, who after three years must leave —"

"Or die."

"Please — one death is enough. But assistant professor," he went on, "that's different. After six years you come up for tenure. And if you are denied tenure, it is always because you have not published sufficiently in the Journals of Gobbledegookia."

"You're making fun of academic writing," she said, feeling on the defensive. "But there is good scholarship and it's important."

"Important! Why?"

"Scholars — answer questions."

"If you say so, Professor. I prefer action." He cocked his head speculatively. "Perhaps Miss Garden would like to make the FBI her second career."

"Her third," said Beth.

"What do you mean her third?"

"I thought you knew. Ida was a nurse before she decided to go to graduate school."

"A nurse! Where?"

"I don't — it was a long time ago. In Montreal — something Memorial. Did she say an Intensive Care Unit?"

Gil put down his beer with a bang. "An ICU? You're sure? What kind?"

"Yes — no — let me think."

She remembered only one conversation — it must have been at least a year ago — and Ida had talked mostly about how doctors exploited nurses. What else had they talked about? She tried to think, while behind her the law students quizzed each other on manslaughter and across the table Gil stared at her impatiently. "Yes," she said finally, "it was an ICU, something to do with neurosurgery."

Gil whistled, took out his notebook, and began writing rapidly, all the while muttering under his breath about spinal cord units and pressure points.

"You're being silly," she said, as he put the notebook away. "Everyone knows karate." She pointed at the bulletin board behind him.

Tilting his head back, he began reading the notices aloud. "Biking — Wisconsin. Hiking — Indiana dunes. Friday night, *The Hound of the Baskervilles*. Wrong case," he said, " — some scholarly groaning, maybe, but so far no baying at the moon."

"Keep going."

"Summer lifeskills courses. Tap dance. Wine appreciation. Relationships and sex!" he said enthusiastically. "Maybe we could audit."

"Oh my God! The *bottom* row."

"It's much more than self-defense." His voice took on a note of excitement. "Midwestern Karate Club. Come for a demonstration class. Karate is a great way to get in shape. It's an art, it's a sport —" He trailed off and confronted her. "Are any of your friends members?"

"Not now. At one time or other" — she hesitated, feeling like a traitor — "I think almost everyone took it up." She hurried to explain. "Noel and Spence wanted to work off tensions, Livy wanted to observe expressions when they punched and kicked. Arthur said he wanted —" Gil was pulling out the damned notebook " — to perfect his concentration. Not Porter, though," she said quickly.

She wished he would stop writing. "I wonder why Ida didn't tell you she was a nurse." He didn't answer, so she asked how the questioning had gone.

"Did you know," he said, still writing, "that your colleagues aren't nearly as excited about plagiarism as you are?"

"You asked about that? I thought you weren't interested."

"I'm not," he said, putting away the notebook, "and neither were they, none of them, including your chairman. 'Uyuh — most certainly — plagiarism is thoroughly dishonorable. Nonetheless, we will always have some few students who succumb — merely out of confusion. Beth — uyuh — Professor Austin — tends to be — unduly inflexible.'" Gil sat back. "When it comes to plagiarism, Professor, your colleagues heave a collective yawn."

Suddenly she was angry. Porter's remark had stung. She hadn't expected that of Porter. "Yes," she said slowly, "I suppose plagiarism — student plagiarism — does bore them." She sat up straight. "But they would be absolutely riveted if one of *them* were caught plagiarizing. 'Disgrace to Midwestern!' 'Fire the scoundrel!'" The voices in the next booth had stopped. She waited for the law students to continue their conversation and then resumed in a furious whisper. "*That's* what they'd say. And whoever it was would be out on his ear — collecting unemployment before you could say NEH."

"Aren't you exaggerating? They wouldn't sack someone just —"

"Don't bet on it. That's one crime that's not tolerated. Maybe," she said, reviewing her academic memories, "the only one. If Spence showed up for class drunk, they'd say deplorable, but that's all. If Arthur squeezed a pretty girl —"

"Has he?"

"Just campus scuttlebut. As I was saying — anything goes. If Porter ran naked up and down the library plaza, they'd be surprised — but not indignant. You don't get fired for peccadilloes. But plagiarism. Pass someone else's words and ideas off as your own and you're an academic outcast." She paused. "Ever hear of Jonathan Korretsky?" He shook his head. "Professor of English at Columbia. Age 33, and they were already calling him 'distinguished.' He had a list of publications a mile long."

"What does that have to do with —"

"Korretsky was all set for an endowed chair at" — she named an Ivy League university — "and he slipped. Just once. He published yet another long and distinguished article. This particular article, however, was plagiarized, *and* someone found out. Bang. The endowed chair offer was withdrawn. Bang. Korretsky was booted out of Columbia. And now, as far as I know, Korretsky is teaching Beowulf in Cuernevaca."

"Isn't that quite a Waterg — rumpus, over one article? Maybe Korretsky got his notes mixed up. Maybe he read something and it slipped his mind."

"You sound like a plagiarist yourself, Inspector. I'm not talking about a few sentences. I'm talking about ten identical pages."

"But why? He must have known he'd get caught."

She paused. The same question had bothered her. "I'm not sure. Unbalanced, I guess. Or desperate. Desperate," she repeated. "Look, what can you tell me about Marylou Peacock?"

"Why are you so curious? Isn't the paper enough to go on?"

"I'm curious because it's not enough — so far. I still have lots of possibilities to follow up. It's funny. In some ways the writing is so sophisticated. In other ways" — she tried to find the right word — "it's so sophomoric, so *green.*"

"Do you want me to infiltrate Beta Chi? Check the files for a phallic fence?"

"It's not the kind of essay that comes out of fraternity files," she said impatiently.

He gave her an appraising look. "You're serious about this, aren't you? Is it because it's such a challenging puzzle?"

"Partly," she admitted. She hesitated and then said decisively, "But mostly — it's because I prize ideas."

"Okay. I respect that. And I respect you," he said, giving her an admiring look. "But I wonder if you're taking too academic an approach?"

"Meaning what?"

"Did you ever think of going up to the girl's study and looking inside?"

"Undergrads don't have carrels."

"That may be. But Sunday night Marylou Peacock was typing in carrel 5710 and —"

Beth had stopped listening. She had formed a mental picture of Five South and was walking around the circle. "That's Arthur's carrel!" Gil nodded. "What was she doing in there?"

"You tell me."

"Sometimes," Beth said thoughtfully, "Arthur uses his carrel as a carrot." Gil asked what she meant. "When he and Penelope go to England," she said, "they get a student to house-sit, but they don't like to pay —" She thought of Arthur and the vague research project that always kept him at the library. "Then where was Arthur?"

"Reading in the poetry room, he says. So far I can't find anyone who saw him there."

"Why didn't he tell me he knew the girl?" She felt cheated. Who else had known Marylou Peacock and hadn't bothered to say anything? "Did you notice if there was —"

" — any Mark Twain literature in the carrel? No. I looked. All the material was Hewmann's."

"You're sure? Well, thanks for looking." Then it struck her — "Then you do think it's important!"

"Important," he admitted, "in the sense that — I'm worried about you." His voice suddenly was very low.

"Hello Beth — Bailey." Noel slid into the booth next to Beth and put an arm around her shoulders. "How's the computer search?"

Beth leaned back almost gratefully. It felt comforting to rest a moment against Noel. She looked at him. In profile, with his distinct French movie star features, he resembled a young Louis Jourdan. Then she thought how Noel, who took such pride in his Illinois origins, would smile if he could read her mind. "It's coming along," she said, and he gave her a friendly pat while Gil looked at him balefully. Noel withdrew his arm and began fingering the cover on his coffee container. "Join us?" said Beth.

"Yes," said Gil, moving over about two inches.

"Thanks" — Noel gave Gil an amused look — "but I'm meeting Spence." He glanced across the crowded room. Far in back, in a huge booth meant for five, sat Spence surrounded by papers and what looked like several hours of coffee cups. While they watched, he wadded up a sheet of paper, threw it across the table, tore off another sheet and began writing furiously. "Spence and I are going to launch an attack on the Walt Whitman chapter," said Noel.

"So far," said Beth, "it looks like the chapter is winning."

"I suspect it only needs some recasting. He thinks it's hopeless —"

"When are we going to start?" Spence stood there, sweaty, wild-eyed. He greeted Beth hurriedly, pointedly ignoring Gil. "Well?" He looked at Noel who rose and pulled two cigars out of an inside pocket. He handed one to Spence and kept the other. "I remember," said Noel, "when my father wanted to think, he used to walk along the river. He'd amble along meditating and smoke a pipe of Prince Albert. Someone claimed he saw him fall in the water, go down, and come right back up with the pipe in his mouth." Noel put an arm around Spence. "Come on," he said. "We'll walk along the lake. We'll smoke a cigar, we'll talk."

"ANYWAY," BETH SAID WITH SOME SATISFACTION, "HE ISN'T your thief — that's obvious."

"Who? Frazier? Why is it so obvious?"

"He'd hardly be so friendly, if —"

"Friendly — that's an old ploy."

Beth, who ordinarily would have defended Noel against the implied accusation, suddenly remembered. "What happened to Marylou Peacock's work? And how do you know she was typing?"

"I don't know to your first question. To your second — the one thing everyone agrees on is that the sound of erratic typing was coming from that study. Oh yes, and occasional rings from Goldberg's carrel — I must follow that up."

"Don't bother," she said, laughing. "Spence keeps a kitchen timer in there."

"So that's — for God's sake, why?"

"He sets it for fifteen minutes. 'Rrring' — stop revising. 'Rrring' — start another page." Between bursts of laughter, she mumbled something about baking cookies, while Gil looked at her as if she had taken leave of her senses. "What about the others?" she asked. "Where were they?"

"Like Goldberg. In their studies, picking and choosing their way through crucial literary questions: Is it 'That's my last Duchess'? or 'That's my *last* Duchess'? Does Prufrock wear the bottoms of his trousers rolled because he's old and shrinking —"

" — or because he likes cuffed trousers? I know, I know," she said. "But still, you're very hostile to academia."

"Let's just say I agree with Henry Kissinger's observation that academic politics are so fierce because the stakes are so small." His tone made it clear that the subject was closed.

"Anyway," said Beth, "Noel's carrel is on Four South so he's still ruled out — and Ida, too."

"I don't have to tell you the layout of the library, Professor. Five, four — it makes no difference. Except for Hub, every tower has a back stairs. Slip out of your study, nip up the steps, and you're on the next floor. Melt into the shelves, keep an eye out for Marylou, follow her when she leaves the carrel, or maybe —" he stared into the distance for several seconds " — maybe get out of the tower ahead of her." He looked at Beth intently. "I gather your friends leave their carrels often. Take Livingston Potter. In and out. What's he looking for?"

"Livy," she said, "is always in and out because he's looking for *people*. People moving — sitting — talking. Talking, especially. He studies the head movements. Livy could have been out hunting conversations."

Gil cocked his head. "How many conversations are there to hunt down on a Sunday night?" He hesitated. "There's bigger hunting in books."

"Then more are missing? Are they valuable?"

"Valuable enough," he said cheerfully and got to his feet. "Coffee?" Beth said yes and he walked away, directly — she caught her breath — in the path of a highflying beachball. He snapped up the ball like a pro, dribbled, weaved in and out, and looped it back in the direction it had come from.

Beth sat back, listening vaguely to the jumble of bar exam talk behind her. "Weak on those plaintiffs — you know what I mean?" " — difference between larceny and robbery? — can never remember." A loud cocky voice: "I'm really into association. I always connect something."

Beth wished *she* could connect. Her head was spinning like a kaleidoscope. She imagined someone crouching behind a bookshelf. Ida? Livy? Or — Porter? Someone slipping into the ladies' room. She thought of Spence, of Noel — of Arthur. Round and round she turned the faces, but try as she might she could not adjust the picture. Long ago — she must have been in grade school — she had turned a picture puzzle round and round, looking between the vees of branches, peering at upside-down castles. She could still remember her delight when she had discovered every hidden face — like the satisfaction she felt when she finished a crossword. She was in her apartment — could it have been only yesterday? — writing in the last words, putting it together finally because she had seen the —

Steam floated from the coffee in front of her. She looked up eagerly. "Gil — patterns!"

He looked blank.

"The missing books —"

"Oh. Of course there has to be a pattern." He shoved the tray over and sat down. "That's what makes this case so daffy," he said. "Usually a thief specializes."

"But maybe there is a pattern. The missing Dickens volumes don't rule out mysteries. Lots of his novels are really mysteries. Now" — she searched through her bag, found a scrap of paper to write on — "exactly which books are missing?"

"It's a bit more than mysteries, Professor."

"What do we have then?" she asked, her pen poised over the paper.

"*We,*" he said with ironic emphasis, "now have *The Masque of the Red Death,* a special edition — with signed lithographs. *We* have John Papworth's *Hints on Ornamental Gardening* — with handcolored plates." He broke off, took a penny from the change on the tray, and studied it as if it were a gold doubloon. "And," he said with a sigh, "we also have Francis Parkman's *The California and Oregon Trail*—just possibly in the original wrapper. Those three alone, with the take-off in prices, could bring from $10,000 to $30,000." He flipped the penny in the air, caught it, and turned it over. "On the other hand," he said briskly, "*we* are also missing Perelman's *Dawn Ginsbergh's Revenge*, worth $350 at most, if it's in mint condition."

Beth looked over her notes, groping for a common denominator. "The thief," she said slowly, "likes authors whose names begin with *P?*"

"Nice try. Also missing are *Nineteen Eighty-Four, The Grapes of Wrath* —" again the sigh — "first editions, both of them, if the catalog is correct. And don't try *O* through *S*," he said, watching her draw diagrams, "because they're all from different sections of the library."

That of course was exactly what she had been thinking. She studied her notes. Gardens. California. So ridiculously random. Well, sometimes you had to wait for the pattern to emerge, let it rest a while — till the tank fills up again, she thought wryly. She dropped the notes in her bag and smiled at him. "Elementary, Bailey — your thief is a bibliomaniac with a passion for gardening, who wants to ride west —"

"What about *The Masque of the Red Death?*"

"The thief is also a hypochondriac —"

"And the Orwell?"

" — who worries about the future."

"Great. What do you do with *Dawn Ginsbergh?* Look, I have to leave. You're really going to work? I'll pick you up at your study." When she told him that she was perfectly capable of getting home safely, he laughed and helped her into her jacket.

The library loomed before them, stark, and somehow inimical. Way up in one of the towers she could see someone standing at the window. "By the way," Gil asked, as they crossed the plaza, "who did your plagiarist — Korretsky — copy from?"

"Korretsky?" she said absently, while she rummaged for her keys. "Oh, he copied from one of his students, someone who transferred from English to Business."

18

THE CIRCULATION DESK ON LEVEL ONE WAS A BULLPEN OF desks and filing cabinets, occupied tonight by a lone student reading a book. He did not look up when Beth reached the counter.

"Can you locate *Twainiana Annotations?*" she asked.

"Have you tried LOCUS?" he said, his eyes on the book.

"LOCUS," she said with more authority, "says it's out. I need to know — is it charged out to a carrel? If it's in the library, I'd like to see it tonight."

He pulled a comb from the pocket of his plaid shirt, marked his place in the book and lazed over to the computer. "What was that call number?" A moment later — "That book is charged out to a closed faculty carrel."

"Whose?"

"Let's see" — he glanced at the screen. "It's in —"

"No!" said a sharp voice, and the student cringed and swiftly tucked his book under the shelf. Coleman Lenites marched up to the counter. "You must know, Professor Austin, we don't give out that information."

"Come on, Coleman —" He stiffened. Uh-oh. She should not have used his first name. "I *need* the book," she said, hating her wheedling tone.

"You know the procedure," he said, extending a hand. "You *do* have your faculty card, or is it in the coffee machine?" He tossed Beth's ID into a drawer and ordered her to wait. Slapping a ring of keys into the boy's hand, he told him to retrieve the book. "Be back here in five minutes!"

The boy took off like a shot, so eager to escape, Beth saw, that he had forgotten to press CLEAR. Now if she could just get a look at that screen. She had an overwhelming wish to know who was reading obscure Mark Twain literature. Taking a position opposite the counter, she pretended to be absorbed in a display case. Our of the corner of her eye she watched Lenites.

He was standing near the computer, scrutinizing a bulletin board plastered with photo-stamped student IDs. He tacked up another ID and looked around suspiciously, as if searching for other criminals to take into custody. He glanced sharply at Beth. She put on an act of trying to get a better look at something inside the case, and watched Coleman under her lashes. He eyed her for a few seconds, then walked to the farthermost counter and, muttering under his breath, gathered up a stack of books. As he began sorting books into bins, Beth stepped forward to a display case that offered a better vantage point. She could almost make out the words on the screen.

From the back offices came the sudden ring of a telephone. She peered through the glass case, saw Coleman was moving away. Then she saw him catch himself and walk back to the computer. So much for that chance, she thought glumly, as she watched the screen blank out.

She waited until Coleman had opened the door to the back offices and then, walking swiftly in the direction the student had taken, she ran to the escalator. On Two, where the escalator ended, she searched the corridor. Only a man at the drinking fountain. The boy had disappeared. Which way could he have gone? She was about to start up the stairs when she caught sight of the plaid shirt in the lounge. The boy was eating peanuts, looking aimlessly out the dark window. She leaned against the wall and waited.

"But Madame — how the dress is *jolie*." Beth groaned inwardly. She knew the man at the fountain had looked familiar. Trotting joyfully toward her was Ferdinand Drôlé, her French department suitor, always lying in wait to woo her with questions about grammar. He halted just in front of her, puffing a bit. "So Madame" — he smiled happily — "tonight you are toiling. You should not tax yourself so," he said, waggling an admonitory finger.

Beth tried to retreat — unsuccessfully, since her back literally was to the wall — and said something about catching up on research.

" — but since you are here, can you perhaps do me the very great kindness" — he gave her a look full of meaning — "to explain what is the difference between this *affect* and *effect?*"

Trapped was trapped. *"Affect,"* she began, while Drôlé gazed at her tenderly, "is usually a verb, and it means —" she glanced toward the lounge. "To influence," she said. The boy tipped up the bag of peanuts — "or to pretend to have or to feel" — tossed the wrapper and cup toward the wastebasket. *"Effect"* — the boy sauntered past them — "is used chiefly as a noun, and it means" — and opened the door to the stairs. "Result or consequence" — Drôlé gaped as she stuttered incoherently about something she had forgotten, and ran.

She was just in time to see the plaid shirt exit on the next floor. Then whoever it was had a carrel on Three, not Four or Five, as she had expected. She scrambled up the stairs, opened the door, and saw the boy enter the South Tower. She hesitated a second, then started after him into the stacks, so determined not to lose sight of the plaid shirt that she almost tripped on a carpet edge.

Three South was unpeopled, the empty chairs casually tipped back on their pedestals as if engaged in silent conversation. She caught sight of the boy and saw that he was headed for the far side of the tower. She waited to see which door he would open. But he ignored the carrels, continued half way around, and disappeared into the back stairway, letting the door bang shut behind him.

Beth ran for the stairs, then paused, her hand on the door. Had there been something? a noise? a movement? She had the same sense of being followed she had felt earlier in the day. Could Coleman be trailing her again? That would be embarrassing, but she could always tell him that she had decided to do some work and come back later for the book. Cautiously she looked over her shoulder, almost afraid of what she would see. Nothing. For the moment, she was all right. Softly she opened the door.

The stairwell was like the inside of a madhouse cell. Walls of cement. Metal pipes for rails. Scattered scraps of index cards torn by some desperate prisoner. By the dim light of one bulb she could make out the graffiti scribbled on the walls. She side-stepped a rain puddle and began climbing. Above her she could hear the boy's sandals clattering forward. He was singing softly — "So nice . . . I feel so nice . . . like sugar and spice." The song echoed down the concrete stairs. She peered up, saw him pass the white FOUR. She moved up a few more steps and stopped dead. Again, she had the powerful sense of someone following. She wheeled around, her eyes traveling nervously down the steps. Around the turn. Was that a shadow?

Just then she heard the door bang above her. The boy must have gone out on Five. Hurry. But she could not lift her feet. She pulled one shoe away from old gum, then the other, and stumbled on, skidding in a puddle of water. She caught the rail and started to move on. Behind her. Someone tiptoeing?

She paused uncertainly and then, keeping her eyes on the white FIVE, she plunged ahead, running now.

At once she heard a pop like a small firecracker. The light. What had happened to the light? Close behind her in the darkness, she thought she could hear someone breathing. Her heart pounding, she reached out instinctively and clung to the rail, trembling. Don't stop. Tentatively, she put one foot up, then the other. Take it step by step. Like a blind man, she felt her way upward.

A split second later something whisked her hair — like a bat wing. Screaming, she threw up her hands. Another bat wing brush just grazed her shoulder. She cried out, twisted away and crouched in the darkness, paralyzed with fear. The rail. Where was the rail? She reached out desperately, felt cold metal, pulled herself up. Suddenly from below, she saw a gleam of light. She turned her head, saw the white THREE moving toward the wall. "Madame?"

At that instant she sensed another movement. She veered around. Above her — something spotted, like leaves or waves — raised for a blow. She screamed, clutched the rail. Something gave her a mighty push and she pitched forward, crying out in pain as her knees collided with concrete.

She lay still, dimly aware of a crashing noise above her. "Madame? *Dieu!*"

19

WHILE BETH WAS WAITING AT THE CIRCULATION DESK, GIL was emerging from the tunnel that led from the new library to the old. He paused to admire the vaulted ceiling in the old reading room. Then he climbed the worn steps, caressing the curve of the oak banister, and entered the silent chapel of Special Collections.

The head of Spec greeted him enthusiastically. "You're here to see more of our collection!" he cooed. "Or" — he looked worried — "does this visit have something to do with the missing books?"

"A bit of both," Gil replied. "Your catalog shows a rare S. S. Van Dine — *The Pow Wow Murder Case* — could I have a look?"

"Certainly, Mr. Bailey —" he pursed his lips. "Just a moment," and he walked over to a researcher and plucked a pen from his hand. "Only pencils here," he whispered severely. Then he hurried back to Gil. "Or do I call you Agent Bailey?"

"Mister is fine," said Gil.

"And I," the head reminded him, "am Goddard Gibbs."

Gil waited, looking up at the ceiling, where Erasmus' coat of arms was carved in oak, high above the researcher at the table. He looked at the researcher more closely. The book he was perusing was bound in fine leather embellished with delicate gold leaf swirls. The man was turning pages too carelessly, Gil thought, too engrossed in erudite hair-splitting to see the beauty of the lovely thing he held in his hands.

Gibbs returned and handed him a thin volume. "How long have you been a collector?" he asked, watching Gil examine the dust jacket and title pages.

"Since I was a child," Gil said shortly. He thanked Gibbs, started to leave, changed his mind at the door. "Mr. Gibbs!" The librarian, who had been standing at the desk surveying his domain, turned around. "I believe your holdings include the six-part edition of *The Mystery of Edwin Drood?*"

"Indeed they do" — Gibbs nodded proudly — "part of a legacy to Midwestern."

"Sure it's still in?"

"Now you're making me an itsy bit twitchy." But a few minutes later he returned triumphantly. "Just where it should be. We take great precautions. Now this one" — delicately he tapped the book Gil held — "Professor Austin came in to see this, when she was researching her — Have you read her book? — *Dickens, The Reviewers Unmasked.* A very fine —"

"Do you realize," Gil interrupted, "that there are books as valuable as this in the open stacks?"

Gibbs jumped back. "Oh I *know,* but there's a glut — so far behind — so short staffed" — he threw up his hands. "Sometimes I walk the stacks myself, at random you know, just trying to spot anything *old*-looking."

Anything old-looking, thought Gil, as he made his way back to the new library. Would Gibbs think an 1823 Papworth and an 1849 Parkman looked old? He moved into Three North, and stopped at the bound periodicals. Would he think — Gil seated himself in a cubicle — an 1849 *Harper's* looked old? He had bought a set of these at an auction, and here they were, out in the open, worth a fortune now, irreplaceable. He handled the journals cautiously, but still the fragile brittle pages disintegrated as he turned them. He glanced at ads for Burnett's cocoaine hair restorer, for Sands' Sarsaparilla for curing scrofula. *Old* — it was a miracle the etchings were still intact. Why did they keep these journals here, anyway? They should be under glass, like stamps, or jewels. No, you don't look at a book the same way you look at stamps or jewels. Just the same, they ought to take some security measures, he thought, as he replaced the *Harper's* and took down *Ladies Home Journals* from the early 1900s.

For some time he sat looking at illustrations, N. C. Wyeths, Maxfield Parrishes. One Parrish woman made him think of Beth. Beth had the same grace, the same firm tilt of the head. He gazed at the picture, then reminded himself guiltily that he was forgetting why he was here, and began to turn pages again. If the criminal is marketing illustrations, he thought, he is missing a gold mine.

He moved to the 1940s, turning carefully from magazine to magazine, where debutantes coaxed him to try Pond's and other ads invited him to have his first post-war love affair with a Waterman's pen. The Rockwell covers, he noted with relief, were still unscathed. He stopped, and swore under his breath. A slug of pages, razored out — and further along, another chunk ripped out. The torn paper was just hanging there. This wasn't the thief. This was students, or anyone passing through — barbarians — savages — in too much of a hurry to photocopy, so they just cannibalized. Damn it, he thought, as he left the stacks, they should chain the books to the walls the way they did in medieval libraries. They should mount cameras on the ceiling, he thought, striding angrily along the corridor.

"Mr. Bailey! Wait! I've been looking for you." A plump girl in shorts ran up to him. "Here's today's," she said, handing him a computer printout. "Up-to-date — as of seven tonight. Okay?"

"Excellent," he said, glancing over the list. "On your way home now?" he asked, noticing how tired she looked.

"Home? Oh no — I've got to work on my dissertation," and Gil shook his head in a show of sympathy and rolled up the sheet.

Three South was all but empty — only a janitor tacking carpet down, and a small wiry-looking man, wearing a narrow shirt, a European cut. Italian, Gil wondered, or French? He watched the man tiptoe from carrel to carrel, stopping at each door to peer in the window. Whatever he's looking for, Gil decided, it is not books to steal. Is he a Peeping Tom? Standard procedure required looking for odd demeanor, but everyone he saw looked odd.

He continued around the silent shelves, moving past American drama and American poetry, halting occasionally to take out a book and put it back. At fiction he stopped, unrolled the computer sheet, and hung it over a shelf. For some time he stood there, comparing the list with the books on the shelves. He frowned at an empty space, and verified it against the list. He saw another empty space, and again checked the list. He swore silently. Mysteries, California, gardens, and now — the thief had switched subjects again.

But why leave a rare edition of Frost — it had been there plainly, only a few shelves away — and take — The randomness was maddening. If only, he wished for the hundredth time, the Boston bookseller had at least saved the paper the book was wrapped in. Well, he thought, I'll have to start concentrating on how. *How* was the thief getting past the checkers? He reached for the list, and stopped short, hearing a bang that sounded like a door hitting the wall.

"Au secours! Au secours!" The cries were coming from behind him. *"Au* — help!" Gil dropped the shelf list and sprinted toward the back of the tower.

The odd-looking man stood at the stairs, screaming frantically. "There! In there!" He pointed inside the stairwell. "*Vite!* Quick!"

Gil pushed past him, looked into the dim light and saw Beth above him, leaning against the rail. He was at her side in seconds. "Beth" — she looked deathly pale — "are you all right?"

"I'm — okay," she said uncertainly, and started to get on her feet.

"Wait — don't try to walk." Ignoring her protests, he bent and lifted her in his arms. "What happened?" he asked, as he carried her down the stairs.

"I'm not sure. I think" — she looked up toward the next floor — "there was — someone."

He carried her out on Four, the odd-looking man trotting next to him, cautioning him, asking if she could be moved without danger. He's not Italian, he's French, am I holding her more closely than I need to, this is my fault, would I be holding her this closely if she were someone else — a hundred reproaches ran through Gil's mind in the few seconds it took to carry Beth to the center of the tower and rest her on the sofa. "Wait for me," he said. "And you" — he looked at the Frenchman — "stay here."

A janitor was scanning his flashlight into the stairwell. "What's going on?" he asked Gil.

"Just hold the light there," he said and ran up the stairs. The few people on Five looked up from their books and stared at him blankly. No, they hadn't noticed anything. No, nothing.

Too late, he thought. Too late. Whoever it is has melted into the woodwork. I should have known, he told himself, as he moved down the stairs. I should have known she'd be in danger. I've been behaving like some tyro. Well, no more of it. At least he could see to that, he thought, as he grimly noted the broken bulb.

The Frenchman was hovering over Beth solicitously, too solicitously. "Who are you?" said Gil.

"Who are *you?*" said the Frenchman.

"FBI. I want to ask you some questions."

The Frenchman read Gil's identification carefully. Then he drew himself up. "You may proceed," he said. "I myself am ready."

20

"YOU'RE SURE YOU'RE ALL RIGHT?" GIL ASKED.

"Quite sure," said Beth. "Nothing broken." She extended one leg, winced, suppressing a cry at a sudden sharp pain in her shoulder.

They were in the lounge, at the same table Livy had occupied in the afternoon. She had to rest somewhere, Gil had said, before she tried to go home. Dismissing her protests, he had taken her arm, led her down to the lounge, and brought coffee. She picked up the cup, noticed with surprise that her hands were shaking, quickly put it down again.

"You're giddy," said Gil, who had been watching her. "Take some deep breaths. Come on, *in* — deep." She took a short breath, muttering that he sounded like an X-ray technician. "*Deep* — what do you have against X-ray technicians? — *hold* it. Out. *In* — deep. Good. That's right."

So silly, she thought, as she breathed in and out, her eyes wandering. She noted how quiet it was in the lounge. Usually evening break was an event, students sprawling on the platform sofas, sitting two deep at the small round tables. Tonight the long narrow room was like an echo chamber, and the chatter of the law students, who had set up camp in the far corner, carried clearly. "How can you study that long?" one of them was saying. "I'm a total zombie by ten." "I've been giving some very strange responses," said another. "My biorhythms are off today."

Maybe my biorhythms are off, Beth thought, shifting uneasily in her chair. She was feeling pretty strange herself — but she wanted to conceal it from Gil. There has been enough commotion for one evening, she said to herself, aware that Gil's eyes were on her.

She thought about Gil, about the way he had carried her.
His shirt, she remembered. She had liked the feel of his shirt.
Just a shirt, just a man's shirt, she told herself, and an inward
voice protested that it was not any man's shirt, would she
have liked the feel of Drôlé's shirt? Ridiculous. Why was she
thinking about shirts, when she ought to be thinking
about. . . . How had this fiasco begun? She retraced her
steps, saw herself at the circulation desk, watching Coleman, waiting for him to leave — "Gil! I never found out
whose carrel the Mark Twain book is in."

"You're still thinking about that?" he said. "What a per-
sistent woman you are," and she saw in his face a look of
worry, and something else — respect? admiration? — she
wished she could read his thoughts. "Relax, Professor. It's
charged out to someone in music. Lenites tells me it's been
there for months, someone researching American
spirituals."

Music faculty. Not what she had expected. She wasn't sure
exactly what she had expected. "You're sure," Gil was saying, "you didn't see who pushed you?"

"No. . . . It was dark. . . . I only saw Drôlé." She thought
about the French professor, standing like Napoleon, his hand
inside his shirt, haughtily explaining to a bemused Gil that he
had been searching for Madame's study. When Gil reminded
him that Madame's study was on Five, he had replied irritably
that he always suffered great difficulty finding his way in the
library. "The plan — so *illogique* — they play tricks," he said.
Having mistaken the floor, he had himself decided to ascend
the stairway, and — "*Tiens! tenez!* — he had just then perceived Madame. But had he seen someone else, someone
following Madame? "*Peut-être* — perhaps" — a Gallic shrug
— he could not be certain. He was concentrating on

Madame. Beth laughed out loud, remembering how Gil had stared, disgusted, while the Frenchman stared back defiantly. "Drôlé," she said to Gil's look of inquiry. "He looked so funny when you were questioning him."

"Is he a particular friend of yours?"

"Not a friend . . . a suitor — of sorts."

"As long as it's only of sorts," said Gil. "You're sure you didn't see anyone else?" he asked again.

"I only heard Drôlé. I didn't actually *see* anyone —" She paused, remembering the spotted something, like waves, or more like leaves. But what was she going to say — that she was hit by a bush? "Maybe I wasn't pushed," she said. "Maybe I fell."

"You were pushed all right, Professor. I think you know that."

"Then who pushed me?"

"The same person who broke the light bulb. The same person who ran out on Four. You heard the door bang, and so did Drôlé. The killer is after *you*."

"After me?" She started to drink her coffee, but found suddenly that her fingers were powerless to hold the cup. "Just because I was following a student who might lead me to a plagiarist's source?"

"Not because of the plagiarism. It's something else." He mused for a moment and then said slowly, "There has to be a connection."

"I don't understand."

"Whatever you're doing with your Mark Twain research — something connects."

"Connects with what?"

"With the book theft —" He paused, looked at her thoughtfully, his face grim. "Without knowing it," he said, "you've run down something that points to the thief. Furthermore," he continued, anxiety in his voice, "you've been hanging out with me. The thief may be afraid that given enough time, and enough talking with me about what's going on, you'll see the connection. Maybe you're anticipating the thefts. You *were* on Three South this afternoon? You didn't by any chance take *Puddn'head Wilson* and *The Innocents Abroad* to your carrel?"

"Of course not. They've got nothing to do with what I'm looking for. Why?"

"Those are the latest."

"The latest what?"

"The latest missing books."

"But what's so special about them? The library must have a dozen copies."

"Of course — but these are first editions. They aren't charged out — and they were on the shelves earlier today." He stopped, gave her the same earnest look. "I'm sure of it, Beth. Somehow, you're stumbling on something, and you've got to stop — for your own safety. . . . Try some more coffee," he said more casually, as he took out a long paper — she saw it was a computer printout — and unrolled it across the table.

"For my own safety?" she said, watching him make check marks on the sheet. "Why would he — she — want to attack me, just because I'm on to the book theft?"

He looked up, frowning. "You're forgetting," he said, "the thief is also the killer. I don't want to frighten you — but until you started chasing around odd corners of the library, no one tried to lay a finger on you."

She turned away from his glance, thinking about the ladies' room, wondering if, after all —

"There hasn't been anything else?" he asked quickly, looking anxious.

She shook her head.

"All right, as I was saying, you're getting too close — and the killer wants to stop you from getting closer. The attack on you proves it."

"I think it proves —"

" — what?"

She didn't answer. She had started to say — proves the killer wants to stop me from finding Marylou's source, but she did not know why the idea had popped into her head.

What *did* she know, she asked herself, while Gil continued to go over the sheet. First, a girl had written a plagiarized paper. What ought to have been easy — finding the source — was turning out to be bewilderingly difficult. Next, the more she continued to hunt, the more someone — assuming someone *had* been lying in wait in the ladies' room, assuming the same someone had pushed her — wanted her out of the way. But why did this someone — X — want her out of the picture? It was conceivable Gil was right, that Marylou had a faculty friend. Could X be a friend who didn't want it known that the girl had plagiarized? She considered this possibility and rejected it almost immediately. Why kill Marylou and then kill someone else to protect Marylou's reputation?

Then suppose, her mind raced on, suppose X was *not* protecting Marylou. Suppose X was protecting himself. Could Marylou's faculty friend have helped her write the paper? What kind of a writer had Marylou been? If only she could see some of her writing. "Gil!" He looked up, smiled at her. "Could you give me the Peacocks' telephone number?"

"Forget it." He turned back to the computer sheet. "No phone numbers."

"Why not?" she asked, indignant.

"Why not?" He looked at her in disbelief. "For one thing, you've already spent God knows how many hours on this. Even if you do find what you're looking for, what will you have proven? That Marylou copied? You know that already. . . . For another thing," he went on, "the Peacocks don't know anything. They've been questioned by experts, and if they knew anything that could help us we'd know. For a third —" He hesitated, as if hard put to think of a third. "I will not," he said finally, "allow you to invade their privacy —" He stopped, looking at Beth whose face she knew had turned a bright red. "Don't get involved," he said more quietly. "I don't want — something could happen to you."

Trying to keep her voice under control, she said, "I only want to talk to them."

He sat thinking, as if he were struggling to make up his mind about something. Then, leaning forward confidently, as though he had made a decision, he said, "Come on, Professor, if you won't think about your own skin, think about your scholarly standards." He gave her a challenging look. "Aren't you exhibiting what academicians call *hubris?* You're assuming that your goals are so important you have the right to interfere where you're not needed. If that's not hubris —"

"You only have hubris," Beth interrupted, "if you're wrong."

He gestured impatiently. "Why don't you take a sabbatical from plagiarism? Do what other scholars do in the summer. Study paradigms. Figure out a way to reduce Shakespeare to Morse code."

"And why don't you," said Beth, openly furious now, "stick to searching for Hummel figurines? You've drawn a blank on your book thief, you've struck out on your killer, you've failed —" She saw him start to say something, change his mind. "Maybe," she said, watching him spin his pen round and round on the table, "you could track down another Hansel and Gretel, *if* they left you a trail of breadcrumbs!" It was hard to read his expression. It might have been anger, or worse, much worse, it might have been patient indulgence.

"You're exhausted." He rolled up the sheet. "I'll take you home."

"I'm not exhausted," and she rose so quickly she tipped her cup over. "Good night, Bailey."

"Wait!" — he yanked the printout away from the rivulets of coffee dribbling over the table — "you can't go home by yourself."

"Who says I can't?" she replied. "You don't have to worry that I'll be in any further danger, because —" she reached for her briefcase, accidentally brushed his shoulder. He reached up and trapped her hand. "Because," she said, pulling her hand away, "I won't be seen hanging out with *you!*" She seized her briefcase and without looking around, limped with as much dignity as she could muster, past the law students and out of the lounge.

Never, she thought furiously, as she moved along the corridor, her ankle stabbing with every step, never will I take up with another man. "Hold it!" she called and watched helplessly as the doors joined themselves, and the elevator clanked downward. She gave DOWN a vicious push.

After what seemed like an hour of protesting clanks, the elevator creaked up again. She leaned against the wall, looking around angrily. SOMETIMES I LIKE BEING ALONE — someone had scribbled this sentiment on the inside of the elevator door, and someone else had amended, BEING

ALONE CAUSES CANCER. Not for me, she wanted to say.
Being alone makes me glow with health.

She would find the source. She would never give up.
Giving the revolving door a decisive push, she went out of the
library and walked the few blocks to her apartment in a fury,
daring anyone to attack her.

When she opened the door, she saw the light blinking on
the phone machine. Gil, she thought, limping rapidly to the
desk. He called to apologize. She would never call him back.
Holding briefcase and unopened mail under one arm, she
reached for the button. REWIND, she noticed with satisfaction, ran for a long time. Good. It must be a five-minute
apology. Would he say he was sorry about hubris? Eagerly,
she pressed PLAY. The tape was filled with messages, the
cleaning lady telling her to buy Hoover bags; Ida asking her to
call if she got in before ten, she wanted to borrow a book; and
a woman who had called the wrong number and thought she
was leaving a message for her chiropodist. She kept the tape
running for a good ten minutes, but there were no more
messages. She clicked the machine off in disgust.

Lewis Carroll and I, she thought in the bathtub, have
parted company. Tuesdays are not what they once were.
Cautiously, she lifted a leg out of the water and studied the
bruise that had started to form on the side of her knee.

She couldn't sleep. Her shoulder ached. Her ankle ached.
Her side ached. She couldn't stop thinking. Over and over
she reviewed the dark stairs, the bushy figure, the missing
books. And Gil. Most of all she thought about Gil. She kept
revising the lounge scene. This time she exited gracefully,
without knocking anything over. This time she made several
stinging replies to his gibe about hubris. After an hour of
composing increasingly clever retorts, she got out of bed and

searched for something to read. It was three o'clock before she switched the light off. As she puffed up the pillow, she remembered. Coleman still had her faculty ID "Damn it!" she shouted at the pillow. "Damn it and damn him!" It was five o'clock and the Vinetown sky was getting bright before she turned the light out again.

21

SUMMER QUARTER WAS IN FULL SWING AND MARYLOU PEA-cock's murder was stale news, displaced by the controversy about whether Midwestern should get out of the Big Eleven. Weeks of unremitting ninety degree weather had made the campus an oven, and students wore swim suits everywhere, going from class to the beach. The more daring faculty exchanged jeans for shorts, and even Porter DeMont was seen in the lecture hall (from which he ordered a boy in swim trunks to leave) in shirtsleeves and tie. In the older buildings ancient fans wheezed; in the newer, the air conditioning worked overtime. A power alert was called and notices were sent out to conserve electricity, but in the end Common-wealth Edison — doing underground maintenance work that caused a cable to explode — created the twenty-four-hour outage much enjoyed by students. "It's weird," said a dorm resident quoted in *Prairie Gust,* the campus newspaper, "trying to take a shower in the dark. Sometimes you're not even sure if everything is clean."

At the library the outage had lasted only an hour, but those who suffered — the faculty whose electronic typewriters and word processors were paralyzed, the personnel whose com-puters were down, the tour group trapped in the elevator — were not amused. Marge had been trapped with the tour group, but as she said to Beth, it could have been worse, much worse. She could have been in the john when the lights went out. A man was using the second floor ladies' room, she was sure of it. Had Beth noticed that one toilet seat was always up? A hermaphrodite probably — or did she mean transvestite? "Couldn't your hunky FBI man," Marge had asked, "do something about these perverts?"

As for the FBI, progress with stolen books was no better, apparently, than with the murder. To Beth, who had been keeping a cool distance, it appeared that Gil had been doing some exit-watching but not much else. The story of the thefts had leaked, and newspaper publicity had prompted a few conscience-stricken former students to mail in books that had been missing for years, but these tended to be volumes of Shakespeare or outdated chemistry texts. Marge had told Beth privately that valuable books were still disappearing even though a new deactivating system had been installed at the check-out counters.

It was Gil who had ordered the new system. This Beth learned from Livy at the Hewmanns' annual garden party.

All the faculty were gathered on the flagstone terrace, which to the east offered a view of the lake, to the west the Hewmanns' Tudor garage and twin Mercedes, one wearing Arthur's IQ200 license plate, the other Penelope's IBID. Whether it was the heat, the humidity, or the presence of the FBI (for Gil had been invited) they were none of them at their best. Porter sipped sherry and quoted Samuel Johnson endlessly. Noel, who could when he was bored be very sarcastic, kept making caustic remarks about "the coming event," referring to the literary game that Penelope always devised for the party. Arthur bustled among his guests, interrupting conversations to hand out copies of *My Harvard* to which he had contributed an essay.

Livy seated himself next to Beth and poured out a stream of hostile gossip about the Hewmanns, insisting that Penelope's dress had been delivered by Brinks, claiming that Arthur had invited Gil because he was so impressed. "You've heard of Fettle Cereals?" Livy asked. "Beatrice Fettle was Bailey's aunt. It's true," he said, looking at Beth hopefully.

Seeing that he was not going to dig out a response, Livy tried another tack. "Did you know Bailey ordered the new deactivators? They'll never do any good."

Beth, who was watching Gil talk animatedly with Arthur, asked why not.

"No electronic system will beat this thief," said Livy. "Do you know what I think? I think he's taking them out in gift-wrapped packages."

Beth, more aware of Gil than anyone else, knew he was looking at her, waiting for her to look back. She kept her eyes on Livy and asked if he really believed that.

"Well, something like that," said Livy. "The *Purloined Letter* method, you know. They shouldn't be looking inside briefcases anyway, they should be looking at the people —" and he began to brag about how expert he had become in body language nuances. "Notice Goldberg," he said. "Very tense."

"But he looks so relaxed," said Beth, thinking to herself that Spence (alone, because Marilyn couldn't get a sitter) must be on his fifth gin and tonic.

"You're quite wrong," said Livy. "Observe the face — the tight expression, the features — almost fossilized. Observe the posture — spine like a ramrod. He's a bundle of nerves," Livy said with certainty, as they watched Arthur offer Spence a tray.

"Caviar!" Spence was saying. "Very insensitive of you to remind me." Arthur asked what he meant, and Spence, laughing loudly and mirthlessly, said, "My electric bill had a black border this month." He glared across the terrace where Ida had plopped herself down next to Gil, and then, tapping the silver dish with his glasses, he asked, "How many books would you have to sell to buy a jar of this?"

"Are you finished yet, Goldberg?" Arthur said hastily.

Spence, who appeared to have forgotten completely about Arthur's power on the tenure committee, replied in a nasty tone, "When I finish my book, you'll be the first to know."

"I was referring," said Arthur, "to your drink. But I have changed my mind. I will instruct the bartender to serve you no more. Since *you* mention your book, however, I refer you to my dictum: 'Never let domestic problems interfere with a day's writing.'" He placed a copy of *My Harvard* on the table and walked away, taking Spence's glass with him.

Noel covered the awkward silence with reminiscences of Quincy, Illinois and everyone listened peacefully, including Beth, who was determined to take no more notice of Gil, until from across the terrace they heard Ida's high voice say "Marylou Peacock."

Suddenly Beth saw that Porter looked pale and ill. The heat, she thought. He shouldn't teach in the summer. She was even more worried a few minutes later when Dot swept in. "Professor DeMont," she said, "you forgot your pills."

"Uyuh — indigestion." Porter looked around uncomfortably and quickly put the plastic bottle in his pocket.

"I hope you're staying?" Noel asked Dot, who was watching Porter with great concern.

"I wouldn't play one of those games if you paid me," said Dot, and just then Penelope appeared, her handpainted silk dress a mass of humidity wrinkles, in her hand a stack of typewritten notes.

"Charades!" said Penelope gaily. "Charades everyone! This year the theme is — *Ancient Mariner!*" Spence groaned and complained he wanted another drink. "Partners!" said Penelope, sounding like a square dance caller. "Choose your partners, everyone!"

Beth saw Gil look at her, saw him start to get out of his chair, and then she saw Ida take a powerful hold on his arm. "I've got my partner," said Ida, " — Robert Redford!" Arthur looked intensely annoyed.

The game was a disaster, with Spence maintaining at the top of his voice that the lines he wanted to act out were "And every tongue, through utter drought was withered at the root," thus inspiring Beth's partner, a visiting nephew of Penelope's, who had been indulging freely in the mulberry wine punch, to leer at Beth and say *he* wanted to act out *The Lay of the Last Minstrel.*

Afterwards, they sat picking at cold eggplant and lobster, discussing a recent novel recalled from the bookstores because it had been discovered to have striking parallels with *Farewell To Arms.* This led to mild teasing of Beth about her plagiarism case. After listening to more jokes about the sleuth of the stolen line and the bloodhound of the borrowed idea than she could endure, Beth decided it was time to leave. Ida, who had driven her to the party, looked at Gil coquettishly and said must they really leave now.

"I'll take you home," Gil said to Beth. He jumped to his feet and moved to her side. His eyes met hers but she looked away.

"Allow *me*," said Penelope's nephew and she quickly accepted.

The overjoyed nephew all but coasted down the Vinetown streets. When they arrived at her apartment, he planted himself outside the door, insisting it would be to both their benefits if she invited him in. Finally she slammed the door on him as he was saying, "But you won't be sorry. We can talk about plagiarism — "

Helping Hand Research, Inc. to Miss B. Austin

Dear Miss Austin:

We are sorry that we do not offer a paper on *"Tom Sawyer,* an Oedipal Adventure: The Case of the Phallic Fence." At present our files include "The Importance of the River in *Huckleberry Finn"* and "Sexism: Does It Occur In The Works Of Mark Twain?"

Should you desire to order, please send a money order. We do not accept personal checks.

> Yours truly,
> R. Smith
> Research Assistant
> HHR, Inc.

Writers Investigative Assistance, Inc. to Miss B. Austin

Dear Miss Austin:

We regret that our catalog does not contain *"Tom Sawyer,* an Oedipal Adventure: The Case of the Phallic Fence." As a substitute may we suggest from our catalog:

> *"Huckleberry Finn:* The Raft as a Symbol of Libido"
>
> "Pornography and American Literature"

The charge for the above titles is $3.50 per page.

If you prefer, we can research the topic you inquire about. Our charge for this service is $10 per page. Please advise.

>   Sincerely yours,
>   M. C. Brown
>   WIA, Inc.

"No," Beth said vehemently, "I would not prefer that you research the topic I inquire about." She laid the letter flat and began to fold it, then drew back her arm and threw ferociously. The paper airplane soared above the desk and darted toward Dickens until, deflected by the breeze from the fan, it turned sharply, crash-landed on *Mark Twain, Man and Legend* and skidded to rest next to a stack of articles.

Her desk was littered with articles, all of them about Mark Twain, none of them any help. After weeks of research, she was up to her eyes in Mark Twain, so steeped in his childhood she could have drawn a map of Hannibal. She had gone on possum hunts with the young Sam Clemens, been lost with him in McDowell's cave, almost fallen through the ice with him when they skated too far from the Missouri side of the frozen Mississippi. She had read biographies, critical texts, articles. Marylou Peacock still had her stumped. She was as certain as ever that the girl's prize-winning paper had been copied. She was also certain there was nothing like it in print.

She folded down the corners of another letter and hurled it aloft so powerfully that it went spinning over the record player where it hovered a second, then nose-dived onto the

Mikado which had been lying there for weeks. She tossed the airplane away and put on the record, then sank down on the window seat and listened abstractedly. . . . Yum Yum danced joyfully with her schoolmaid friends, Nanki-Poo consented to be beheaded in one month provided he could marry Yum Yum. . . . Beth's thoughts drifted to Marylou Peacock. Her mind seemed incapable of resting on any other subject.

On the low table in front of her, pinned down under a glass of root beer, was a copy of Marylou's paper. She brushed off the water ring and began to leaf through the pages. She could have recited the essay, from first sentence:

> As a resolution of father-son conflict, *Tom Sawyer* is *sui generis*

to last:

> In writing *Tom Sawyer*, Sam Clemens had cut down his "pa" and risen up his own strong oaken branch to become the fearless Mark Twain.

She had compared these sentences and all the others with every relevant piece of writing, yet she was no further along than she had been on the morning when she had first seen the paper. Nagging at her was the feeling that she *knew*, that if only she thought hard enough she could name the writer of the original.

She gave a sigh of frustration and listened halfheartedly to the music. . . . Yum Yum was refusing very sensibly to be buried alive with Nanki-Poo. "With a passion that's intense, I worship and adore, but the laws of common sense we oughtn't to ignore."

"But the laws of common sense," Koko affirmed, "you oughtn't to ignore."

"The laws of common sense," Beth said aloud, as if to remind herself they were still in operation. Marylou's pages went flying as she bounded out of the window seat and banged open a desk drawer. A few minutes later she held a newspaper clipping aloft and read the caption under the photo: "Clement Peacock, President of Hexagon Corporation, and his wife, Diane, at their Elystane Hills, Connecticut home."

"Directory Assistance," said the voice. "What city?"

"Can you give me the number of Clement Peacock in Elystane Hills?" Beth picked up a pen and began to scribble on the note pad. *"Marylou Peacock & Mark Twain. MP + MT."* She studied the initials and outlined them with an elaborate heart.

"Sorry," said the voice. "We do not have a listing for Clement Peacock."

All right, she told herself, think. She turned off the record player and began to pace up and down the room. After some time, she snapped her fingers and moved to the telephone.

"Who?" said Thorpe McBride. He sounded as if he had been sleeping. "Oh, Professor Austin . . . I was going to call you." Thorpe, it seemed, had given up the stage, and was going to strike it rich instead. Could she write him a recommendation for the Harvard School of Business?

Gradually Beth brought the conversation around to Marylou. "Do you remember," she asked, "when she made that remark about 'contented corpse'?"

"Yeah," he said, his voice wary.

"Did she say anything about Mark Twain?"

"Mark Twain?" he said, surprised. "No, nothing like that."

"Listen, Thorpe — do you by any chance have Marylou's telephone number?"

"Hey, no."

"Do you think you can get it?"

"I'll try. There might be someone around. Call you right back."

By the time the phone rang, she had covered several sheets with rows of initialed hearts. "Hey," said Thorpe. "I'm sorry. I've turned this place upside down."

So that was that, she thought. Or was it. She was too close to give up. She sat tapping her pen on the note pad and then picked up the receiver.

"This is Professor Austin," she said authoritatively to the voice at the other end. "I need a student's home telephone number. Yes. Yes, I know. I understand. But I have some papers of hers and I think her parents would —" It was so easy, she thought a few minutes later, as she wrote down a number. She should have thought of it a long time ago.

In the registrar's office, the secretary looked up a number and reached for the telephone. "Mr. Bailey? You wanted to be notified. There's been an inquiry for Marylou Peacock. No. It was a woman. A professor."

23

THE PHONE RANG, AND RANG AGAIN. *ANSWER,* BETH SAID silently. She visualized a pale blue telephone on a French provincial bedside table, a white telephone beside a swimming pool, and on a massive walnut desk a conference-equipped telephone, all ringing in chorus.

Please answer, she said, addressing the newspaper photo and scrutinizing it more closely. The Peacocks were in evening dress, but Diane Peacock, tan, hair in a decorous page-boy, looked as if she felt more at home in a golf skirt. She plays golf at the club every day, Beth speculated, and in the evening she works needlepoint pillow covers. Golf is his game, too, she thought, turning her attention to Clement Peacock. No, not golf, squash, more intensely competitive. She continued assessing the Peacocks with half her mind, her concentration on the telephone. Twenty-nine, thirty, thirty-one, she counted the rings, thirty-four, thirty-f — almost simultaneously two voices said hello and Beth started, nearly dropping the telephone.

"Oh," she said, "is this Mrs. Peacock? Professor Elizabeth Austin here — of Midwestern University. I am so sorry to bother you." Beth plunged into the explanation she had planned, feeling that at last she was on the verge of unraveling the solution.

"Research project?" The voice was a woman's, the accents cultivated. "My daughter never mentioned collecting primary or secondary material for that topic," said Diane Peacock, and Beth's social register matron faded rapidly away.

"It's entirely possible that she wouldn't have —" Beth began cautiously.

"Are you from WYTZ?" the woman asked.

"No, Mrs. Peacock. I'm Professor Austin, from —"

"I don't know that name. Are you from the newspapers?"

"Wait, Deedee" — a man's voice, surprisingly young, almost boyish. "She said she was one of Miffy's professors. Why don't we talk to her?"

"Don't tell me to talk to her, Clem. And don't you say anything!" Her voice rose nervously. "Professor, whoever you are and I don't think you are" — she talked rapidly, excitedly — "we will *not* talk to you. We've cooperated — my God, how we've cooperated," said Diane Peacock, and Beth could hear the tears in her voice. "What more do you want from us? You — you're *vultures.*" There was the sound of sobs and then a click.

Feeling horribly ashamed, Beth let the receiver hang in her hand and waited for the inevitable second click.

"Professor?" Quickly Beth put the receiver to her ear. "Are you still there?" said Clement Peacock. She began apologizing, and he said, "It's all right, perfectly all right. But could you just hold on a moment?" There were sounds of muffled sobbing, then voices, one loud, despairing, the other lower-pitched, soothing. Then it grew quiet and she heard the sound of the telephone being picked up.

"This is Clement Peacock. What is it you wanted to know, Professor — ? — is it Audley?"

He sounded so nice, so decent. He made her feel like such a rat that she almost felt like breaking the connection. Then she decided she could not let her guilt and pity keep her from one last try. "Austin," she said, "Elizabeth Austin. Marylou and I were working together." She had not known she had it in her to lie so wholeheartedly. . . . "It was quite an important project," she finished, "and I think Marylou might have kept some articles and notes I lent her."

"Miffy did keep a lot of notes —" said Clement Peacock. "She did — ?"

" — but I don't know about Mark Twain. Funny, she never said anything about Twain and we, the three of us — my wife majored in English — used to talk about literature a lot. We — we always —" He faltered and when he went on his voice was husky. "You asked about notes, Professor. Miffy did bring some notes with her — to Hawaii. We met her there — for Spring Break. That was the last time —" he stopped abruptly.

"Marylou had some notes?" Beth said softly.

There was a silence and then he said with a forced brisk-ness, "Miffy brought a box with her. Notes and papers, she told us, that she wanted to keep, so — of course," he said, his voice almost inaudible, "we brought them home for her."

Beth closed her eyes and said almost involuntarily, "You took the notes back to Connecticut?"

"Yes, we — we haven't had the heart to open the box. We've both — my wife has — you'll have to forgive Deedee," said Clement Peacock, so simply and artlessly that Beth felt more wretched than ever. "My wife hasn't been able to work. She has a small business — bookbinding. Does very well at it, too, very high quality —"

"The notes," Beth said very gently, "I wonder, could you —"

"Yes, of course. I'll look for them. Where can I reach you, Professor Austin?" he asked, businesslike now.

"When will — will you be calling soon?" said Beth, trying to conceal the urgency she felt.

"You really *are* concerned about these notes, aren't you?"

"I hate to bother you — but, well, yes I am. You might say they're essential."

"I'll look for them immediately."

Beth gave Clement Peacock her number and put down the receiver. Feeling more optimistic than she had in a long time, she rose from the desk, picked up the empty glass and carried it out of the room. As she put the breakfast dishes in the dishwasher, she suddenly realized she had forgotten about lunch. She could not possibly eat anything now.

She moved out of the kitchen and down the hall, the parquet cool under her bare feet. She stopped at the etchings and glanced appreciatively at John Stuart Mill's calm receptive face. In the living room she wandered about, collected books from the loveseat, the sofa, the tables, and returned them to the shelves. She stood for a moment, gazing at Dickens. We've almost got it, she told him silently. But what was taking so long, she wondered, looking at the telephone.

She crossed to the bay, threw herself on the soft cushions of the window seat, and stared out blankly into leaves tinged with late-summer gold. She sat up suddenly, walked to the desk and picked up the note pad. Then she sprawled on the window seat and began writing, *M. T. + M. P.* With great care she traced a heart around the initials. The telephone rang and she bolted to the desk.

"Chemistry. Philosophy. Poetry," said Clement Peacock. "Nothing about Mark Twain."

"Nothing? You're sure? Nothing from any lit course?" said Beth, looking glumly at the heart-filled note pad.

"Nothing about Mark Twain," he repeated. "Lots of notes about Walt Whitman."

"Whitman?"

"Yes, from Professor Goldberg's class — and a paper about Whitman, too. Miffy got an A on it," he said, a note of fatherly pleasure in his voice.

"You must be very proud of your daughter," said Beth, trying not to sound disappointed, thinking it was just as well he did not know how his daughter got her A's.

"We are proud of her — always have been. It's not just that Miffy's a fine student," he said judiciously, as though it was important to render an exact picture. "She — she was such a decent person. She likes people, really likes them, and they liked her," he said. "Miffy was friends with everyone. The mailman, her teachers, her classmates."

Beth murmured assent, thinking that his daughter had other qualities of which he was unaware.

"And Miffy's so honest," he was saying. "A real square shooter. Do you know, once when she was down five-four in a tennis tournament, the umpire called her serve good and Miffy corrected the call. Said her serve was out —" Beth sat perfectly still, watching the play of shadows on the rug. "It cost her the match," said Clement Peacock. "She was only fourteen then, and she wanted to win, very badly. But she was like that, never wanted anything she didn't deserve."

"She sounds like — a champion," Beth said miserably.

"Oh, Miffy had her faults," said Clement Peacock, appearing not to notice Beth's unease. "But it was herself she'd get angry at. She set such high standards, always saw a way to make something better. She stayed on campus late because she wanted to rewrite a paper, get it just right —"

"She was working on a paper?" Beth leaned forward on the edge of her chair. "Do you know what it was about?"

"I did know — but I'm afraid I've forgotten."

"It would help so much if you could remember," said Beth, forgetting it was notes she was supposed to be interested in. "She didn't talk to you about it at all?"

"Yes — yes, she did. I think —"

"Could she have been writing about Mark Twain?"

"No — not Twain. It was poetry. She was writing about a poem," he said. "Something — I know it — about music. It will come to me."

"A poem?" Beth sat back dejectedly, her mind a confused jumble.

"Can you tell me why you're really calling, Professor Austin?" Clement Peacock said suddenly. His voice had changed, less confiding now, an edge to it. "You never worked on a research project with my daughter," he said, not reproachfully, just stating a fact and expecting a response.

"You're right, of course," she said, wondering if he would break off now.

"Then why — ?"

She had to tell him the truth, no matter how he reacted. She owed him that. She took a deep breath. "It began some time ago, Mr. Peacock. On the — some weeks ago I was given a paper of Marylou's. . . ."

"I hated lying to you," she said a few minutes later, "but somehow — I can't explain it — I know it's important."

There was a long pause and then Clement Peacock said very firmly, "Miffy would not have done that. I know it."

"I know it, too," Beth said swiftly, and the instant the words were out of her mouth she realized she had meant what she said. She no longer believed Marylou Peacock had plagiarized.

"But you think — there's some connection with — her murder."

"I'm positive," Beth replied, realizing she meant this, too, and that she felt her responsibility to Marylou more keenly than ever.

The long silence was broken finally by Clement Peacock. "I want my daughter's murderer found."

"So do I," Beth replied. "Oh, so do I," she said, wanting desperately to say something consoling. "I know how you loved her —"

"Prufrock," he said.

"Prufrock?" She wondered if he had suddenly gone over the edge.

"The Love Song of J. Alfred Prufrock. That's what Miffy's paper was about."

"You're sure?"

"I'm certain of it."

She told Clement Peacock that she would be in touch with him, put down the receiver and picked up the note pad. She sat looking at her doodles of *M. P. + M. T.* Then she drew a single angled line across the center of a heart. She began slashing lines across the page and did not stop until she had canceled every heart.

24

"*The Love Song of J. Alfred Prufrock?*" said Spence. "What are you talking about?

"About Marylou Peacock's paper," Beth repeated, looking around for a place to sit down. The painters had finished but the English office was still in disarray, the furniture hidden behind new file cabinets and cartons of supplies. She removed a stack of textbooks from a carton, sat down, and looked up at Spence. "*Did* you include Eliot?"

"Did I include Eliot — ?" Spence began indignantly. He stopped and surveyed the room, as if ready and waiting to defend himself against anyone who dare accuse him of failure to uphold the standards. He cast a piercing eye at Livy, who was studying a book of photographs, and Dot, who was feeding the copying machine, then turned back to Beth: "You know how I teach C-102. Naturally we read some Eliot."

"Well then?"

"I told you — I only saw her Whitman paper." He stood there looking uneasy, as if he wanted to say something more.

Finally he sat down on the carton, took off his glasses and began polishing them with quick nervous swipes. "If you must know," he looked down at the floor, "she did write other papers. Nothing I assigned," he added quickly. "She was one of those students who are always writing forty-page essays they want you to read." His face reddened. "Who has time?" he said loudly, as though Beth had been pressing him for an explanation. "Papers! Meetings! Committees! I don't have the time to read outside work — Dot! When do those checks get here?"

"Hold your horses," said Dot, as she gathered up a stack of papers. "The mail gets here when it feels like getting here."

"But Spence," Beth said bewildered. "Why didn't you tell me she was in your class?"

"For Chri — I don't tell you about every student I ever had."

"But you knew I —"

"Oh —" Spence pounded a fist into his hand. "Let me alone, can't you!"

"Hey, Goldberg — pipe down!" Dot looked at the closed door of the chairman's office. "Professor DeMont is trying to work."

"What about me?" Spence jumped up and began stuffing papers into his satchel. "I can't sit around here all day," he raged, as he fumbled with the clasp. He gave up and stormed out of the room, slamming the door so hard Beth thought it would fall apart.

"Sonofabitch!" said Dot, looking again at Porter's door. "Why does he have to whoop like a rooster?"

"Changes in pitch," Livy said wisely. "The loud voice signifies anger."

"No kidding," said Dot. "You can tell he's mad. You sure are savvy," she said. Livy shrugged his shoulders and moved away.

"You'll appreciate this," he said, coming up to Beth. "Do you know that in *Nickleby* I found five examples of the false smile?" He took a breath and went on eagerly. "The implications —"

Beth kept her eyes on Livy's face, not really listening. Why was Spence so reluctant to talk about Marylou? She felt confused, uneasy. She had to find some answers. Identifying the writer of Marylou's essay was crucial, she was sure of it. But she did not have a glimmer of what to do next. She leaned back, resting her head on a file cabinet, and tried to think.

"Austin, wake up! Are you listening?"

"Yes, Livy," she said wearily.

"*As* I was saying," he went on, "the implications are enormously significant. Only the other day I saw someone in our department bare the teeth in what was clearly a false smile. I had just mentioned Mark Twain and —"

"What was that?" Dot said suddenly. She disappeared into the inner office only to return a moment later with mutterings of where the hell's the mail, could have sworn she'd heard the door. "Hey, Potter, what was that you were saying?"

"About what?"

"That smile stuff. What do you mean false smile?"

"Aha!" Livy looked pleased. "I refer," he said, "to the smile as a mask for deception. The timid smile that camouflages arrogance. The friendly smile that conceals raging hostility. The smile of humor," he went on, warming to his subject, "that —"

"Oh," Dot interrupted, "a fourflusher, you mean. I knew a guy like that. A real Jekyll and Hyde. The Twins," she said darkly, and when they looked at her uncomprehendingly — "He was a Gemini," she said, as if that explained everything.

"Forget horoscopes!" Livy shrieked. "I'm telling you, you can figure a person out by looking — you don't believe me," he said to Dot, who stood watching him, hands on hips. "Okay, watch this." He moved to the far end of the room, paused a moment, his hands to his eyes. Then he drew up his body, turned, and began to walk up and down between the file cabinets. It was an erotic walk, virile, predatory — a swagger really, sensual, inviting — and it was so out of line with Livy's personality that Beth could not help laughing.

"Pretty sexy," Dot said slowly. Then a look of surprised recognition crossed her face. "I know who that is. It's

Hewmann. A mite exaggerated, mebbe, but that's the way
Hewmann walks." And when Livy indicated smugly that he
had proven his point, "Hey," she said, "that's pretty good.
You mean" — a ribald laugh — "old Artie is saying I'm avail-
able, baby?" Livy nodded happily. "Bet he's a Scorpio," said
Dot, "or a Scorpio-Sagittarius."

"You don't need horoscopes!" screeched Livy, looking
ready to jump up and down in vexation. "It's people! *People*
give themselves away." He turned imploringly to Beth. "*You*
see what I mean," he said.

"I think so."

"You can't disguise yourself," said Livy. "Your walk is you.
Your talk is you. You do understand, Beth?"

"Your walk," she said slowly. "Your talk — yes, I do
understand," once again overcome with the feeling that the
answer she wanted was in the back of her mind. She thought
hard while Livy elaborated enthusiastically on message
movements and language signals.

"Just the same, Potter," Dot interrupted, "when's your
birthday?"

"Oh, for —" said Livy. "October fifth."

"Uh-*huh*. Libra. The Balance." Dot went to her desk and
got out a magazine whose cover, emblazoned with scorpions
and bulls, proclaimed, "ALL SIGNS: YOUR MONTH
AHEAD." She read intently while Livy discoursed to Beth,
then closed the magazine abruptly.

"Well?" Livy turned to Dot.

"Skip it."

"Let me see that," said Livy, tearing the magazine from
her hand. "What page? — oh, I see — 'A word of warning.
Planetary influences are too strong for even you to swim

against the tide. Be cautious. The danger is real.' Rubbish,"
he said, but he looked shaken.

"They're not always right," Dot said consolingly, as Livy
paged through the magazine. "Look at what that seer said
about the White Sox."

"Listen to this," said Livy suddenly. "'The long battle to
maintain your professional prestige will come to an end
around the time of the Full Moon.' Rubbish," he said with
more conviction. He turned the page and snickered. "'Dear
Counselor,'" he read in falsetto tones, "'Everything has
turned out *exactly* as you said it would, and I am so happy.'
Trash." He tossed the magazine back to Dot.

"Go ahead," she said, "laugh. If you read *Rhythms Of The
Universe* you'd laugh out of the other side of your mouth."

"I've got to leave," Beth said abruptly. They watched,
astonished, as she tore out of the room, muttering something
under her breath.

"What was that she said?" asked Dot.

"I'm not sure," said Livy. "I thought she said something
about — it doesn't make sense — the tank starting to fill up
again. Strange."

"Strange! You ain't just whistling Dixie!" Dot shook her
head. "I don't know. Everyone's acting mighty peculiar.
Maybe," she said speculatively, "the Sun and Mars are in
opposition. Oh well —" Ignoring Livy's furious look, she
moved to her desk and began to type. "Dig this," she called
out a moment later. "'This course will examine extraordinary
sociolinguistic patterns in old English.' Did you ever hear
such malarkey? I'm sick of this literature crap. When I come
back I'm going to be a country singer. How about you,
Potter? What do you want to come back as?"

But before Livy could reply — "I'll tell you," said a voice from the far corner. Dot and Livy jumped as Ida emerged from behind a file cabinet. "I'll tell you," she said again, staring at them wildly.

"Have you been there all the time?" said Livy. "What are you playing? Hide and Seek?"

"When I come back," Ida said loudly, ignoring him, "I'm going to be" — she paused dramatically — "*Blooody Maaary!*" She drew out the words in a tormented howl, while Dot and Livy gazed at her, appalled.

The silence was broken by a loud rumbling noise from the hall.

"It's about time," said Dot, heaving a sigh of relief, as the door banged open and Campus Mail entered, wheeling a dolly across the tiles. He rested his canvas sack on the desk, started to unbuckle it. Ida hurtled past him and the sack slid off and thudded to the floor like a lifeless body.

"Well, for —!" Dot stared at Ida's retreating back. "What in hell is her problem?"

Some time later Dot said to Livy, "Maybe it's not Mars."

"Maybe what's not Mars?" he said impatiently.

"Whatever it is that's making everyone act like they lost their buttons. I bet it's the murder. No one talks about it anymore, but it's sure making everyone goofy. I wonder who did it," she said, as she sorted paychecks into the mailboxes. "Who killed that Peacock kid and why?"

25

It was mid-evening, the working period at the library. Exam week was approaching, and the whole of Level One surged with procrastinators, punching the computers, slamming the catalog drawers. Up on Five, the South Tower had settled into labor. Only the whisper of a turning page, the rustle of a felt tip pen gliding over paper, and the muted cricketing of a dozen typewriters sounded softly through the stacks. The carrel doors were closed, their windows oblong patches of light.

Beth stacked *Three Keys to Language* on top of *Language in Thought and Action* and looked wearily at the books that remained. Unintentionally, Livy had embarked her on a program that was more exhausting than any so far. In this new territory, she felt like an ignoramus. Sighing, she got out of her chair.

A fog was coming in, a real Chicago special, swiftly eclipsing the campus. As she watched, a man and woman strolling arm in arm suddenly disappeared into the mist. Swallowed up, she thought, as if they had never existed and involuntarily she shivered.

One seminar room and two carrels away, Porter DeMont leaned an immaculate hand against the window frame and stood watching the fog blot out the neatly angled towers. Shaking his head impatiently, he moved to the desk where pens, paper clips, and scissors reposed in their proper receptacles and just above, on shelves labeled 18TH CENTURY DRAMA, 18TH CENTURY BIOGRAPHY, 18TH CENTURY NOVEL, the books were lined up in militia men rows.

His eyes slid to the calendar, each square filled with notations in his small, neat writing. He read the note for today,

then opened a black leatherette case and took out an ancient
Underwood.

> I am writing [Porter typed] to urge that the plan
> for demolition of the old music hall be
> abandoned. The callous indifference on the part
> of certain administrators toward this barbaric
> plot

No, no. Too strong. He pulled the sheet from the typewriter
and, folding the paper into halves, fourths, eighths, he let it
fall into the wastebasket. He sat thinking a while, then with a
nod of his head turned back to the Underwood.

> Finally, it behooves us to remember that our
> students shall not pass out of Midwestern
> insensible of its history. Let me press the point
> home with Leslie Stephen's words on Dr.
> Johnson: "The most interesting part of most
> men's lives is the early struggle in which their
> intellectual gifts are developing."
>   As with lives, gentlemen, so with buildings.

Yes, Porter decided, that was the effect he wanted. However — frowning, he contemplated the final sentences. Was
that precisely what Stephen had written? He was feeling
somewhat fatigued. Nevertheless, the passage must be verified. Heavily, he rose from his chair and removed his suit
jacket from the hook.

FREE ANGELA! NIXON MAKES SLAVES! The yel-
lowed clippings tacked to Spence's bulletin board struggled
out between the wobbly columns of books and cartons that
reached from floor to ceiling. From the desk, jumbled with
grimy index cards and old coffee cans sprouting dried-up

pens, the litter cascaded downward. There remained on the carpet a narrow channel from door to chair and Spence lay there in a sound sleep.

Somewhere outside a door slammed. He gave a start and sat up, rubbing his eyes. Still half asleep, he stared groggily at the shambles around and above him, thinking how Ma used to warn him he was getting like the Collier brothers. Groaning, he pulled himself off the floor and slipped his glasses on. His eyes moved from the DADY drawing to his manuscript, then back again to the drawing. Giving a huge sigh, he put the manuscript away and drew from a concealed niche under the counter a crumpled set of notes. Then he climbed on the chair and retrieved the typewriter which teetered crazily on an upper shelf.

Resolutely, he set the timer for thirty minutes. Now! Where the hell was some paper? He searched among the litter, vaguely aware of a faint knocking from the next study.

Arthur Hewmann opened the door and stared. "Well?"

"Please — can you tell me — ?" The boy looked confusedly at Arthur's bulletin board where a Mensa certificate, a Harvard banner, and a framed enlargement of a bookjacket — A NEW TRANSLATION BY ARTHUR HENRY HEWMANN — were tacked side by side with photos of an Ikebana container and a Japanese tea strainer marked late Edo period. "Is this the center for Oriental studies?"

Arthur pointed fiercely to the door. "Can you read that?"

"THIS . . . IS . . . NOT" — the boy stumbled through the sign — "AN . . . INFORMATION DESK."

"Downstairs," Arthur roared.

"I only thought" — the boy looked at the photos.

"Out!" Arthur slammed the door shut, then glanced at his watch and muttered angrily. Almost a whole evening down the drain.

One floor below, and three doors along the circle, Noel Frazier poured water, plunged an immersion heater into a mug. He drank his coffee and gazed around him. A photograph of Oxford spires. A dish filled with gray and white stones. *A Critical History of the Novel* by William F. Frazier. Noel picked up the book and leafed through to the acknowledgments. "With thanks to my son for his lively participation in the research for this study."

Humming a tune to himself, Noel took up a yellow legal pad and began to write, stopping frequently to consult his notes.

In the next carrel, jammed indifferently to the rear of the desk, was a framed snapshot of smiling nurses. A younger Ida towered in the back row, looking happier than the Ida who was scowling at the headline — TWELVE TO RECEIVE TENURE THIS YEAR.

Ida wadded the *Prairie Gust* into the wastebasket and picked up a folder. If this was torture yourself day, she might as well get all the raw deals up front: "The editors have not had a chance to review your article, 'Solution to the He-She Pronoun Gap: Use "She" Until Women Catch Up.' While we were intrigued — impressive research — did not find suitable —" "We return herewith 'Executive Wage-Equality: If the President were First Lady' — thought-provoking — topic unorthodox — trust you will find another —" "The Tenure Committee regrets — This decision is in no way a reflection on your —" Scrupulously Ida reread each letter. Then, forming the letters into a sizeable stack, she ripped them to shreds.

Savagely, she crammed paper into the SCM. "OUR BOTCHED UP WORLD," she typed. "OF COURSE GOD IS A MAN." She whacked the keys. "Men — overweening —

Men — duplicitous — Men, like raccoons, are vicious when
cornered."

On Five South, in the carrel directly above Ida's, Livy bent
excitedly over a book, stopping every few seconds to high-
light passages with a yellow pen. Extraordinary, he murmured to himself, pausing to reread a sentence. Too good, he
thought suddenly, to take risks, and he jumped up and tiptoed
to the door in stocking feet. He smiled and nodded to someone outside and watched the person move away. Curious, he
thought. Defensiveness? Guilt? He pondered the walk until
the person was well out of sight.

Then he returned to his desk, took from an upper shelf a
diary-like notebook and turned the key in the lock. He flipped
past scores of closely-written pages, found a clean one.
Copying carefully from the book, he wrote, "'. . . Charity to
be sure,' returned Squeers, rubbing his knees.'" Livy under-
lined *rubbing his knees,* added *Nicholas Nickleby,* Volume II,
Chapter XXXIV. He transcribed several more passages,
then settled back in his chair with an air of satisfaction.

His eyes fell on a clipping. If Beth hadn't left in such a hurry
— he had meant to tell her about this.

> TWAIN LETTER DISCOVERED,
> PURCHASED THIS WEEK, BOSTON'S
> BRATTLE BOOKSHOP . . . "But I give myself
> only five years longer to live," wrote Mark
> Twain, "and in that time I must finish certain
> books for the betterment of the human
> race. . . ."

Livy stopped reading and surveyed his study — the rows of
marker-filled Penguins — the open diary.

Abruptly, he sat up straight, gave a quick over-the-shoulder glance at the door. He took a deep breath. "I give myself five years," his voice boomed in the quiet study, "to finish developing the full significance of nonverbal communication in Charles Dickens — in order to — " He looked at the clipping in his hand. " — for the betterment, that is to say — "

There was a sudden loud clicking noise, like a gigantic grinding of gears, and Livy stopped short. The fan flopped to a halt, and the carrel was plunged into darkness. He waited quietly, lost in thought. A minute or so later, the lights went on again, and the fan resumed its whirring. At the same moment, hearing a noise behind him, Livy dropped the clipping and wheeled around so fast he knocked the chair against the desk. The diary key rolled under the typewriter.

"Ah," Livy said jovially, as he swung the door open. "It's you. I'm afraid we don't have much time. Do sit down," he said, clearing a space on the other chair. "Take off your — why gloves? What were you working with?"

Quickly, without waiting for an answer, he began to cover his notes. "You startled me," he said. "I was sitting here daydreaming, and then, 'While I nodded nearly napping —'" He spotted the key, bent to retrieve it, all the while continuing his nervous chatter. "Makes you think of Poe," he said, as he fumbled under the typewriter, his back to the visitor. "'Suddenly there came a tapping, as of someone gently rapping, rapping at my —'"

A short time later everyone was filing out of the library. "A real London particular, a fog Miss," Spence said to Beth. "Help you carry your books?" He looked, Beth thought, more cheerful than he had in weeks.

* * *

Next morning the fog had cleared. The sun shone down from a cloudless sky and set the tower windows gleaming. It warmed the ramp where Vinetown boys leaped their bicycles into the air, and made death-defying plunges toward the library entrance.

Just inside the bookchecker halted a student. "You can't go in," he said, pointing to the clock which stood at 8:21. "The library doesn't open until 8:30." Turning his back on the restive group inside the entrance, he stared impassively at the steps that led up to the lounge on level two.

On the second floor, the vending machine man removed a bundle of dollars from the bill changer. There was a loud Las Vegas clanking as he refilled the machine with quarters, dimes, and nickels, crashing the bag against the machine until every coin was out. "So," he said to the janitor who sat on the window sill watching him, "they're going to move Angel to the chapel."

"Yeah," said the janitor, "he'll be over there buffing the chapel."

"Nice guy, Angel," the vending machine man ventured, "but not much upstairs."

Silence.

He wiped off the front of the next machine and unlocked the glass door. "When are they going to lay the new carpet?" he asked, as he stacked Snickers bars in the empty row.

"They laid it."

"They laid it! I thought it was padding."

"Oh, everyone loves this oatmeal color carpet," said another janitor joining them. "Reminds them of breakfast in the morning."

"What have we got? What have we got?" A stocky man, chewing a half-smoked cigar, entered with a jaunty air. He was wearing a Cubs cap. From one back pocket a red rag flew out like a distress signal; the other bulged with a walkie talkie.

"Whadua say, Ange? We ain't got nothin."

"Nothin? Man, you better —" Angel cut off his riposte and looked down at his hip pocket where the walkie talkie was emitting loud crackling noises. It gave a few more preliminary croaks, then burst out with "Fifth floor wastebaskets have not been emptied for several days."

There was a roar of laughter. "Go to it, Ange."

"In due time, in due time," said Angel, as he brought out a Dunkin Donuts bag. The other blue-uniformed janitors lit cigarettes and settled in. Behind them the bulky vacuum cleaners and floor polishers, heavy red cords pooled on the tile, formed their own intimate group.

"Man, they don't stop harassing," the vending machine man said a few minutes later. "Now take my daughter." He drew a coffee for himself and gazed at it deliberatively. "A very nice looking girl, I don't say it because she's my daughter — tall, very shapely. Every time we go somewhere —"

"Okay, okay. Knock off the yackety-yack." There was a flurry of cigarettes being stubbed out and a move toward the equipment. "Man, you guys have been screwing off all week." The super looked sharply at Angel who stood chewing a doughnut. "What do you think you're doing?"

For sure, they have a soft time of it, Angel was thinking, as he moved grumpily from carrel to carrel, dumping papers, wrappers, cardboard cups into a kingsize wastebasket. Now this wise guy — Swearing, he got down and picked orange peels off the carpet. He should report him. Moving out of the carrel, he tripped on an umbrella. By God, he would report him.

How much do they work? he asked himself, as he rolled the cart along. A couple hours a week. Man, if he could latch on to a pushover like that.

At the next door, hearing a whirring noise, he knocked halfheartedly and waited. A few seconds went by. He knocked again. When there was no answer, he peered inside. "For Chrissake," he muttered. "What next? Must have been here all night. Man, he knows how to make himself cozy when he takes his beauty sleep."

Angel took out his key and opened the door. "Want your waste — ?" He took a closer look at the face and backed off. "Jesus — God!"

26

WHILE THE JANITORS WERE HUDDLED AT THE VENDING machines, Gil was in the stacks, making the motions of going over a shelf list. He had got to bed late, but could not fall asleep. At two o'clock he had been staring out at the fog that enveloped Lincoln Park, while he reviewed every stolen book, every blind alley. "You've drawn a blank on your book thief, you've struck out on your killer" — suddenly Beth's words had come echoing back and he had leaped out of bed and fled downstairs. For some time he had roamed about the study, removing a book from a shelf, putting it back, taking pleasure in the fine-grained cloth of one cover, the golden design on another. Gradually his mind had calmed, and pulling a winter robe over himself — he kept the temperature at a book-preserving chill — he had settled down with *Bouillabaisse for Bibliophiles* and dropped off over a dialogue on "The Evils of Circulating Libraries."

He had dreamt he was at an outlandish cocktail party. A group of elderly bibliomaniacs were gathered in a booklined drawing room, cackling over their acquisitions. "I bought this for pennies," shrieked a graybearded codger, brandishing a leatherbound book ornamented with dollar signs. "Now it's worth thousands!" Gleefully he flung the volume at an old crone who caught it one-handed and hurled it back contemptuously. "You call that a bargain?" Tumbling books out of the shelves, she began to pelt him with first editions, while the other guests cheered and joined the fray. Soon the air was alive with books and Gil, powerless to move from where he stood, dodged this way and that as books piled up to his ankles, his knees, his elbows. Foundering, he fell to the floor and an instant later was submerged. He heaved at the books,

breaking spines, ripping pages, tunneled a small opening —
and saw Beth, trapped under an avalanche of books, oblivious
to the menacing figure behind her. He battered the books that
wedged him to the floor. "Beth — watch out!"

His own voice had jolted him awake, and he had found
himself in the chair, the lamp burning, the sun streaming in on
the glass-fronted cases. He had closed the curtains to protect the books and fifteen minutes later, having showered,
gulped down coffee, glanced at the *Tribune* (swearing at an
anti-FBI headline), he had been on his way to Midwestern.

Now his attention was diverted from the shelf list by two
graduate students talking outside an open carrel.

"Whenever I come to *Hamlet,* I sense an aesthetic sta-
bility —"

"You're conflating the notion with the question of muta-
bility. My sense of the dichotomy —"

All summer Gil had observed academia, listened in on its
talk. It had remained, he was resolved, exactly the same. He
stared absently at the shelves above him — T. H. Huxley,
Science and Education, Technical Education. He contemplated the titles, remembering. Well, he thought, shifting
restlessly in his chair, that had been a long time ago and in the
interim he had put in a good many satisfying years with Squad
Two. The Hummels, the Fabergé eggs, the Meissen cabinets, at least they were real — not academic bullshit.

"That's a collectible?" he remembered asking Houlihan, as
they examined a photo of a lifesize Majolica heron.

"Sotheby's," Houlihan replied without blinking an eye,
"calls it an object of virtue. Anyway," said Houlihan, who
went all the way back to Dillinger days, "it's not our job to
calculate if they're worth what they're going for." He slapped
an Interpol report in front of Gil and asked angrily: "Who

would have figured that 'A letter from Vanessa Bell apologizing for an outburst about the servants and expressing gratification that her sister will lend her the cook' would be worth in the neighborhood of $500? Who the hell is Vanessa Bell?" Virginia Woolf's sister, Gil told him, and Houlihan glared.

Houly had a place in Michigan now and divided his time between bird-watching and bridge tournaments. But before he retired they had worked together on every kind of theft: the Art Institute's Cezannes, the Napoleon letters, and — as the prices had gone skyhigh — books. Fifty-thousand dollars-worth once, from Downstate U, and for a while it had them baffled. "You don't know Plutarch?" Houly had said to him then. "Surprised with your background you don't know Plutarch." Reaching under *Day of the Jackal,* he extricated his dog-eared *Bartlett's* and put on his glasses. He read Chicago-style, converting *th's* to *d's:* "'Themosticles replied that a man's discourse was like a rich Persian carpet, the beautiful figures and patterns of which can only be shown by spreading and extending it out; when it is contracted and folded up, they are obscure and lost —'"

Houly pitched the book aside. "Spread and extend," he said, thrusting out his arms like a football referee. "That's the game plan," and eventually they tracked down a pick-up truck hauling half a million dollars-worth of material "borrowed" from universities from the Great Lakes to the Mississippi Valley.

All right, Houly, I'll spread it out. Gil took out a long sheet and unrolled it on the desk. It was a master list of the stolen books, compiled with the help of the Acquisitions librarian.

Thomas Bailey Aldrich — *The Story of a Bad Boy*

Louis Agassiz — *Contributions to the Natural History of the United States*

Henry Alken — *The National Sports of Great Britain*

Wystan Hugh Auden — *Poems*

Arnold Bennett — *The Old Wives' Tale*

Niels Bohr — *Drei Aufsaetze ueber spektren und Atombau*

Charles Robert Bree — *A History of the Birds of Europe*

Benjamin Butterworth — *The Growth of Industrial Art*

Samuel Clemens — *Innocents Abroad; Puddn'head Wilson*

Wilkie Collins — *The Moonstone*

Charles Darwin — *On the Origin of Species by Means of Natural Selection*

Charles Dickens — *Bleak House; Pickwick Papers; Edwin Drood; Our Mutual Friend*

Sir Arthur Conan Doyle — *A Study in Scarlet*

Ralph Waldo Emerson — *Essays*

Sir Alexander Fleming — *On the Antibacterial Action of Cultures of a Penicillium*

Sigmund Freud — *Aus der Geschicte einer Infantilen Neurose*

Oliver Wendell Holmes — *Autocrat of the Breakfast Table*

Carl Gustave Jung — *Wanderlungen und Symbole der Libido*

John Maynard Keynes — *A Treatise on Money*

George Orwell — *Nineteen Eighty-Four; The Road to Wigan Pier*

John Buonarotti Papworth — *Hints on Ornamental Gardening*

Francis Parkman — *The California and Oregon Trail*

S. J. Perelman — *Dawn Ginsbergh's Revenge*

Edgar Allan Poe — *The Masque of the Red Death*

John Steinbeck — *The Moon is Down; The Grapes of Wrath*

Giles Lytton Strachey — *Elizabeth and Essex*

William Targ — *Bibliophile in the Nursery*

Sidney Herbert Williams — *A Bibliography of the Writings of Lewis Carroll*

Edward, Duke of Windsor — *A King's Story*

Frank Lloyd Wright — *The Natural House*

Gil propped the master list against the back of the cubicle and brought out his *Values* sheet. Once again he scanned the figures, hoping to find something to set his thoughts in motion.

Aldrich — $50, in good condition
Agassiz — $140
Alken — L830
Auden . . .

Only what he had noted before: an absurdly wide price range, from Orwell's *Wigan Pier* which catalogued at $35 — too low to log with BAMBAM* — to the Conan Doyle, a first edition

---

BAMBAM. Bookline Alert: Missing Books and Manuscripts. A national system for reporting stolen and missing items.

which had auctioned last year in London for L2500. The broad spectrum could mean the thief was desperate for money. It could also mean, Gil thought, tearing a sheet from his notebook, that he didn't know what he was doing.

Travel — 1
Psychology — 2
Sports — 1
Autobiography — 1 . . .

The new list yielded a similar hodgepodge. Among fiction, conceding Beth was right about Dickens, there was a prevalence of mysteries, but how to fit in the Steinbecks, the Aldrich, the Orwell. Eclectic taste? Or — thinking back wryly to his conversation with Beth — a bibliomaniac?

Spread and extend, Houly said insistently. Gil looked speculatively at the master list and brought out his pocket calendar.

Before June — Dickens, Doyle, Collins
June 19 — Clemens (2), Perelman, Parkman,
Papworth, Poe, Orwell, Dickens
June 21 — Steinbeck (2)
June 25 — Aldrich
June 26 — Bennett
June 30 — Auden
July 2 — Emerson
July 6 — Holmes
July 9 — Agassiz (2 vols.)
July 12 — Agassiz (2 vols.)
July 14 — Bree, Darwin

July 17 — Butterworth
July 19 — Fleming
July 22 — Freud, Jung
July 24 — Targ
July 25 — Williams
July 28 — Alken
August 3 — Wright
August 6 — Strachey
August 7 — Windsor
August 10 — Parkman
August 12 — Keynes (2 vols.)
August 13 — Orwell *(Wigan Pier)*

About the timing before he had been called in, he could not be sure. The exact number of days, if any, between the Dickens, the Collins, the Conan Doyle remained a question. Since then, it was certain that the thievery had been steady, a book or two filched every few days. But no pattern: The thief had no preference for either a Monday-Wednesday-Friday sequence or a Tuesday-Thursday. Excluding Fourth of July, he attended every day of the week, including an occasional Saturday and Sunday. There was no predicting what day he would choose next or what books would take his fancy. Or her fancy, he reminded himself, as he crumpled the paper and started to toss it away. Struck by a thought, he smoothed the paper out again.

Interesting. Here was something he hadn't seen before. During the initial period, the stolen books took in a scramble of subjects. But later, after the twenty-fifth of June, there appeared to be large but discernible categories. Fiction, poetry, essays added up to literature. Nature, ornithology,

evolution merged into science. Almost — he studied the dates
and titles — a rough Dewey Decimal order? Quickly, he tried it
out, bracketing dates and adding major classification numbers.

	June 25 — Aldrich
	June 26 — Bennett
800-899	June 30 — Auden
	July 2 — Emerson
	July 6 — Holmes
	July 9 — Agassiz (2 vols.)
500-599	July 12 — Agassiz (2 vols.)
	July 14 — Bree, Darwin
600-699	
	July 17 — Butterworth
	July 19 — Fleming
100-199	July 22 — Freud, Jung
000-99	July 24 — Targ
	July 25 — Williams
700-799	July 28 — Alken
	August 3 — Wright
	August 6 — Strachey
900-999	August 7 — Windsor
	August 10 — Parkman
300-399	August 12 — Keynes (2 vols.)
	August 13 — Orwell *(Wigan Pier)*

Gil felt a surge of hope. Clustered within time periods
were distinct Dewey groups. First, a week of pillaging from
Literature, Dewey's 800 classification. The following week a
looting of the 500s, Pure Sciences — life sciences, paleontol-
ogy, zoology. Then a few days of 600s, Technology (Applied
Sciences), with subdivisions from medicine to manufactures.
A brief foray into the 100s, Philosophy and Related Disci-
plines — psychology, ethics. Half a week with the 000s,

Generalities, which included bibliographies and book rarities. Up again to the 700s, The Arts, from civic and landscape to recreational and performing. Further up to the 900s, General Geography and History, taking in travel and biography. The clusters were there, definitely. But — his excitement faded — he did not know what to make of them. And there was no getting away from the fact that the books came from every floor, every tower. Except for Asiatica the thief had ranged (or perhaps stumbled was a better word) over the entire library.

So much for spreading it out, he told Houly. I defy you to find a pattern. Maybe personal shopping? he could hear Houly ask. Stealing on order? Fine, great, on whose order? With that assortment he has a whole slew of customers, and who are they? BAMBAM hasn't reported anyone trying to sell.

Why? *Why hadn't anyone tried to sell?* Maybe the thief was building up a stockpile. Maybe . . . Gil stared at the khaki green walls, trying to reason it out. A few chalked scrawls on the freshly painted surface arrested his thoughts, and he scanned the names and initials, the vapid slogans. Something orange on top of an open dictionary caught his eye. He looked closer, saw it was a heap of orange peels and was filled with disgust. At that moment, a student walked past, threw a carton toward the wastebasket, missed and went on. Gil started to call him back, changed his mind. "Damn their eyes," he muttered, got up and put the carton in the waste-basket. Returning to the cubicle, he looked at the list again.

It was no use. His mind was a clutter of dates, subjects, locations. He could wait — the cunning bastard was bound to make a mistake. But he wanted to *do* something. Abruptly he stood, crammed the notebook in one pocket, the lists in another, and made his way to the main entrance where, as he had countless other times, he watched people exit from the library.

At this hour most people were coming in; but a few were going through the exit — students drifting out after early classes, faculty returning to their offices — and for these the bookchecker interrupted his studying to open booksacks and Osco bags. He was also opening faculty briefcases, and this Gil noted with some satisfaction. He had spent some time re-training the checkers, and he particularly remembered the boy at the exit now.

"Frat guys, that's who I look out for. They think they're beyond the law, that Daddy can buy them out of anything. Oh sure, I can tell them easy. They're tall, because that equals success and to get into a frat you've got to look like you'll be successful. Another thing, they look rich, you know, preppy, pink buttondown shirts, bermudas. The shoes — that's the giveaway. You take Topsiders that have only been on the sidewalk — the soles are worn. But if the soles are still in good shape and the top is worn, you know, with waterstains, that means they've actually been on a boat.

"Nah — I don't check faculty. Just people from 'outside.' Outsiders, they dress, you know, normal, not collegiate. Profs are bad dressers. Like they wear the kind of clothes no one ever buys. The jackets and pants don't match. The ties are too wide. And they've got bad bodies, you know, over-weight, like they've been sitting around.

"Hey, I couldn't do that! Ask faculty to open their brief-cases? Like, hey, you could be a thief? You mean even some-one I've had for a class? Well, I suppose — oh all right, if you say so."

Just then an older woman, a high school teacher, Gil guessed, swept past the checker. Instantly the bar went up and the beeper exploded with sharp little blasts like a miniature factory whistle. Gil saw the checker point to the sign, saw the woman open her carryall, saw the boy look over her books, which must have been charged out, for he pushed them inside the bar along the counter and waved her on. Suddenly something tugged at Gil's mind and he stiffened to attention. He should have thought of it before. A hundred-to-one shot, but worth trying. He waited until the checker finished dealing with a departing surge of touring parents, then went up the short flight and asked him a question.

"Well, you seldom get that," said the boy. "But I always ask them to —" He stopped suddenly and Gil turned to see what had produced the look of astonishment on his face.

Lurching toward them along the corridor, his tie askew, his vest unbuttoned, was Coleman Lenites. "Bailey?" he called, as he hurried past the LUIS terminals. He puffed up to the bottom of the steps. "Five," he said breathlessly. "There's been — another — go up to — Five. You can — take the staff elevator —" But Gil was already in motion.

Rejecting the elevators, he covered the escalator in three strides, leaped forward and banged open the door to the stairs. He raced the steps, leaving people hugging the walls as he tore upward. Was it Beth? Was he too late this time?

On Five he was almost propelled backwards by a plunging crowd of exiters from 10 A.M. classes. Regaining his balance, he forced his way through the door and pressed forward, regardless of buffets and jabs from booksacks and sharp briefcase corners. At the South tower he found himself in another crowd which, sensing that something was swarming toward the back of the tower. Through this second crowd he elbowed a clearing, then sprinted the circle.

Two university police officers stood outside the farthest carrel, trying ineffectually to get the crowd away. On a sharp order from Gil, the crowd retreated, with the exception of a stocky man in a Cubs cap and janitor's uniform. Gil showed the police a card and they moved from the door. He looked inside and quickly turned back again. "It's Potter," he said almost involuntarily.

"The police are on the way," said one of the officers, looking at him curiously.

"Has anyone else been inside?"

"Just us. And him" — he gestured toward the janitor who was sagging against his cart. "He found him."

"All right. Close the tower. Send someone to get people out of the carrels."

"Okay. We'll shag everyone out."

"Wait! Did you touch anything?"

"No," one of them said, finally. "Well — we just got him off the typewriter — but we didn't touch anything. At least I'm pretty sure," which probably meant, Gil thought, as he turned to the janitor, that they had.

"I heard this whirring sound," said Angel, "so I looked inside. Thought he might have left his typewriter on. Sometimes they forget when they flick the lights."

"Flick the lights?"

"You know — the closing signal. When they turn off the main switch."

Gil asked a few more questions, then told him he could go, that he would want to talk to him again later.

"I'm a little nauseous," said Angel. "His face! Dju see his face? *Geez*, why would someone —" He staggered off, pushing the cart, using it to support him, like a walker.

They had picked Livy Potter off the typewriter and propped him up in the chair. He was slouched back, his body turned so that it faced Gil. The skin over the eye socket was torn, the edges of the wound ragged and black — where he hit the typewriter, Gil guessed. He stared at the face. Marbled, grotesque, the nose and cheek were patched with white; the lips were the mottled blue of someone dragged out of icy waters. The rest was a brackish purple, spreading from the forehead, to the ears, to the front of the neck.

Gil looked at the body, his expression grim. Dead before he hit the typewriter. He would bet on it. And he would bet on what the ME's report would be. Someone had come at him from behind — the edge of the hand to the back of the neck.

The whirring fan jarred into his thoughts and he turned away from Livy to survey the study. No signs of a struggle. The litter on the desk was a typical scholar's disarray. He picked up one note card, then another.

ARM-FACE — *OUR MUTUAL FRIEND*
    Mr Podsnap had even acquired *a peculiar
flourish of his right arm* in often clearing the
world of its most difficult problems, by sweeping
them behind him . . . with those words . . .
'Not English,' when PRESTO! with *a flourish of
the arm, and a flush of the face,* they were swept
away.

WALK-HANDS-INVASION OF SPACE — *OUR MUTUAL FRIEND*

. . . a gentleman came *cooly sauntering* toward them, with a cigar in his mouth, his coat thrown back, and *his hands behind him.* Something in the careless manner of this person, and in a certain lazily arrogant air with which he approached, *holding possession of twice as much pavement as another would have claimed.* . . .

Gil dropped the cards and turned to the shelves. Automatically, he looked for missing books. Dickens, plenty of Dickens. But no Nonesuch editions. His eyes glided downward to the silent typewriter. He caught a gleam of something beneath it, slipped a hand in and fished it out.

Sometime later, when the police had finished, Gil watched the body being removed. "What do you mean this tower is closed?" The complaining voice was Hewmann's. He wanted to talk to him — and to the others, too.

* * *

Beth, hurrying toward the library, saw them carrying the stretcher out and stopped short, overcome with a horrible *deja vu.* "Who?" she said faintly, seeing Dot.

Dot's face looked all wrong — vulnerable. "It's — Potter," she whispered. "Can you beat that?" she said, tears rolling down her cheeks. "Hey!" She grabbed Beth's arm. "Don't *you* keel over on me."

*KUP'S COLUMN . . . A REPORTER'S
REPORT. . . . They're wearing their hearts at
half-mast at Midwestern U, where memorial
services were held today for T. L. Potter, professor
of English, nationally known expert in kinesics.
The FBI is involved in the mystery, increasing
speculation that the case is linked with the
unsolved murder of a Midwestern co-ed.*
     Chicago Sun-Times

INC . . . ON THE CAMPUS BEAT. . . .
Everything is very hush-hush on the
Midwestern campus where the football team is
warming up for another losing season and
Vinetown police are investigating the death of
Professor T. L. Potter. Hush-hush that is except
at FBI headquarters where they're screaming
that their top agent got his fingerprints mixed
up with the victim's. A source close to INC says
the official cause of death is a martial arts clip to
the cranium, and the chief suspect is a member
of Midwestern's English department, the *creme
de la beaucoup eggheads*. INC hears that the
professors are afraid to be alone with each other
among the tomes and *belles lettres*.
     Chicago Tribune

News of the second murder shook the campus and beyond.
Terrified parents called their offspring home. The students
who remained filled out transfer forms and clung to room-

mates with whom, before the murder, they had maintained a warlike coexistence. Together the new inseparables visited Vinetown Hardware, fought for the last deadbolt lock on the shelves, and barricaded themselves in their rooms.

SAFEGUARD OUR CAMPUS, yelped *Prairie Gust* in a full-page editorial. Specifically: the president should step down, the campus police should have foot patrols, and exam week should be canceled. "Gustoes," the letters column, was packed with indignant queries: Why didn't they turn up the wattage on the path along the lakefill? Why wasn't there an escort service for people who studied late at the library? Campus Constabulary, the all but defunct crime-watchers group, started a recruitment drive and signed up seventeen members, to the wrath of the director of campus police: "They just like playing policeman and scaring people." Another controversy broke out when the campus Marxists circulated leaflets saying Livingston Potter was an underpaid tool of the ruling class, his murder the result of a sick capitalist society which provided schooling for the bourgeois elite. Young Americans for the Constitution replied by marching on the library, carrying American flags and signs: BOURGEOIS PROUD OF THE CAPITALIST SYSTEM. They were all home well before dark.

The general bad temper showed up most of all at the library. The announcement the day after the murder that the university president had taken the unparalleled step of closing the library to all but Midwestern students and faculty was received calmly, even in some quarters with glee. But the following day, when it was announced that the library was to be closed at night, there were howls of outrage. At closing time a dissertation writer was found hiding in Archives, proofreading her final chapters, and had to be dragged from the library. To make matters worse, at all hours of the day there were long waiting lines at the exit counter. For some reason which no one could understand, the bookcheckers had suddenly started behaving like customs inspectors.

"I thought that kid was going to undress me!" Dot said, grabbing Porter DeMont as he entered the library. "Get a load of that!" She nodded twice and pointed to the boy at the exit who was just then prodding someone's extra-full sweat shirt.

Porter condoled with her a few minutes, and then moved on, pondering: Now that could be used to exemplify correct usage of an adverb he detested. Automatically he put his thought in textbook form. WRONG: *"Hopefully, that kid will undress me."* RIGHT: *"I thought that kid was going to undress me,"* she said *hopefully*. He was still framing sentences when a woman he had seen somewhere about the library leaped in front of him.

"Professor DeMont! Please! Do you know if it's true?"

"If what is true — uyuh" — Porter groped — "Miss Westwood."

"I don't know — everything!" Her fear outweighing her awe of Porter, Marge grabbed him by the arm — he recoiled — drew him aside, and poured rumors into his unwilling ears: "They say the killer was wearing a janitor's uniform. Maybe it *is* a janitor. Or maybe that's what they want us to think! They say strange cars have been cruising the campus, they say there was a funny mark on the wall of Professor Potter's carrel —"

Porter looked mystified. "Mark? Cars? What — uyuh — precisely do you mean?"

"A gang killing!" Marge said frantically. "They say gangs are taking over the library —"

At that point Porter, who had been prepared to wait until evening if necessary for Marge to spin herself out, suddenly came to life. "Gangs!" he bellowed. "What of the library? Pilfering! Looting! Vandalizing manuscripts —"

"But manuscripts are kept in —"

" — decimating the shelves! A league of barbarians! I will not have it! Let the underclassmen swill beer in the Poetry Room. Let underclassmen fornicate in Microfiche! But — "

"That's just what I mean," Marge interrupted. "There's a rumor of rape." Porter stared. "You know, a — a pervert." She tightened her hold on his arm. "They've got to *do* something," she whimpered. "We need more security guards — alarms —"

"Alarms? But — uyuh — surely, we have —"

"Not like in the East!"

"In the East. To be sure," said Porter, wondering how to escape from this gibbering madwoman whom he now perceived to be suffering from anxiety hysteria. "Uyuh — yes, most assuredly," looking about bleakly, "in the East." He brightened. "Then you must tell Professor Hewmann. Something in the East, Hewmann!" and with surprising finesse, he deftly extricated his arm from Marge's grip and hurried away.

"Harvard?" Arthur called. But Porter was out of earshot, or pretending to be.

"Harvard?" Marge looked at him blankly. "They may have one. I'm talking about the University of Pennsylvania."

"Oh — *Penn*." Arthur shrugged.

"I didn't think you'd understand. *Here*" — slapping a pamphlet into his hand.

Holding the pamphlet at arm's length, Arthur read: "'The alarm is activated by pulling a cord, which sounds a shrill horn. The system consists of the cord running around the

toilet stalls and sinks, easily accessible from any point in —'"
Arthur gave a sound between a laugh and a snort. "A bathroom alarm system! Exactly what one would expect. At
Harvard such a contrivance would be egregiously super-
fluous. At Penn, however, bang, as the English say, in the
middle of a neighborhood fraught with peril — But, Miss
Westwood —" Arthur eyed her low-cut blouse " — Marge.
Don't you think you're being needlessly alarmed?" He
chuckled. "No pun intended."

"I am not," Marge said, "the only one. Coleman has his
application in for a gun. I'm taking karate lessons."

"Karate?" Arthur's patronizing tone made a swift change
to one of consternation. "But why?"

"Why? I could be dead by the time 911 answers. So could
you," she said, with a shrewd glance at the *Tribune* peeking
out of Arthur's briefcase. "You've read INC? Then you're
even more scared than I am."

"Hardly," and giving Marge what he hoped was a look both
distant and cutting, Arthur swaggered off to the elevator. He
waited there alone until someone turned the corner and then,
a look of fear on his face, he edged backwards as if he were
going to leave.

"What's the matter, Artie Academums?" said Ida. "You
look agitated." The elevator arrived, the doors slid open. Ida
drew her eyebrows together. "Come on, Artie. You aren't
afraid?"

"Hold it! Hold the elevator!" It was Spence, tearing around
the corner. The three of them got on. Arthur ostentatiously
took the *Tribune* out of his briefcase and opened it to INC.
Ida, just as ostentatiously, opened her *Sun-Times*. Spence
started to say something and stopped, as the elevator
reached Two and Porter and Noel got on.

"Not a very good picture of Livy," said Spence, for once the first to break the silence.

"Must have been taken years ago," said Noel. He took a closer look at Ida's paper. "What a rag," he said, gesturing contemptuously at the pictures and screaming headlines. "The *Tribune* of course is no better."

"Then you've read about the killer in our distinguished department," said Ida. There were exclamations of disparagement and disbelief. "It could have been one of us," she said defiantly. "It could have been me. I was here — in my carrel the whole time. What about the rest of you?" she challenged, as the elevator stopped at Three. The doors opened and they saw Beth.

She stepped inside and looked at their faces. "What's going on?"

"Simple," said Ida. "It's obvious Bailey thinks one of us is the killer. I'm saving him some time."

"You're not serious," said Beth.

"Not serious — ?" Shoving Beth aside, Ida made one mad spring forward and pushed the STOP button. Instantly, the elevator gave a sharp jerk and began pitching and plunging like an airplane caught in turbulence. They cried out, desperately steadying themselves. Then, with a final convulsive lurch, the elevator bumped to a standstill.

They stared dumb with amazement at Ida who stood facing them, one arm guarding the panel of buttons, the other braced against the wall. "Not serious?" she repeated. "You never, none of you, think I'm serious! Well, this time —"

"Enough," Arthur blurted out. "Come off the Lady Macbeth act."

"Enough," said Ida, mimicking Arthur's effete accents. "Hold it" — as he took a step forward. "Touch that button and I'll scream rape!"

Arthur stopped in his tracks. "You're insane," he said. "No one would believe you."

"Of course not, but wouldn't it make a good story on page one of the *Gust* — and wouldn't that make your department look good?"

"How would it make you look?" someone asked. "It's your department, too."

"Not any more it isn't. What have I got to lose?" Her eyes glittering, Ida looked them over one by one — and came back to Beth. "We'll begin with you," she said. "Where were you that night?"

Beth looked at Ida's hand, fingers outspread on the carpeted walls, and thought of a padded cell. "If you really want to know," she said, keeping her voice calm, "I was in my study."

"Working on what?"

"A linguistics problem," she said, moving forward.

"Stay there!" Ida looked suspiciously at the books Beth held out to her. "Linguistics. That's a switch. What about you?" she asked, turning suddenly on Porter.

Startled, he said, "I was — writing in my study."

"In your carrel the whole time?"

"In point of fact, I departed once — uyuh — to look up a reference. Miss Garden, I resent — am bound to take umbrage —"

"Departed once, did you? How about you, Artie? You going to tell me you were in your study too?"

"I'm not going to tell you anything," said Arthur, his face rigid with resentment.

A bell rang. From above, they heard banging sounds and shouts. "Are you all right?" The voice carried down the shaft.

Ida looked at Arthur and opened her mouth to a scream. "Rraa —"

"All right, Ida, relax," Noel said quickly. "We're okay," he shouted toward the ceiling. "Better answer her, Arthur," he said in a lower voice.

"To think," said Arthur, glaring at Ida, "I almost took the stairs. As it happens," he snapped, "I *was* confined to my carrel. No interruptions, well, one — of no consequence."

"Sure you didn't interrupt yourself?" Ida said contemptuously, before turning to Noel.

"Where was I when the lights went out? In my study — writing. Nothing much — an introduction for a Norton edition."

"Norton-Shmorton — hasn't that project been going on for some time?"

"Now just a minute, Ida," said Noel.

But Ida was looking Spence in the eye.

"Yes, *here,*" Spence said loudly. "Writing an article. Finished it and sent it off that night." His face was a puzzle. Shame? Bravado?

"What — not your book? One article won't get you tenure, my friend. What's it about?" Spence's face turned a bright red and he fumbled nervously with something in his pocket. "Oh, what's the difference," said Ida, and still standing guard over the panel of buttons, she confronted them. "So it seems all our little community were present that night. Funny we didn't see each other. No comradely visits. No scholarly exchanges. Funny," with an ironic little laugh.

The bell rang again. "Keep calm," they heard from above. "The engineer's on the way."

"I don't see it as funny," said Arthur. "We were all endeavoring to advance our research, a task, I must say, which is becoming increasingly difficult —"

"You said it," said Spence, "with these new hours. There's never enough time as it is. Now will you knock it off, Ida?" He sneezed. "It must be over 100 in here."

Research. New hours. Beth was becoming more and more depressed. "What about Livy?" she said. "Doesn't anyone else feel bad?"

"A good question," said Ida.

"Of course I feel bad," said Arthur. "But a true scholar makes a contribution. And Potter's research — what harm to concede it among ourselves? — was worthless."

"Be fair," said Porter. "His work was somewhat unorthodox perhaps, but he often made sense." A pale defense, Beth thought, a sharp contrast to the eulogy he had given at the memorial service.

"And what's your idea of a contribution, Artie?" Ida challenged.

"A definitive text, a new insight —"

"Text, insight — give me a break!" she jeered. "Where's the relevance?"

Arthur muttered, what had she published, relevant or irrelevant.

"The question is," said Noel — he took a step forward — "did Potter's work contribute to make known" — another step — "the best that has been known" — he reached under Ida's arm and pulled the button — "and thought in the world?"

"I heard that, Hewmann!" said Ida, who had made no effort to stop Noel. "Then I suppose you think my — what about discovery of truth?"

"What about literature?" someone asked, and someone else asked what new area of literary history had Livy explored.

The elevator was moving again and they hardly noticed. Livy is dead, Beth thought, and they talk about his research. She stood silent, taking sidelong glances at her colleagues. It was as if she were seeing them clearly for the first time. She looked at Noel and thought she detected behind his modesty a base servility. She looked at Spence and saw cowardice in his constant despondency. She turned to look at Porter and saw behind his drive for perfection an overwhelming egotism. Behind Arthur's pomposity she saw a streak of cunning. And Ida. She studied her face. Behind the apparent righteousness, she saw someone gripped by a terrible inadequacy. Had the whole episode been a sham? Beth wondered. Was Ida a good actress, hitting out before someone could hit her?

The waiting group on Five stared at them curiously. Someone asked what had happened. They hesitated, looking at Ida, who after a hostile glance at Arthur, strode away. Porter waited a moment, then hurried after her.

"You aren't going to your carrel?" Noel asked Spence.

"Think I'll come along later."

"Look at that walk," said Noel, watching Spence move toward the stairs. "Sometimes — sometimes I devoutly wish —"

"What?" Beth asked.

"That Livy were here to interpret."

* * *

Gil sat at the kitchen table, reading. He gave a groan of annoyance, threw INC aside, and picked up the ME's report.

As he reread the fact sheet, he could almost see the County
Morgue, the buckets of formalin, the body refrigerators.

> Cause of death: Fracture of C-1 and C-2 with
> dislocation and compression of the spinal cord
> consistent with a severe blow to the back of the
> neck. Spinal cord removed and studied. . . .
> Evidence of hemorrhage and trauma in medulla
> oblongata . . . livor mortis. . . face. . .

He picked up the telephone.

"Livor mortis?" said the ME. "Simple. The head was
dependent, see, lower than the body. Sooo — there was
gravitational pooling of red cells causing discoloration in the
small vessels of the skin. In not so plain English — livor
mortis. Spectacular color, huh? Saw someone with a tattoo
like that once. The white part? That's where the face pressed
onto the typewriter."

Gil asked another question, and the ME said, "You know I
don't like to fix time. It's a lot more variable than mysteries
make you think. But in this case you're lucky because he died
face down. Raises Cain with the undertaker when someone
dies face down — they have trouble getting the face the
regular color. They can do it, but it takes lots of dyes —

"Yeah, yeah, the time. Livor mortis begins immediately
after death. After eight to twelve hours lividity becomes
fixed — stays where it originally formed, see? The body was
found at 9:30 A.M. and someone turned it over. If it had been
turned over before eight hours, the lividity would have
shifted. Soooo — I'd place it sometime between 9:30 and
midnight."

Gil nodded, thinking about the 11:45 lights-out signal. "What about the blow?"

"No lacerations, nothing to suggest a sharp instrument. It could have been a blunt instrument."

"Or a karate blow?"

"Of course," the ME said cheerfully. "But it must have been planned. Usually someone trained in martial arts doesn't kill out of emotion."

"Thanks for the psychology."

"De nada," the ME said graciously. "Like before, huh? Say, did you read INC? Is that true about the fingerprints? Better protect your bottom, fellow."

Softly Gil hung up the telephone.

WHAT A BUNCH, BETH THOUGHT, AS SHE UNLOCKED HER CAR-
rel. Well, not all of them. Still, it was cruel to disparage Livy
who, as Porter had finally admitted, had often made sense.
He had made sense to her.

But the books that stared at her now looked even more
formidable than the first batch she had groped her way
through. *Bilingual Behavior. Isogloss Bundles.* Her eyes
jumped from book to book, confronting a title, abandoning it,
confronting another and rejecting it as even more abstruse.
The only intelligible title was *Dictionary of American Slang.*
Dislodging it from the pile, she opened the book to the
introduction. She sped through a few pages, checked herself,
and began to read more closely.

> Consider the son of an Italian immigrant living
> in New York city. . . . After leaving high school,
> he joins the navy; then he works for a year
> seeing the country as a carnival worker. He
> returns to New York, becomes a longshoreman,
> marries a girl with a German background, and
> becomes a boxing fan. He uses Italian and
> German borrowings . . . slang with a navy
> origin, and carnival, dockworker's and boxing
> words. . . .

Without moving her eyes from the page, she reached for a
note pad.

> On the other hand, a man born into a
> Midwestern, middle-class Protestant family,
> whose ancestors came to the United States in

the eighteenth century, might carry with him
popular high school terms. At high school he had
an interest in hot rods and rock-and-roll. He may
have served two years in the army, then gone to
an Ivy League college where he became an
adept bridge player and an enthusiast of cool
music. . . . This second man, no more usual or
unusual than the first, will know cant and jargon
terms of teen-age high-school use, hot-rods,
rock-and-roll, Ivy League schools, cool jazz,
army life. . . .

Could she reverse it, she wondered, go backwards *from*
the words to get a picture of the person. She reread the
passage, got out the Mark Twain essay and began jotting
down words and ideas.

"Sui generis" — College education — assumed. Could
mean knows Latin?

"budding sexual impulses"
"schoolboy manipulation"   — Psych background?
"phallic rivalry"   In analysis?

"Pa" — Working class background?

Suddenly the ideas fizzled out. It was no use. She was
fudging and she knew it. Her random observations were
those of an amateur. She needed to talk to an expert. That
linguistics professor — wasn't his carrel in Three North?

* * *

"Then this" — Beth gestured at the *Dictionary of American Slang* — "is no use at all?"

"Well — some, I suppose."

"Then it is possible." she said eagerly, willing him to forge ahead.

Professor Geraldi looked at her closely, somewhat startled, apparently, at her avid interest in what she had called a minor literary mystery. "The idea has some merit," he said slowly. "You could hit a winning streak. Say your culprit grew up in a naval family. That would be easy to spot. He might say 'head.' He might call a wall a bulkhead. I don't suppose there are any words like that?" — he glanced at her. "Right. Of course not, not in an academic piece."

He paused, his jolly face furrowed in thought, his heavy features as sharply delineated as the regions on the map behind him. Beth watched him, waiting impatiently.

"Skillet?" Geraldi suddenly asked, "or frying pan? Cottage cheese — or curd? Fire fly — or fire bug?"

The questions, clearly, were rhetorical, and she made an attempt to look as if she were following his line of thought.

He gave her a broad smile. "Word choice," he explained. "Historically that's always been most indicative of regional background. For example," he said with enthusiasm, "fire fly. That word dominates in the Northeast quadrant of Illinois. In the Northwest, fire bug takes the lead, Winnebago, Rock Island, Whiteside counties —" He swiveled around in his chair and pointed to the map.

Beth read the title — *Dialect Boundaries of Illinois* — wondering when he would finish naming counties and get back to her problem.

"Mark Twain," said Geraldi, and she leaned forward in her chair. "You're aware that in the Preface to *Huckleberry Finn* he identifies seven dialects, five of them out of Pike County, Illinois?"

She nodded and sat back again, watching him tap the map somewhere on the lower left.

"But I'm drifting into the wrong ballpark," Geraldi said.

"It's very interesting."

"And you," he said, smiling, "are very diplomatic. I'll tell you — establishing region is tough going. I've been called in by police departments to listen to tapes and the best I could say was that their suspect hailed anywhere from Denver to Ohio. And that's spoken language. You're dealing with written language which makes it that much harder. After 1425 written language became much more standardized. From 1500 on, it's exceedingly difficult to localize anything. Well, let me have a look. But it sounds to me as if you're back on your own one-yard line."

Quickly, he ran through a few pages. "Yes, just as I thought. Standard literary prose. Mentions Hannibal, but that would be —"

" — from Mark Twain," Beth said regretfully.

"Yes, of course — and Pa, too. Nothing you could call slang. Slang is the least reliable anyway. The media communicate it in no time."

Beth nodded, reflecting on all her trials and errors, the constant barriers, the stumbling blocks.

"Frankly, Miss Austin, it boils down to something other than slang. You have no letters, no publishers' records — your culprit was playing to an empty stadium. I don't like to disappoint you. Still, without external clues of any description, you're left with —"

"Internal evidence," she finished the sentence. The conundrum was back in her hands again — as she had known it would be.

"Exactly — what Altick calls 'idiosyncrasies of style.' However, as Altick says, internal evidence is slippery, very slippery. It's easy to blow a call. Some of our colleagues," he said, in a voice of increasing severity, "may look like they're in the big leagues — but they're strictly bush. I've seen too many foolish attributions based on expressions that are already in the air, terms any duffer should know are part of the general vocabulary."

He frowned disdainfully, looking, Beth thought, as if he wanted to have all the duffers fined and suspended.

"Unique," Geraldi said emphatically. "The images, the allusions, the anecdotes must bear the stamp on only *one* person" — he slapped the pages — *"his* habits, *his* special quirks. They must be as distinctive to your writer as — as — "

" — as a Butkus tackle?" she suggested.

He looked surprised. "A Butkus tackle? Very good. Expresses the idea exactly." He sat back, looking pleased.

"There's something else," he continued. "You must have incontestable proof. Say you have a few skull sessions, find a few repeated turns of phrase — you think you've hit pay dirt. But a handful of parallels is only a warm up." He smiled. "Here, of course, I'm venturing into your turf. As I — and thousands of others — might express it, you're no rookie. I hardly have to tell you that to identify beyond doubt you must steep yourself in the work until you know your player's personality through and through. And as I understand it, there is no way you can compare this" — he tapped the Mark Twain pages — "with works you know to be by the writer."

Beth stood and thanked him.

He stood, too. "You must," he repeated, giving her the essay, "have something to compare."

But perhaps she did have something to compare — that is, if she tested the fantastic idea she had been avoiding all along.

"Remember," Geraldi said, as she started to go out the door, " — unique. Take me. I couldn't play football in college — had a bad knee. So I wrote the sports pages." He chuckled. "Perhaps you could tell?" Then he became serious again. "Unique," he repeated sternly. "You must ask yourself: would only *one* person have said it that way?"

29

"I'LL NEVER FINISH BY FOUR," SAID MARGE, FROM THE NEXT computer.

Beth murmured an absent reply, typed "DeMont, Porter," and pressed ENTER. The list, which filled two and a half screens, was awe-inspiring, and it took her some time to jot down titles; but it gave her a feeling of satisfaction. It was good, she thought, as she typed "Goldberg, Spencer," to be back to research she understood.

NO ENTRIES FOUND . . . "Garden, Ida" . . . NO ENTRIES FOUND. Damn. What she had expected — but damn it anyway. All right, she said to herself, they may not have published, but they wrote. God knows they wrote. How to get her hands on enough samples? Offer to proofread for Spence? Tell Ida she wanted to read her views on — on what? Why couldn't they be on LUIS, she thought, as she gazed at the empty screen, her fingers resting impatiently on the keys. On a sudden impulse, she typed, "Bailey, Gilbert B.," hesitated a moment, pressed ENTER — and stared at the screen, astonished. T. H. HUXLEY AND EDUCATION . . . GILBERT B. BAILEY.

"Boy, he's good-looking," said Marge.

Beth started guiltily. "Who?"

"Bailey, of course. Here he comes."

Beth fumbled with the keys, pushed CLEAR and typed the first name that came to mind.

"Hello." Hearing Gil's voice, she turned and gave him a cool nod. Marge greeted him eagerly, and began firing nervous questions. . . . Gangs, why gangs, Beth wondered, as she listened to Marge. What could have brought on this latest obsession? Marge was starting in again, and she could hardly blame him if he lost patience. But Gil listened sympathetically and gave Marge reassuring replies. As he talked, Beth studied his face. He looks tired out, she thought, harried. There was something else — a tension, she decided, an air of excitement. He was like a runner, poised at the starting mark.

"I wouldn't set foot in Five South," Marge was saying. "That place is haunted. Is it true there was another book missing just outside Livy Potter's carrel?"

"I think you'll be quite safe," said Gil, ignoring her question.

"Look at the time," Marge said suddenly. "I have to be at a meeting." She picked up her folder. "I'll leave you two lovebirds alone," she said, and walked away, pretending she hadn't seen Beth's reproachful glance.

"Don't you think this has gone on long enough?" Gil took the seat Marge had vacated and looked at Beth earnestly. "I miss you."

She met his eyes for a second, then, looking just to the right of his head, she began to study a rather dull exhibit of old posters.

"What are you working on?" he asked, his voice gentle, like the touch of a hand.

"Just — research." He moved to the computer, and she leaned to the side, aware of his shirt just brushing her face. Suddenly she imagined him turning, taking her in his arms.

"Mark Twain!" Gil looked up from the screen. "My God! You're still — ?"

He turned, saw her face — and raised his arms in a gesture of capitulation. "I surrender," he said. "It is important. Ideas. They don't just happen. It takes time. Truce?" He put out a hand.

For one uncertain moment, she hung back. Then, "Truce," she said, reaching out to him. It didn't seem important to be angry, not after Livy. Solemnly they shook hands. "You've had a rough few days," she blurted out, noting the dark circles under his eyes.

"Not too bad. What about you? Read any good books lately?"

She laughed, and they talked away, on the old footing, teasing and joking, until the conversation came around to the inevitable subject. "Livy," she said sadly. "I still can't believe it."

"I can," he said, his eyes suddenly hardening. He looked at her a moment, then reached into his pocket and took out a key. Without a word, he handed it to her.

She held it in her hand, turning it up and down. It was a small key, ordinary, except for the bow, which was formed into a smiling Mask of Comedy. "It's Livy's," she said, giving it back to him. "The key to his diary."

"His diary?" said Gil, looking mystified.

She nodded. "He had it custom-made, with a special lock mechanism. Very Gothic, with secret shutters to conceal the keyhole. He showed it to me once, and I told him it made me think of my teenage Special Secrets book. I don't think he appreciated my taking his diary so lightly. Didn't you find it? He always kept it in his carrel. That's strange," she said, when Gil shook his head. "You must have seen it," she persisted, "a red cover with a Three Little Monkeys design?"

At the far end of the counter, a girl who had been sitting head in hand, staring at her computer, turned her head ever so slightly.

Beth lowered her voice. "The ultimate hand symbol, Livy called it. You know, See No Evil, Hear No — you're sure it wasn't there?"

"No diaries," said Gil, as he pocketed the key again. "No journals. Nothing like one. A diary of what?"

"Of his findings. His insights into nonverbal communication," she explained, in response to Gil's inquiring look. "He was so terrified someone would get wind of his research that he kept his major discoveries locked up. He was proud of his research —" She paused, remembering the morning Livy had lectured to Dot in the English office . . . the last time she had seen him.

"Poor Livy," she said after a moment. "Every time he turned up something new he made a dramatic announcement — I don't think he could help himself. But he never went into too much detail. He reminded me of someone who's afraid he'll get beaten out for the Nobel Prize."

"You're sure that's all he recorded?"

She hesitated. Then she said slowly, "Some of us suspected that Livy jotted down other observations — about people he knew. We used to joke about it. Don't move. One false twitch and you'll be an entry in The Diary. But we weren't at all sure, and now — who would have taken it?"

"Someone he knew," Gil said firmly. "That's certain."

"But why?"

"Now that's the question." Gil's eyes circled Level One, stopping to probe the card files as if they held the answers he wanted. "I think it's very likely — with all his roving about — he made another kind of discovery."

"About the thefts? You can't think he was killed for the price of a few books."

"Not such a small price."

"I've noticed," Beth glanced toward the exit, "you've increased security."

"All over — and it's helped wonderfully. We've apprehended a janitor who was stealing toilet paper, we've nabbed a visiting trustee who didn't know she was supposed to check out books. I'm a complete failure." But he didn't look discouraged. "What about you? How's your work going?"

"I called them — the Peacocks —" She broke off when she saw his expression. "You knew, didn't you? It's okay," she fended off an explanation. "Did you also know that Marylou didn't write that essay, plagiarized or not?"

"I didn't know," he said surprised. "Then what are you — ?"

"Oh . . . I'm trying a new approach."

"Which is?"

"Well — let's say I'm following your path. Like this." She cleared the screen and typed, "Hewmann, Arthur."

"Indeed," said Gil, after a glance at the screen. "Very promising." Casually he looked at his watch. Then he said, "What about dinner? Tomorrow night? Wish I could make it for tonight, but I have another engagement . . . business." Again, she saw the excited glint in his eye.

"Perfectly all right," she said. "As for me, *mon ami* — I labor into the night on my new research. It is completely unimportant. That is why it is so interesting."

"Roger Ackroyd," he said automatically. "All night?" He gave her a worried look. "Don't overwork the little gray cells." He leaned closer and just touched the tip of her nose. "By the way," he said, "you look beautiful."

Beth felt her face turn red. "Don't worry," she said quickly. "If the Vinetown gangs come after me, I'll threaten them with a surprise quiz. . . . There was something I wanted to ask you —" thinking about the title she had seen on LUIS.

"Ask away, anything, but," without changing tone, "not too personal since I see Frazier headed in our direction."

Noel greeted them and asked if they had seen Spence. "I'm moonlighting at helping writers," he explained, perching on the edge of the counter. "Just propping Spence up a bit — the kind of thing we all need." He laughed. "There are times when I wish I had a Maxwell Perkins."

Beth started to protest and Noel cut her off.

"No, I mean it. It's as true for me as for Spence. If I could only give him confidence," he mused. "For some writing, he's perfectly sure of himself, but when it comes to academic writing — he clutches."

"But what other writing — ?" Beth trailed off.

Spence was there, looking dejected as usual. He eyed Gil warily, almost expectantly, before turning to Noel. "I'm ready." He sounded as if he were leaving for his own execution instead of a writing session. As they started off, Beth asked casually if Spence had an extra copy of his dissertation.

"Sure — there's one in the English office. Why? Looking for errors?"

"Just reading up on Whitman."

"Help yourself. You'll be bored stiff," and he hurried to catch up with Noel.

"You were going to ask," said Gil. He leaned forward, resting his elbows on the counter. From behind him came a sudden staccato of beeps. Instantly he turned to look at the exit.

"I completely forgot," they heard Noel say. Embarrassed, he removed a book from the pocket of his jacket and apologized to the checker. "Bad habit of mine. See — I've charged it out. Goldberg," he joked, "it's all your fault. Come on — we've only got an hour or so."

"You're in a hurry, too," Beth told Gil. "My question can wait."

"Tomorrow then . . . I miss you," he repeated, his voice low.

Beth watched him run the steps and go through the exit. Feeling illogically happy, she returned to the screen.

A few minutes later she was scanning Arthur's list. Impressive, she thought, you had to admit it. She began to scribble titles. *"The Waste Land* Revaluated: A Study of Eliot's Rendering of Human Failure."

"I HATE THE BASTARD," GIL SAID.

"Your guest?" said Victor, who was lounging behind his desk, facing the door as always. He took a sip of slivovitz. "Just because of the murders?"

"Of course because of the murders."

"I don't think so. Oh, naturally," he conceded, "you hate for the murders. But you also hate because someone has put over one on you. Why look at me like that? Not to be ashamed. I felt the same way," said Victor, his expression turning grim, "when I discovered my sous chef was a restaurant critic. I caught him raw-handed — at his station in the kitchen! Little cards!" said Victor, in a voice of supreme contempt. "He was writing notes on little cards. 'This is flavored with sorrel, that with cilantro' — can you conceive of it?" He uttered a curse and glared at the framed awards that covered the walls of his private room.

A moment or two went by. Victor composed himself and turned back to Gil. "And you hate," he said, his voice once again calm and assured, "because something you value was stolen. This, too, I understand. I spend months, developing, testing, refining. I create a new dish. And then" — he named a famous chef — "comes in, so friendly, so smiley. He tastes, he makes with the compliments. Then he hastens back to his kitchen — and imitates my couscous! A failure, naturally, a compromise to mass taste. Still, I am furious at even the attempt to steal my creation. And without acknowledgment! When a chef puts a dish of mine on his menu, I expect the credit that is due me. I have made you think of something."

"What?"

"Very well. You do not wish to say. Lastly," Victor ticked off the final point on a finger, "you hate because it is still in part a mystery you have failed to solve."

Abruptly Gil got to his feet and began pacing the room. "It's the damndest thing I ever encountered, Victor. There's no reason to it." He strode back and forth and went over the story point by point, while Victor listened, his eyes half-closed. "Well," Gil said finally, "the whys and wherefores will have to wait." He sat down again, opposite Victor. "I know who it is — and the accomplice. Now I need proof."

"Why not simply search the home?"

"I can't justify a warrant — yet."

"Who says anything about warrants? I know someone, a former maître d' — you shake your head! Ah yes" — Victor gave a scornful shrug — "here it is different. Our methods were better. Bureaucracy! I have no patience for petty officials," and pounding a heavy fist on the desk, Victor launched into a tirade against immigration.

Gil waited until he had finished. Then he said, "I take it you're still waiting for the visas for your new assistant chefs?"

Victor broke into a deep laugh. *"Touché!* All right, my friend Gilbert, what can I do for you?"

"We'll begin with this." Gil produced a package.

Victor removed the wrapping, looked over the contents. "Is this all?"

"All? It's my own — in mint condition."

Victor nodded, handling the object carefully. Perfection he understood.

"Now the timing," Gil began, "that's crucial. . . ."

Victor listened, nodding enthusiastically from time to time. "The idea appeals to me," he said. "I love the duplicity, the element of the unexpected. You startle, you shock, you take by surprise — like a fine menu." He got up, went around the desk and embraced Gil in a bear hug. "Don't worry, Gilbert. It will work!"

* * *

They sat at a banquette in the same private corner Gil and Beth had occupied earlier in the summer and listened to the captain recite the menu.

One of them asked for steak and mashed potatoes.

"May I suggest," said the captain, with the slightest lift of the eyebrows, "the lamb rib eye in puff pastry? The risotto of lobster?"

He was told to make the steak well-done and asked if they had A-1.

The captain left to consult with Victor, and returned sometime later with wonderful looking dishes, rack of veal, poached capon, and steak and mashed potatoes, arranged on the plate to perfection. Next to it he set a cruet filled with A-1 sauce.

Gil played with his food and watched his guests. One was relaxed, at ease. The other, tense, suspicious, glowered at Gil and cast warning looks at the other person, entering the conversation only once to ask if that was Gloria Steinem over there.

"I believe it is," said Gil absently. His eyes were on the other guest. He watched the hands, skillfully cutting the meat, and thought of Marylou Peacock, of Livy Potter.

While one guest sat silent, the other, occasionally using a French phrase or an apt quotation, conversed easily. They talked about travel, about gardens and paintings, about the

Ivy League and Midwestern and through it all Gil saw Livy's
face.

It was getting late. They had started late and, as it was a
week night, the crowd soon thinned out. Finally they were
the last ones left in the room, but there were none of the
usual subtle moves from captain and waiter to hurry them
out. The two guests ate, obviously enjoying their meals.
Victor hovered in the background, motioning to the waiter,
chiding.

Dessert was served, and the conversation turned to Chicago, its politics, its schools, its transportation. Gil made
some comment about lack of air conditioning on the buses.

"'Human life,'" quoted his guest, watching Victor pour
brandy, "'is everywhere in a state in which much is to be
endured and little to be enjoyed.'" He sat back, brandy in
hand, and gazed around with an air of content. "This room is
— superb." His eyes moved from the paneled walls to the
high ceiling. "Admirable proportions. Like an Adam interior. I
remember in London —"

Victor reappeared suddenly. "I have something," he said,
"for you." He brought a hand from behind his back, placed a
book on the table and walked away.

The guest started with surprise. Then, looking pleased,
he put down the brandy snifter, reached out — . *"National
Sports of* — but I have that!" He dropped the book as if he had
been burned. "How did he get this?"

"Shut up! It's a trap! Excuse me, Professor DeMont," said
Dot, "but don't say anything."

From behind them they heard a bellow and the sudden
violent crash of breaking china.

ACROSS THE ROOM STOOD VICTOR, TABLECLOTH IN HAND, looking disdainfully at the shattered remains of a crystal vase. "Why do I pull off the cloth?" he shouted at the terrified waiter. "Because it is askew. We have no crooked table settings here!"

Gil watched the waiter bend to pick up the fragments of glass. Then he turned and looked at Porter. The chairman's expansiveness had melted away. His whole face sagged, as if the features had suddenly surrendered to age. A second or two went by. "It was you, wasn't it?" said Gil.

Porter sat, eyes down, staring at the floor.

"You took them all, didn't you?"

"No, Professor!" said Dot, as he started to speak. "Don't say anything!"

"What does it matter?" Porter murmured, giving Dot a weary wave of the hand.

"Would you care to tell me why?"

"He's a savior," Dot said promptly, looking at Porter as if he were indeed the Messiah.

"Why?" Gil persisted. "When did you first — ?"

At that the chairman lifted his head. For a moment he merely looked at Gil, on his face an expression of restive tolerance, the same look that might appear when a student grossly misinterpreted a line of poetry. "First?" he said. "There was no first. There was an assemblage, an abhorrent accumulation — a monstrousness of destruction. Acid splashed on Sandburg Hall, brick wars in the Tennyson Garden, paint —"

"What did that — ?"

"The vandalism spread — to the library! They defaced the walls, they gashed the tables! They treated the books like playthings, drawing imbecilic pictures, scribbling puerile inanities — they marked up the whole of Chaucer!" Porter was almost shouting now. Gil had never heard him speak with so much energy. "During examination week they ran out of the building with textbooks. And what did the guards do? They filed incident reports — !"

Gil listened, reminded of something — what? In the space of a few seconds, he tried to put his finger on it, gave up, and turned his attention to Porter who was talking wildly about an article in *Smithsonian*.

" — I learned to my shock that plundering university libraries had become big business, even for gangs!" Porter shook his head. "Dreadful. A harbinger. Close on the heels came reports of Audobon prints razored out at Harvard, maps pilfered from Yale, Civil War histories from Duke. And all the while Midwestern still relied on guards. I advised them they must have more sophisticated security. I was told," he said angrily, "there were no funds." Abruptly he stopped, and lost apparently in his own thoughts, he stared indifferently at Victor who stood at the fireplace watching them.

"And then?"

Porter turned his eyes on Gil. "Then came reports, emanating out of the entire country, from Princeton to Stanford," he said definitively, as another person might speak of New York and Los Angeles. "A notorious thief, a scoundrel — passing himself off as a Mormon doing genealogical research — was pillaging academic libraries." Porter sat up straight, seeming to square his shoulders. "They caught up with him," he said in a voice of triumph. "At Muhlenberg they found him out. The rascal had fifteen footlockers of books! When he came up for trial, the judge said that university libraries must be protected from such abominable assaults, and sentenced him to twenty years at Leavenworth. Quite right," said Porter, with a satisfied nod. "And the shameful episode prompted our library to install an electronic system."

"So you had what you wanted."

"So I thought," Porter said bitterly, "until a mangled *Waiting for Godot* was discovered, the cover in one room, the inside in another. Students! Trying to remove the metal tape. Then worse, oh much worse, I learned that we were losing books to professional thieves who knew how to circumvent the electronic system. Report it, I demanded. Call the FBI! No, no, I was told. We must avoid publicity. And thus — our library — a house of prayer — was allowed to become a den of thieves." He paused and slowly looked around, surveying the beautiful room. Then his eyes came back to Gil. "There was only one answer, and I advised them of it.

"We must, I told them, follow the example of European libraries. Make the collection noncirculating. Close the stacks. Bar everyone from the shelves." He was talking rapidly now, the words spilling out like students decamping an 11:00 A.M. class. "Impossible, I was told. We would have a return to the sixties. Students would be so infuriated by the inconvenience they would occupy the administration building. And the expense. The cost of the required personnel would be overwhelming. Nor would they consider my final suggestion, to call an end to unrestricted access and close our library to people not associated with the university. I —"

Porter was interrupted by a clatter of talk. A party of four, carrying theater programs, was being ushered to a table. A look of annoyance crossed Victor's face and he started toward the maître d'. Then he glanced at Gil who made the slightest gesture, did a slow about-face, and returned to his post at the fireplace.

The exchange was lost on Porter. "I was horrified. I lived in a state of dreadful expectation. I would see a beautiful book, an important book — kept in the open stacks because it did not qualify as rare — and the next day I would marvel that it was there still."

I should have seen it, Gil thought. It's me. He reminds me of myself. He's not the one. Then who — ?

"It became clear," Porter continued, "that some dramatic action was required."

Gil brought himself back. "Dramatic action?"

"Something," said Porter, "to call attention to our vulnerability." He hesitated, picked up his napkin and began to fold it. "I had read a report. A Tulane professor — using his credentials to gain admission to libraries — had stolen books and peddled them. I determined it was my duty to follow his example, not for my own gain, but for the gain of all. I myself," said Porter, creasing the napkin into fourths as he talked, "would — uyuh — rip off so many books they would be forced to report the thefts, forced to close the stacks. I began my research."

"Your research!"

"On the science of theft," said Porter, adopting a professorial tone. "As I would for any project, I began to collect material."

Gil imagined him in the lecture hall, telling students that material is of the utmost importance. "But where did you get it?"

"I looked naturally to the primary sources. I found a splendidly edifying article on theft prevention in *Library Quarterly*. *Library Review* also had an excellent piece, offering valuable information with respect to magnets for detecting security devices and instruments for removing tattle-tape. Most instructive," Porter said approvingly. "The *Journal of North American Libraries* provided an admirable discussion of the Von Hoffen electronic system as well as the address of the company — to which I wrote for material. I was still pondering my method when, feeling somewhat unwell, I had occasion to visit my doctor." He stopped and gave Gil a challenging look, as if defying him to guess his secret.

"And you had your answer," said Gil, taking satisfaction at Porter's surprise.

"You know? Who told you?" Porter looked unbelievingly at Dot.

"Great balls of fire!" she shouted, looking hurt. "You know I wouldn't —"

"No one told me," Gil interrupted, noting the inquisitive face of a passing waiter, and thinking of the gossiping and speculating that must be going on in the kitchen. "There's a sign about pacemakers at the exit."

"To be sure," said Porter, with a nod of apology to Dot. "I saw it too. Strange I never noticed it earlier. But not until after — I had feared the worst, but the doctor assured me my heart was sound, that I suffered merely from occasional palpitations. He advised me to reduce coffee intake, to cut out tobacco, and to avoid excitement. In the midst of our discussion, the doctor was called from the room. On his desk was a booklet on pacemakers. I picked it up and it fell open to a passage advising patients as to how to avoid electrical interference. Excitement! It was fortunate the doctor had completed the examination. I was certain he had more — still, I regretted taking the booklet."

"But I wonder what the little green things are?" The high voice came from the theater party, and it was followed by more voices, raised in debate. Then Gil saw the woman beckon to Victor.

"At home," said Porter, ignoring the interruption, "my excitement rose. I came upon a paragraph which dovetailed perfectly with my own research. Airport screening devices, it explained, were unlikely to interfere with the pacemaker, but they might detect the metal in the pulse generator. It was advisable, therefore," said the chairman, looking at Gil as if he had just scored a victory, "for the pacemaker wearer to obtain clearance by presenting his identification to the airport clerk!"

"And the card? Your identification?" Gil said, fascinated with the story, even while the question, if not Demont, then *who*, nagged at him.

"There followed a description of a permanent plastic card, a form for the patient to fill out and send for a new card in case of loss, and the address of the manufacturer. The name. Let me see —" He frowned.

"I'm right, am I not? They are shredded artichokes?" The question was being addressed to Victor.

"Leeks, Madame." Victor motioned to the waiter.

"I have it," said Porter. "Elektramed, Incorporated." That question solved, he continued. "The student guards," he said, "presented no difficulty. I am told, though I do not see it, that I have a certain intimidating quality. I merely showed the student my card. He would examine the books in my briefcase, then switch off the device, and I would walk through the exit with a book in the inside pocket of my suit. If I had a heavy book, I carried my jacket over my arm. In bad weather I could fit several books in my raincoat pocket.

Occasionally," Porter glanced at Dot appreciatively, "Miss Drennan would help.

"She would nod twice for perfect conditions — if a particularly credulous student were on duty, if none of my colleagues were likely to be in the region. As a further precaution, if the opportunity came, she would say I was in my office when I was at the library."

"Yeah," said Dot. "I did it that day Livy Potter — I felt like a louse about that."

"Not at all, Miss Drennan. You have no occasion for guilt." Porter put a protecting hand over hers. "When I had collected what I judged sufficient books to cause consternation, I deliberately sent one off to a bookstore in Boston, someone known to be a reputable dealer. As you know, my hopes were realized. The extent of the loss became known, the FBI was called in. . . ."

"But you still continued —"

"They refused to close the stacks!"

"So you — became a thief yourself," said Gil, his tone expressing more condolence than blame.

"What do I care for disgrace in the eyes of others?" Porter shouted. "'A man's first care should be to avoid the reproaches of his heart, his next to escape the censures of the world. If the last interferes with the former, it ought to be entirely neglected.' Addison," he said, "'Sir Roger at the Assizes,'" and flung his napkin on the table.

"Great balls of fire! Please, Professor DeMont," said Dot. "Calm down. Don't make a federal case out of this, Bailey. Can't you see you're frustrating him?"

"It *is* a federal case," said Gil.

"They're quite safe," said Porter.

"I've got 'em," said Dot, "at my house. I stored them in the basement."

"Good God!" said Porter. "The damp! They'll have to be vacuum dried. *Library Trends* has an excellent article about what to do when disaster occurs —"

"But what was your method?" Gil cut him off. Porter looked puzzled. "Your organization? You must have had some plan."

"Plan? There was no plan. At first I — uyuh — protected at random. I was hurrying to a lecture in the council room and I saw the Papworth. I was on my way to uyuh — the men's room when I stopped to look at the Dickens. The Nonesuch! A crime they're still in the stacks!" and Gil almost found himself nodding in sympathy.

"Thereafter," Porter went on, "as I became deeply involved in revising my study of eighteenth century attitudes, I took whatever came to eye. Naturally, during the beginning stages, I spent considerable time in the literature shelves. Later, my research broadened, the early moments of the Industrial Revolution, the spread of experimental science — I stumbled on the Fleming when I was looking into Jenner's discovery of vaccination for smallpox."

"The Alken?" Gil nodded toward the volume on the table.

Porter spread out his arms in a gesture of inevitability. "One quadrant from the literature on architecture — I was researching the classical designs of the brothers Adam. I came upon the Frank Lloyd Wright," he volunteered, "when I was investigating the Gothic revival of the latter part of the century."

"The Freud?" Gil said desperately.

"A few shelves from Hume's *Treatise on Human Nature*. I had no plan — only to save the books." Porter drew himself up. "'As good almost kill a man as kill a good book: who kills a man kills a reasonable creature, God's image; but he who destroys a good book kills reason itself.' *Areopagitica*. I first read it in the Widener Library."

"And so you were not the one," said Gil, voicing his new conviction more to himself than Porter.

"Not the one?"

"You forget, Mr. Chairman," said Gil, falling for a moment into Porter's formal mode of speech, "we have before us still — I had thought that first Marylou Peacock, then Livy Potter found you out."

"You thought that?" For a moment the chairman looked ready to get to his feet. Then, appearing to have thought better of it, "Kill? Nonsense. I saw Potter, of course, that night."

"You saw —" Gil let out his breath in surprise. "What do you mean?"

"I had occasion to pass his carrel. I was looking up a quotation. And when I returned I saw —" He mentioned a name.

Gil rose. "Why didn't you tell me?"

"I thought it of no importance. It did cross my mind that there was a look of perturbation — but my thoughts were elsewhere. I wanted to quote precisely, you see —"

Porter watched Gil run out of the room. "Perhaps we should leave now, Miss Drennan. I am feeling . . . tired."

"I think," said a firm voice, "to wait would be better." Victor was standing at the table.

In Victor's office Gil held the telephone to his ear, counting the rings. Why didn't she answer?

32

THE CARREL HAD A LONELY EDWARD HOPPER LOOK, THE periphery in darkness, the focus on the desk where the lamp threw a circle of light.

Her back to the door, elbows resting on two piles of articles, Beth pondered the paragraphs in front of her. She glanced at her watch and gave a start of surprise. Why drag it out any longer, she thought, her eyes moving to the list on the bulletin board. A canceling scrawl ran through every name except one. She took up her pen and drew an extravagant circle around the final name, then flung out of the chair. Cautiously she pulled aside one fold of the coat that covered the window.

The campus, under a cloudy, starless sky, was blacked out. Peering down into the gloom, she could just see the deserted quadrangles. To her left, was that a wink of light? She craned her neck. No, the East Tower was dark. Whatever it was had vanished.

She let the fold drop and lowered herself into the chair. She was still feeling stiff from the hour spent cramped under the sofa in the ladies' room. She had listened to the janitors' shouts, heard the crash of a wastebasket, the swish of a mop. Once, the resting room door had opened and she had lay still, trembling. A few cursory shoves of the vacuum, then she had heard the sound of eager feet leaving. She had forced herself to count out the minutes, waiting until she thought it was safe to leave. In the corridor she had halted once, her heart skipping a beat at the dark shape that loomed ahead. Gradually her eyes had become accustomed to the dim light, and she saw she had almost stumbled into a dolly, packed with chairs. They were stacked on their backs, legs in the air, like

lions rampant. After a gingerly detour around the dolly into
the tower, she had sighed with relief when she reached her
carrel. She had been inside ever since, reading, comparing,
checking names off the list.

Why, she wondered, as she poured coffee into the cup. She
could not explain it, but of this she was certain: the writers
were one and the same. Shoving the thermos out of the way,
she picked up the Mark Twain essay.

> . . . Father Polly aiming her switch at Tom,
> keeping him from other boys, turning his
> Saturday holiday into captivity at hard labor. No
> approval is ever shown by Father Polly. Tom
> must stage his own death to hear a good word
> of himself.
>
> The passions and problems of *The Adventures
> of Tom Sawyer* inevitably lead one to think of
> James and John Stuart Mill. One thinks of James
> setting John to Latin at age three, Greek at age
> 8. . . . The most extraordinary point of all is
> that John never raises his voice against his
> father. . . .

Putting the essay aside, she scanned the article on Samuel
Butler once again.

> . . . Ernest Pontifex, entirely under his father's
> thumb. Before Ernest can speak well, Theobald
> sets him to lisping the Lord's Prayer. Before
> Ernest can crawl, Theobald decrees that he
> learn to read. When Ernest forgets a word,
> when he says 'tum' for 'come,' Theobald whips
> him and shuts him up in a closet. Ernest's entire

childhood is fear and shrinking. Yet he never
kicks back.

The passions and problems of the father-son
relationship in *The Way of All Flesh* inevitably
lead one to think of James and John Stuart Mill.
One thinks of James setting John to Latin at age
3, Greek at age 8. One sees James flying into a
rage when John stumbles over a line in Plato.
One hears James proclaiming that there will be
no children's books, no boy companions, no
holidays. The great James Mill never praises his
son, and he guards against John's hearing praise
from anyone else. . . . Above all, what strikes
the reader as extraordinary is that the son never
raises his voice against the father.

There was, in the second article, a depth and confidence that
made her think it had been written later, perhaps years after,
the Mark Twain essay. But the same writer, surely, had
authored both.

She wondered if the Mills came into articles by the same
writer on Gosse and Ruskin. That would be the logical place.
And conclusive proof — even Geraldi would grant her that.
There was no hurry, she thought, contemplating the walk
through the dark library to Periodicals. She could put it off
until morning — but the last thing she wanted was another
wait. Fumbling among paper clips and staples, she fished her
flashlight out of the drawer. Suddenly her fingers tightened
around the flashlight. She stared at the door.

Again she heard it. A little scraping sound followed by a
metallic clink. She sat perfectly still, imagining fingers, groping in the dark. Then she heard the click of a key, the subdued

rattle of tumblers sliding back. The study door banged against the wall.

Silhouetted in the doorway, a camouflage design parka over an arm, was the last name on her list.

"Working late, Beth?"

She drew her eyes away from the parka. "Just — catching up," she said, with an effort at lightness. "Is — is that why you're here?"

"Catching up?" said the visitor. "I suppose you could call it that," and walked straight over and stood in front of her. He gave a casual glance at the bulletin board, then looked down at the desk. She watched him, as he stood quietly, examining the pages she had been reading. He finished, and began flipping through the discard stack. "Ah," he said exuberantly, and pulled out an article. "Let's have a dose of Arthur!"

With one arrogant move of an arm, the books were swept off the other chair. The visitor sat down, legs comfortably crossed. Holding the pages high, he declaimed a few lines. Then, with an exclamation of disgust, he flung the article into the heap of books on the floor. "The man can't write a decent sentence! I can write better blindfolded." He stared at the desk. "I can also," he said, "write worse."

Beth followed his gaze to the Mark Twain essay.

"Dreadful, isn't it?" said Noel.

33

It was very quiet as they sat facing each other, Beth bolt upright, Noel lounging in his chair. Framed in the open doorway, he looked the picture of a gentleman, cultivated, slim, not Gil's wiry thinness, she thought inconsequently, a polished slenderness, almost dandified.

"You have to understand," he said, as if he were bringing forward a fundamental point, "that piece is out of my salad days."

She looked a question. He made a self-effacing gesture and said. "I wrote it when I was a grad student. I thought it was so brilliant I zealously sent it around to all the journals. I might have saved the postage. It was mailed back promptly every time. ' — needs focus — too diffuse — immature —' There was some merit to the criticisms — especially the last. Still, it was a natural for a boy from Quincy." He eased himself into a more comfortable position and began to hum the tune she had heard so often.

She tried to keep her voice steady. "Where exactly is Quincy?"

"You don't know my home town? Quincy, Illinois —" he bent an arm " — elbow of the state."

Suddenly she thought of Geraldi, tapping the edge of the map.

"You should take a drive there sometime," Noel was saying. "Nothing to it. Go south on Highway 66 to MacLean and from there you head due west. Put your foot on the pedal, go as far as you can without crossing the Mississippi — and you will be in Quincy. Peaceful, droning Quincy. It hasn't changed. Even the Elks Club is the same. That's where they held our high school reunion. Do you know, out of my whole class I was the only one who left. 'We've jest stayed here in Quincy,'" he drawled.

He smiled. "But I'm getting away from your grand tour. Have a look at the town square. You'll see benches around it and old men, loafing, chewing their plugs of Union Leader. Oh, and you have to go down Main Street. There's an arch of elms over it and along both sides are mammoth old Victorian houses — widows' walks way up on top, big roomy porches down in front. Summer nights you can hear the chains creaking while the Quincy folks rock in their swings and watch the world go by." Suddenly his voice took on a higher pitch. "'There goes Billy Frazier's boy — not quite so tall, mebbe, favors his mama. Pour me another lemonade, will you deary?'"

Noel smiled at her. "Don't look so terrified, Beth. The place is out of the past, a backwater. Let's take a kayak," he sang softly, "to Quincy or Nyack, let's get away from it all."

She thought how absurd it was that Noel should be singing in her carrel, at God knew what hour, and at the same time she thought, so that is the tune.

He stopped singing and leaned back in his chair, a faraway look in his eyes. "Just a mile or so south of Quincy sits Marblehead. Ever hear of Marblehead? That's where the quarry is and the Quincy wits made much of it. If you wanted to say that someone was stupid, a real moron, you said, 'Oh, he's from Marble head.'"

Noel's face turned a faint red. "Once — once my father called me a marble head. He was going over a paper I'd written — line by line — the way he always did. Then he stopped reading and looked up at me under his glasses — I can still see that look — as if he wanted to kill me. '*One* of

Hamlet's famous soliloquies!' he said. 'Is *that* the best you can do? You — you marble head!'"

There was a silence. Then Noel laughed and said, "He was right, of course. I keep a dish of stones from that quarry in my study. To remind me."

"But Mark Twain?" she asked. For some reason, one she had no wish to discover, she was afraid to hear any more about Noel's father.

"Geography, my dear. Just across the Mississippi is Missouri — Missoura, they say in Quincy. Drive over the bridge — sometimes you'll still see a big paddleboat on the river — and you're in Hannibal. Compared to the metropolis of Quincy, Hannibal was a village, but it was famous because that was where Mark Twain grew up. There's Becky's house, and across from it, with the picket fence around it, Tom's house — Mark Twain's really. You could almost say I grew up with Mark Twain. Every chance I had I did what he did. I stole watermelons, I explored the cave. I skated the Mississippi — at midnight," Noel said exultantly, "without permission."

She had a momentary vision of Noel as a small boy, escaping — from what?

"I copied his breakfast — steak and coffee. I copied his curses." Noel gripped the arm of the chair. "You quadrilateral astronomical incandescent son of a bitch!" he shouted, and Beth jumped.

He chuckled. "I tried that one out on my father many times — not to his face of course."

All right, she thought, fighting an urge to jump and run, there was some tension between Noel and his father. It had nothing to do with the essay in question. She got hold of herself and spoke out: "I still don't understand, Noel. How did something you wrote get into the essay contest? Was there some mixup?"

He gave her a broad grin. "That's amusing. No, Beth. There was no mixup. I put it there."

"You!" she cried out. "But why?"

"Why? You've only been at this a few years. How could you understand?"

"Try me. I mean just explain, Noel. There must be a simple explanation," she said, suddenly realizing how much she wanted this to be true.

He looked away from her stare, turning a handsome profile. It was almost a habit to turn that profile, Beth thought distractedly, and wondered how many times he had used it effectively.

"As if there were simple explanations." Noel's voice broke into her thoughts. "As if I could say it without sounding clichéd. Well, the clichés are true — and even that's a cliché. Publish or perish. You know the pressures. They forget — there are other pressures."

He looked at her sternly, almost, she thought, the way his father must have looked at him. "Do you think I want to be like Arthur — lecturing from yellowed Harvard notes? Intellectual apathy, my distinguished father would have said, a failure to my calling." He paused a moment. Then he said, "It's *Left Hand, Right Hand!* all over again."

"Left hand, right — ?"

"Really, Beth," he interrupted, "for such a book-wise lady, you have surprising gaps in your reading. I'm speaking of Osbert Sitwell's autobiography."

"Oh — Sitwell. It's a strange title."

"But apt. It comes from those soothsayers who look at your hand and read your future."

"You mean — palmists?"

"Exactly. Give me your hand. Give it to me! No! The other one." He caught hold of her left hand with a force that made her lurch forward in her chair. "You're cold, my dear," he said, patting her fist.

"Such a small hand." He forced her fingers back. "So beautifully formed. If you ever give up this trade, you could be a hand model. Let me see —" Beth shivered as he moved a finger along her palm. "Pride — intelligence — audacity. Too much of the last perhaps. Too bad. You can never change it." He dropped her hand abruptly.

She moved away from him. "Can't change what?"

"According to the palmists, my dear Beth, the lines of the left hand are incised at birth." He heaved a sigh and looked at the pages on the desk.

"And the right hand?" she asked finally, unable to endure the silence any longer.

Noel looked at her blankly. "The right hand?" He roused himself as if coming out of a dream. "That, Beth, is the hand we own. We change the lines of the right hand by our actions, and environment, and the life we lead — so the palmists say. Perhaps. But it always comes back to this."

Noel held up a nail-bitten left hand and studied it as if it were an object that belonged to someone else. Then, turning, so that she could see his palm, he began to trace the lines. "These," he said, "are the hidden roots that can strengthen, just as they can on occasion enfeeble the character. Our determinants, our heritage, our birthrights — our wrongs. You know my father?"

She hesitated. "I — I know something of him."

"William Frazier, Rhodes scholar. He made a brilliant record at Oxford, could have gone wherever he wanted. But he chose to return to Quincy where he became the sage of Crockett College. Oh, he was one of the great teachers. One of his students became a Supreme Court justice." Noel was speaking so softly now his voice was barely audible.

"I didn't know it was Crockett — I still don't see," she went on, determined now to get the answer out. And then, her mind ran eagerly ahead, they could both leave, and get the sleep they so obviously needed.

He gave her a calculating look. "No?" he said. "You still don't see? You will. Let us return, gentle reader, to late spring. I had been asked . . . to take on a project." He stopped abruptly, his voice suddenly losing its confident note.

She forced herself to think back, and called up a memory of Noel, rushing about the stacks, gathering armloads of books. "An introduction, wasn't it? But you never —"

"Never said what? I didn't, did I? It was a new edition of Eliot's *Poems.*"

She stared. "You were asked to write an introduction of T. S. Eliot?"

"Why are you so surprised? I said Norton, but it was Cantbridge Press that asked me. A great honor." He looked down at the books piled in front of his chair.

When he began to talk again, his voice was weary. "Weeks. For weeks I worked on that introduction." He met her eyes, almost pleading. "You must know what it's like. You write, you rewrite. No matter what you try, everything comes out hackneyed. . . . One day — the worst day of all — I couldn't write a line. I'd been locked in my study for hours, cooped up like a prisoner. I wanted to get out — to run, to smack a tennis ball. But I couldn't afford to leave. I had already missed two deadlines."

He stopped, giving her the same pleading look. "I knew what they expected from me," he said. "Something original, something that hadn't been said before. But you see, my dear Beth, I couldn't think of anything original.

"So I sat there, not thinking really, just looking around, at the books, the photos — all the scholar's accoutrements and memorabilia. And then suddenly I knew. I was looking at that damn dish of stones when it came to me. I never was going to find something new to say. I wasn't up to it. I packed up my notes. I'll get out, I thought, I'll play some tennis. Maybe then I can think. I slammed out of my carrel. And my problem was solved."

"But how?"

Noel gave a sudden laugh. "Marylou Peacock. She was standing just outside the door."

Beth's stomach tightened. "You knew her?"

He smiled. "Marylou was an old friend. I met her one day on the tennis courts. Then from time to time I'd see her in the stacks. I used to talk to her, listen, rather, while she prattled away. Pretty girl — but tiresome. She had the typical fervor of the undergraduate English major." He broke off and sat thinking, letting a foot roam over the books on the floor.

She looked at Noel's face, pale in the shadowy light. How handsome he was, she thought. How he must have captivated Marylou. How thrilled she must have been that a famous professor had time for her. She pictured the girl gazing up at him, as they stood outside his carrel.

Suddenly Noel kicked out savagely and sent a book crashing to the wall. "I can still see her silly smile! 'Oh,' she said, 'Professor Frazier! I was hoping —' She was off and running, confiding her latest infatuation. 'T. S. Eliot. He's so amazing. I just had to get what I felt on paper. I haven't shown it to anyone — could you?' She watched me read it, kept asking, 'Do you think it's any good?'"

Noel looked at Beth thoughtfully. "It's funny," he said, "the way students sometimes blunder into a genuine insight. I encouraged her, told her it was wonderful, as indeed it was. Just what I needed. I offered to submit her essay for the prize, and" — he turned his eyes on the Mark Twain essay — "I substituted that pathetic effort of mine. . . . Who would have believed it would win?"

He shook his head. "Never trust committees. I was still trying to think of some way to convince the department the essay was ineligible — it ought to have been ineligible, god-dammit! It wasn't written for a class."

He sat up straight and glared at Beth. "Where was I? Oh yes, I ran into the minx on campus. She rushed up to me, babbling away. 'Thank you, thank you, it's so wonderful. I'm so *ecstatic* I'm going to work all night.' Someone had leaked the news her essay had won — who I wonder? She wouldn't say. It doesn't — didn't — matter. I had no choice. She had said she had one more paper to write, but the dorm was so noisy, everyone getting ready to take off, it was hard to concentrate. So I suggested, not to mention my name, but that she ask to use Arthur's carrel." Noel paused and gave Beth a conspiratorial look, as if he hoped to draw her into a different discussion. "I knew," he said, "Arthur would never be able to resist that body."

She ignored the bait, met his eyes and said, "No choice?" knowing how he would answer.

There was a second's pause. Then he said matter-of-factly, "Of course not. I had to kill her."

Beyond him through the open door she could see the darkened stacks. Surely someone, a janitor, a night watchman, would be coming around. She felt Noel's eyes on her. He had moved to the edge of the chair. Keep him talking. I've got to keep him talking. "Couldn't you," she threw out, "tell everyone the whole thing was a mistake, a joke?"

"Dear Beth." His voice was amused. "You're such a romantic. Who would have believed me?" He shrugged. "Even if they did believe me, she was bound to find out the winning essay wasn't hers."

"Would that have been so bad? You would have been forgiven. You're a wonderful teacher. You spend so much time on their papers." She stopped, realizing the insane truth of what she had just said.

"How right you are," Noel took her up. "I think that I shall never see, a teacher lovelier than me. But if the teacher doesn't print, he'll never get another stint. That's original — made it up myself — and it's the truth. Forget the flattery, Beth," said Noel, rising out of his chair. "If the girl had found out, it all would have come out."

"What all — ?" she asked desperately.

He stood looking at her. "You still don't see — ? Think about it, Beth." He sat down again. "What if the Mark Twain story began to circulate? Give it enough publicity and some of my former students might have been inspired to look over my publications." He studied her face. "I see you do understand now."

"But not — not everything?"

"I'm not a complete dolt!" Noel brought a hand down on the chair. "Of course not everything. I only started when —" He caught himself and stopped short, staring in front of him.

Dazed, overtaken by fear, she watched him. He had killed Marylou. He had — he must have — killed Livy. And now, the thought struck at her, he is going to kill me. She braced herself to make a run for it — suddenly Noel looked up and fixed his eye on hers. She sat rigid, afraid to move, as Noel, with the urgent air of someone who must justify himself, began to talk.

"My beginnings were so bright, Beth. I remember a time when I could blast out a book every couple years. I worked like a galley slave of course. Far harder than anyone else ever had to work," he said, looking at Beth as if he expected some protest.

"But then came the rewards," he went on, when she made no reply. "Tenure. Promotion. An endowed chair. The triumphs piled up so fast I astounded myself. God knows," he said, his voice hardening, "my father would have been thunderstruck — had he been alive to witness my achievements. . . . But you get older. You're still expected to publish. But you don't get the leisure you have a right to expect. And it takes me twice as long to write as anyone else. *You* can do it," he said, glancing upward at the shelf which held a copy of her Dickens study. "You must have turned that out in a year."

"But that's not true," she said, moving forward impulsively. "I worked on that book for five years. And I was never sure I could bring it off."

He hooted. "Don't talk rot!" he said, in a voice that verged on hysteria. "You've never known the feeling of being in over your head." She started to protest and he cut her off. "I started with —" he named an early essay that she knew well.

"Not your — ?"

He gave her a defiant nod. "Based on a paper from a pre-med. That was a good article, wasn't it? Brilliant, they called it. Innovative. It worked out so impeccably I began to orchestrate my assignments. When I was bogged down in an article about Tennyson, I assigned 'Discuss the distinctive features of the poet's use of myths.' When I was struggling to develop a philosophical point, I assigned 'Compare the Doctrine of the Imperfect in Browning and Ruskin.' They wrote; I refined. Just little loans," he said. "I never forgot to phrase — praise them." He stretched out his lips grotesquely in what was meant to be a winning smile.

Yes, she thought, it's believable. She imagined him standing at the head of a seminar table, handing out papers and compliments, head cocked to the side, a charming smile on his face. "Loans?" she asked, a challenge to her voice.

"That's all. I did my students a favor. What kind of readership did they have? Without me their paltry notions would have been buried forever. I gave their ideas publicity. It was . . . like giving them a medal of honor."

"You call that an honor?" she blurted out. "When no one knew the ideas you published were theirs?"

He looked stunned. "What right did they have to publish? What had *they* done? I had proven myself. I had, I might add, made a name for Midwestern."

"So you were above acknowledgment?"

"Why should I acknowledge?" he exploded. "Did Stravinsky footnote Schönberg? Did Matisse footnote Picasso? Did Picasso — ?"

"You're talking about influences," she interrupted furiously.

"Influences! I made them. I took their shopworn phrases and clumsy sentences and used *my* gifts, my training and technical skill, to make them part of a greater idea. I jumped them to the head of the line! No one could have done it as well as I did."

"In other words, sometimes you paraphrased, sometimes you took whole segments word for word."

A look of anger flashed across his face. "Quite the gumshoe, aren't you, Beth? Everyone lifts a little. You know that." He paused, the slightest break in his voice. "But everyone doesn't get found out. If I had been found out, what would have been left for me?" He gazed at her intently. "Even assuming I was lucky enough to be retained, my reputation would have been destroyed. Every book, every article, every word I've written — even the ones I wrote myself — would have been discredited."

He is right, she thought, looking at him. She saw the beginnings of lines around his eyes, the faintest limpness under the chin. In a few years, she thought, it would have been harder to charm the students.

"Worst," he said, "the humiliation. You know what they did to Jonathan Korretsky. Long Jon Korretsky. Crooked Korretsky. Imagine the fling they'd have with me! Frazier the filcher. Light-fingered Frazier. Noel Frazier — no phrases. There's no end to the quips they could hatch up — I'd be the marblehead of Midwestern."

"You could," she said, and it was almost a question, "teach somewhere else."

"You know better," he shot back. "Who would hire me? Wherever I tried they'd know. I'd be the university man without a country, barred forever from teaching and scholarship. I don't want that, Beth. I love this life. There are times when I wake up in the morning and think how lucky I am. This is too good to be true. I don't deserve it. It can never go on. But it can," he said, looking at her in a new way.

"Of course it can. I haven't told anyone —" She stopped at the glint in Noel's eyes. "But why Livy?" she said.

He hesitated. "Livy?" he said softly. "I was outside the English office that day — when Livy was lecturing to you and Dot. Don't you remember?" he said. "The false smile? Mark Twain and someone in our department? I stood there listening and I thought, he *must* mean me. Somehow — who knows what his crazy theories might have led to — somehow, he must be on to me."

From outside came a rumble of thunder. Noel paused a moment, his face tense, before he went on.

"I waited for Livy to leave. Then, pretending an avid interest in kinesics, I made an appointment to talk with him. The rest was easy." Noel smiled ironically. "I had my father to help me."

"Your father!"

"William Frazier," he proclaimed, as if he were pleased that he had astonished her. "The James Mill of the Mississippi Valley. Lessons, I had lessons. Piano. Tennis. Karate — my father thought I would learn the self-discipline I needed so badly. So little Noel was sent to the Quincy Academy of Karate, where he was taught concentration — and basic kicking and punching techniques.

"I had the devil of a time getting the diary open. And then, nothing. Just a catalog of head waggings and shoulder shruggings — all from novels. I was wrong. We were all wrong about Livy's observations about us," Noel said. Then he was at the window tugging at the coat to cover every inch of the glass.

Beth looked around wildly at the open door, at the desk — the thermos, a few inches away. She edged her hand toward it.

Noel swung around. "Why didn't you give up?" he said. "I had my eye on you, Beth. I watched you in Hub that night and then I did my best to discourage you." He took a step to the desk and stared at the bulletin board.

"You — you were the one who left the message?" The thermos was still warm. She kept her eyes on him and pried at the stopper.

"Of course I was. Didn't you ever suspect? For a while I even supposed you had given up. But when I saw Arthur's name on the screen and when you asked to see Spence's dissertation — why wouldn't you give up? What if I did borrow a few banalities?" he said — suddenly he reached past her and tore the list off the bulletin board. He ripped it to shreds and stuffed the paper into a pocket.

With the faintest pop the stopper was out. She gripped the thermos. "They couldn't have been so banal," she said. "Look what you milked out of them!"

He glared at her with such a burst of loathing that she reeled back. "Bitch!" he shouted — and lunged.

She thrust her hand up high and coffee spewed out of the thermos into his face.

He screamed and his hand flew to his eyes.

Instantly she was out of the chair.

34

INSTINCTIVELY BETH THRUST OUT A HAND, SLAMMED THE door behind her, and plunged between the shelves. Running headlong toward the center, she jammed into the sofa. Caught off balance, she stumbled and fell. She remained on hands and knees, looking at the red exit sign. Did she dare move into the corridor?

All at once from behind her, she heard a door crash. Without a pause, she crawled into the stacks. Taking refuge behind a three-sided cubicle, she crouched, listening. Silence. She waited a moment, then peered around the cubicle.

The only source of light was the suspended fixture at the tower's center. Beneath it were signs with arrows, TO STAIRS, TO ELEVATORS. Beyond she could make out bookshelves angling off into the darkness like a spooky study in perspective. Suddenly a roar of thunder pounded the tower.

There was an instant's hush, like the catch of a breath, and then the steady sound of rain drumming against the building. Nearby she could hear water splashing, into a wastebasket, she guessed. She moved slightly and something revolting, wormlike, touched her hand. She gasped and pulled back. Then she looked down and almost laughed hysterically. She had been touching a satin ribbon, a book-marker. Quickly she concealed herself, knocking into the cubicle with a thud that seemed loud enough to rattle the windows. . . . Footsteps, padding on the carpet, somewhere in front of her. Molding herself against the cubicle, she waited, keeping perfectly still.

Which way was he going? She hoped that, thinking she had left the tower, he would go into the corridor. Then he would have the whole library to search and she could wait him out, through the night if she had to. The footsteps moved closer and she risked another look between the shelves.

A few yards away was Noel, heading toward her slowly, as if he had all the time in the world. In his hand was a flashlight, and he was swinging it back and forth, casting its beam between the rows. She watched the light flicker over the books, veer to the opposite side, then swerve back again, closer to her hiding place. When he got to her row, one glance to the left and he would see her. She looked behind her, hesitating. Should she retreat further into the stacks? No, he would surely catch up with her.

As quietly as she could, she crawled around the cubicle and began inching her way outward. Something cut into her knee, and she suppressed a cry of pain. She felt down into the darkness, grasped a metal book-end, pushed it away and went on, left hand touching the carpet, right hand tracing the edge of the shelf. When the shelf ended, she stood trembling, watching the moving light. Then the flashlight beam caught her row in a blaze of light.

She let go of her shelf and sped out of the tower. She ran to the elevator, put out a finger to push the button, and stopped, remembering that at night the power for the main elevators was off. Hearing the tower door open, she turned and dashed across the corridor. Next to the chair-packed dolly, she came to a sudden halt. Between her and the stairs stood Noel, feet planted apart, like someone at the end of a hunt.

For a second they remained motionless, staring at each other. In the few minutes since she had run out of her carrel,

Noel seemed transformed. No longer the elegant man of letters, he had become the enemy, on his face a menacing grin she had never seen.

Then he yelled and ran toward her and she threw up her arms protectively. Her hands came up against the dolly. She got a hold on it and pushed. The dolly remained immobile. Desperately summoning all her strength, she shouldered the dolly and shoved. Like a train released from its brakes, the dolly gave a violent jerk and lurched forward, driving directly into Noel's path.

He gave one look of surprise, then leaped to the side but a second late. The dolly caught his leg as it shot past him. He screamed and went sprawling to the floor, the flashlight spinning out of his hand. She watched long enough to see the dolly, caught in the crazy angle of the flashlight beam, collide against the doors, pitching its load of chairs into the glass with a shattering crash. She turned and ran.

A rush of heat came out to meet her as she entered the stairwell. For a moment she hesitated, looking downward. No, he would expect her to go that way. The roof. If she could just get out on the roof. There had to be someone on the quadrangles she could call out to. Careless of the click of her shoes on the concrete, she tore up the steps and pulled the knob of the door to the roof. She tugged harder, bracing her hand against the cement wall. The door refused to budge. She looked around the landing, her eyes darting across the stairwell to the window slit, dark with rain, then down to the deep fall into the shaft. A wave of panic rushed over her. Just one flight below was Noel. In another few seconds he would be coming out the door.

She stampeded down the steps. Four. Three. Nearing Two, she heard the metal bang of a door and rapid footsteps descending the stairs.

She held her breath, creaked the knob around and slipped into Level Two, easing the door shut behind her. But it closed with a click as loud as a pistol shot. She knew he must have heard it. She rushed to the left toward the student lounge, then stopped, disoriented.

A wall of corrugated steel confronted her. The fire doors were down, turning the passage into a prison. Panicked, she swung in the opposite direction and shot into the main corridor.

Near a sign, QUIET PLEASE, PROGRAM IN PRO-GRESS, she slowed, mentally reviewing the faculty lounge, the narrow entranceway, the large open room, like a vast foyer, and as quickly gave it up. Her best chance was Hub. Down the corridor she raced, to the North tower, opened the door and crept through the entranceway.

Inside, Hub was very quiet, very dark. NO FOOD OR BEVERAGES PERMITTED. She could just see the white letters on the sign. She pushed the metal bar and stumbled ahead, keeping her hand on the catalog files until her fingers reached into nothingness. A few faltering steps to the center and she halted at the balustrade, staring down at a ghostly theater in the round. Surrounded by velvet chairs, illumined by the dim light of the central fixture, the middle was an exposed pit, the flight of stairs at either end for a spectral audience to make its way to their seats. She waited a second, then descended into the pit and down another flight to the lower level.

She had made a mistake. Downstairs there was nowhere to hide. She looked at the round tables, their bare metal legs leaving the space underneath exposed, at the group study rooms, doors gaping, like open traps. She started around the circle and stopped, holding herself tense.

Above the noise of the rain beating against the windows, she heard a crunching sound. She ran to the windows and saw the night watchman. Hunched down against the rain, water streaming off his hat, he was trudging along the gravel path that led around the tower. She screamed and pounded the window. The watchman put up an arm and wiped his face. She battered her fist against the glass. He paused, a puzzled look on his face. For a second he seemed to be staring directly at her. Then he shook his head and shambled on and she watched in despair as he disappeared around the corner. She raised her head. Someone — Noel — rushing down the steps.

Like a mad person, she tore around the circle, scrambled up the two flights of stairs and fled into Reference. Behind the shelves where she had sat so often, she stopped and caught her breath. Here, above the windows, the only sound was the hum of air-conditioning and a high-pitched fluorescent wail. She remained still, looking at the clock, its hands showing twenty minutes past midnight. Then she heard the thud of a book dropping to the carpet. She wheeled and saw Noel emerge from behind a free-standing book display.

She reached above her to the highest shelf, dislodged a heavy index. It crashed down, bringing with it dictionaries, histories, volumes of quotations. Almost simultaneously, at the other end of the shelf, one volume toppled, then another, then all of *Encyclopedia Britannica* avalanched between them. At once she slipped back and around the shelves, sped past the counter and burst through the exit bar. Some sixth sense made her stop and turn. Noel was coming up fast behind her.

She couldn't make another run. She would never outdistance him. Her eyes lit on a pacemaker warning sign. She reached over the post, snatched a book from the wagon, then, remembering what Marge had done, flicked the alarm switch to ON.

When Noel was almost on top of her, she shouted, "Here! I'm in here, Gil!" Noel looked up a second, then came barging toward the bar. A moment before he reached it, she threw the book in his path. Instantly the bar flew up and, too late to stem his onward rush, he pitched into the metal rod and took a brutal punch full in the stomach. He staggered and dropped.

Then she was out of Hub and speeding along the passage. Through the copying room she ran, into a small room whose floor was lined with book-ends and nests of plastic baskets. Along the wall next to the staff elevator was a metal draw-bridge that extended to a dumbwaiter apparatus. She ran to the elevator and pressed the button, alert for any sound from the corridor. Slowly she became aware of a grinding noise, a ceaseless clanking, coming from reaches far beneath the book conveyor. She thought of an underworld river, an infinite Styx of books. Repeatedly she jabbed the button, her eyes darting nervously to the sign on the wall.

> Place the container on conveyor load station.
> Dial destination.
> Do not change dial setting after the container
>   has been placed on the conveyor load station.
> Do not withdraw or move the container from
>   inside of conveyor load station for any reason.
>   1 — First Floor Service Desk
>   2 — Second Floor
>   3 — Third Floor
>   4 — Fourth Floor
>   5 — Fifth Floor

From the corridor came the sound of pounding feet. She jammed her finger against the button. A moment later she heard footsteps crossing the tile at a clip. Without a pause, she turned the dial to One, climbed on the ramp and crawled inside the conveyor. She reached out to push the button and caught a glimpse of Noel in the doorway. Then he was in front of her, thrusting his arm inside the conveyor. His fingers slipped over her wrist. She wrenched her hand from his grasp and shrank back as far as she could. Suddenly she heard him swear and saw his hand yank itself free. A split second later the conveyor door cleaved down like a guillotine.

She was inside a monster oven. She could see nothing, could hear only a steely uproar. The conveyor began rocking and swaying, taking her with it. Then a pulverizing din blasted her ears. The conveyor gave one tremendous bump that threw her against the door — and plummeted. Downward it roller-coastered, bowling her from side to side. She hugged her arms around her head, thinking, even as she was hurtled back and forth, what would she do if the door remained shut when the monster reached One. How long could you survive without air? Suddenly the conveyor literally ground to a halt. Her ears were ringing, but she was not sure if the noise was real or a clangorous echoey aftermath. Dizzily she put an arm out in front of her, heard a threatening roar, and quickly drew back. There was a long pause, and then the door rasped upward, admitting a dazzling brightness. She leaned forward and found herself staring into a sea of books.

Everywhere, under the ramp, next to it, were bins, overflowing with books. Banked along the opposite wall was a row of shelving carts, fronts marked with Dewey numbers, insides packed with books. She was behind Library Privileges, in Circulation.

Half crawling, half sliding, she moved onto the ramp and down the incline. Shakily she got to her feet and swayed against the ramp. The floor seemed to heave beneath her.

From behind her she heard a loud report. She whirled and saw on the near wall a time clock. As she watched the hands reached a point and clicked again. In exactly seven hours and thirty minutes the room would come alive. Students would be perched on the three-legged stools, sorting books for return to the stacks. Someone would be behind the desk whose brass stand read *Stack Supervisor.* She contemplated a glassed-in area beyond the desk, marked Stack Control. Unsteadily, she crossed the room and looked inside.

A multitude of signs leered at her. NIGHT WEEKEND SECURITY. "CRITICALLY IMPORTANT." WHEN YOU SHUT DOWN THE COMPUTER AT NIGHT, TAKE PLASTIC COVERS AND COVER THE TAPE DRIVES AND THE DISK DRIVES . . . WE NEED EMPTY TRUCKS . . . WEEKEND CLOSERS: "REMEMBER TO SIGN OUT BEFORE GOING UP." Below was a desk, on it a gold bag of Godiva chocolates, and an open book, face down, as if someone had left it momentarily. Of the trained grad student and his beeper that the tour guide had mentioned, there was no evidence. She tilted her head to get a look at the book — *The Student Entrepreneur's Guide.*

What was she doing? If Noel could read a dial, he would know where to find her. She went out the door and found herself in a narrow corridor with a network of passages branching out. She chose a passage and ran, then veered into a wider hall bordered with glass-partitioned rooms. At once she realized she had picked up the path she had followed with the tour group. She pressed on until she was gasping for breath and came to a stop outside the data center.

The room was empty, silent. Some of the machines were covered, but not all. On the uncovered units, the lights were dimmed, as if the machines were at rest. At the front of the massive central processing unit, lights blinked on and off, but the gigantic tape wheels were dead still. The inactivity made her focus on the walls, hung with framed photos of spring gardens, autumn landscapes, and prints of leaves and flowers, as if the people who worked in the windowless room craved some nature. On one desk was a vase of flowers, on another, a plant. Then she saw, next to the plant, a telephone.

She looked ahead at the doors to the loading dock, looked behind and saw that the corridor was empty. She was still safe. She opened the door marked AUTHORIZED PERSONNEL ONLY, ran to the desk, and picked up the phone.

There was no sound. The line was dead. She threw the receiver down in frustration and tried to think what to do. To escape by the loading dock was hopeless. She was almost certain you needed a key to unlock the doors from inside. To hide in the main section of level one meant retreating down the corridor and risk encountering Noel. She felt exhausted, all the energy drained out of her. Could she take refuge here until morning?

The hum of the cooling system filled her head as she stared groggily at the cartons of copier rolls strewn over the floor. Then her gaze was drawn across the room to a gigantic metal locker that towered over the central unit. THIS EQUIPMENT CABINET IS PHYSICALLY UNSTABLE. USE EXTREME CAUTION WHEN MOVING. Ponderously, like someone taking a test, she read the sign. Then she moved toward the cabinet. Something beneath a terminal caught her eye. She looked down and saw a blue-jeaned leg emerging between the rubbery bunches of electrical cords.

Quickly she went around the terminal and saw a boy prone on the floor. She gasped "Thorpe!" His eyes were closed, his face pale as death. She knelt and took his wrist, felt a weak pulse. He moaned. She saw a beeper lying next to him. Just as she picked it up she heard someone call her name. She turned and froze.

Noel was standing there, blocking the doorway. He looked at her and smiled. Then he began to whistle softly, a snatch of the same little tune.

She put her mouth to the beeper, pressed the button and shouted, "Help! In the data center — !" At once Noel leaped forward.

The beeper flew to the floor as she got to her feet and took three running steps to the cabinet. Putting her hands flat against the metal, she gave a mighty push. For a second or more the cabinet teetered in space. Then it lurched downward. Noel yelled something, she did not know what. I've got him, she thought, then saw him dodge and saw the cabinet topple, like a felled tree, into the CPU.

Lights and noise. Above her, lights dimming, flickering off and on. From somewhere in the wall a terrific clanging. A shrill whine, like a shriek of pain, came from the mangled machine. Then its lights blanked out. She looked around, dazed, and saw Noel coming toward her. He raced forward and stopped. From the severed wires beneath the machine, sparks were shooting out in all directions. Noel hesitated an instant, then vaulted over the wires.

Her head swam. It crossed her mind that this was all wrong. Noel and I should be joking about all this state of the art technology. She opened her mouth to say so and he hurled himself at her.

Suddenly voices, Gil's, shouting, "No! The other way!" Then she saw Gil followed by a crew of running men.

JUST BEFORE TEN BETH JUMPED UP AND TURNED ON THE television. Then she stretched out on the floor next to Gil and nibbled on pizza, watching the screen. A few seconds later a voice said, *"The* ten o'clock news. Coming up — details of the extraordinary story of the library murders. Stay with us." The screen shifted to a glistening glimpse of tangled bodies. Simultaneously a husky voice whispered, "Abandon — the fragrance that throws caution to the winds."

Somewhat self-consciously Beth held the carton out to Gil. "Have the last?" she asked. "No? You should. It's symbolic."

"Of what, Professor?" said Gil. He reached out and gently brushed back her hair, gazing at her in a way that made it impossible to meet his eyes.

She looked at the screen, saw the commercial was still in frenzied swing. Turning back to him, she said as briskly as possible, "Symbolic of the main event of the day. Too bad all your activity kept you away from the library."

"The library! What now?"

"At precisely 5:30 P.M.," said Beth, "Vesuvian Crust delivered a pizza to Coleman." Remembering the scene, she began to laugh. "They called him out of his office and he was in a fury. He marched up to the front desk, like — like —"

"Like Soapy Sam Wilberforce going out to debate Huxley?"

"Bishop Wilberforce?" She registered the reference. "Very good," she said slowly. "Anyway," she went on, "Coleman stood there glaring at the boy. 'Yes?' he said, his voice dripping icicles. 'Mr. — uh — Leprous?' the boy said. 'Lenites. Coleman Lenites.' 'Oh yeah — this writing is hard to read. Here you are. Behemoth Special — pepperoni, mushroom, and jalapeno.' I wish you'd seen it," Beth said, "Coleman holding the carton as if it were filled with snakes, screaming he hadn't ordered anything. The boy shouting yes he *had* ordered it, that he'd taken the call himself, and Coleman owed him $12.50."

Gil threw back his head and laughed. "Who arranged it?"

"Thorpe."

"Then he's home now?"

"Not yet — he called in the order from Student Health. But he's going to be fine. I went to see him today. He's been accepted at Wharton and he's preparing for big business — says he has an idea for a food service that caters to libraries during exam week."

"Naturally, I trained at Harvard." The familiar accents came from the television.

They looked at the screen and saw Arthur lounging behind the news desk, looking very pompous. "Then Marylou Peacock was a student of yours?" the reporter asked.

Arthur cleared his throat portentously. "Not," he said, "in the classroom sense. But in a more profound sense, yes, she was my student, as are all students at the university. I find it curious that so many of my colleagues fail to recognize that teaching is not *intra muros* — within the walls only. At Harvard we learned that teaching extends beyond the classroom." Arthur paused importantly. "For me it was not a question of *meums* and *teums*. I saw it as my professional duty, indeed my obligation, to give her the use of my carrel." Arthur paused again, this time to give the interviewer a brief but obvious onceover.

"What a phony," Beth said. "Look at him leer!"

"Not surprising," said Gil.

"What — the leer? Why not?"

"Hewmann has — a weakness for —" Gil drew a shape in the air.

She laughed. "Are you telling me that Arthur goes for big-busted types, with large — what Hardy calls 'attributes'?"

Gil nodded. "No doubt he was persuaded to lend his carrel less for his dedication to scholarship than for his fascination with Marylou's — attributes. Her attributes might also account for Hewmann's fling with Ida — hey!" Gil caught the plate before it slid to the carpet.

Beth sat up, staring at him. "Arthur had a fling with Ida?"

"Briefly. Then he dropped her."

"Dropped her," Beth repeated, still trying to take in the idea of an affair between the department's devoutest male chauvinist and its most ardent feminist. "But — when?"

"When she came up for tenure. He was afraid that if he recommended her as he'd promised, he would ruin his reputation."

Beth shook her head, wondering how Ida could have been attracted to Arthur. She thought a moment. "That explains the English office episode. Ida must have thought Arthur made a practice of — flings."

Gil asked what she meant and she told him about the argument between Livy and Dot, about Livy's sexy mimic of Arthur. "Dot told me that after I left Ida stormed out from behind a file cabinet, mad as hell. I thought that for some reason Ida was furious with Livy and that she must have been the one who — I had thought — it might be Spence."

"Why him?"

"No reason — except he was always so hostile to you."

"Goldberg was hostile all right — because he had two secrets he didn't want to reveal. One I'd already found out, the other I guessed. I was almost certain he was the one who told Marylou she'd won the prize."

"Spence! Then why didn't he say so?"

"He was afraid. When he was a freshman in college, he was arrested with a group of demonstrators — and he thought, since he had a police record, that if he admitted he'd told Marylou we'd leap to the conclusion that he was the killer. His wife finally made him come out with it."

"I'm not surprised — what did you think of Marilyn?"

Gil glanced at the television where Arthur was still droning interminably, then said, "Marilyn is out of a completely different package. Definitely an efficient type. And proud of her husband. 'I'll have you know, Spencer sleeps with a humidifier every single night of the winter!' — she seems to think that his allergies make Goldberg the equivalent of a Nobel Laureate."

Gil grinned. "'You know how they say someone makes a house a home?' she asked me and she picked up some papers he'd thrown on the piano. 'Spencer turns a home right back into a house again.' Then she walked over to him, patted him on the head. 'Now Spencer,' she said, 'just *tell* Mr. Bailey.' Not that his confirmation that he'd told Marylou made any difference," said Gil. "I still had a puzzle on my hands."

"You said Spence had two secrets," said Beth.

"Remember when Frazier said that for some kinds of writing Spence was okay, that for academic writing he clutches? It was the other writing."

"What do you mean?"

"Let me return to the question of literary scholarship," said Arthur, and Gil looked at the screen.

"Come on," said Beth, " — tell me!"

"Can't you guess? The kitchen timer in his carrel is a clue."

She shook her head impatiently.

"Goldberg picks up extra money writing cooking columns, culinary trends, that kind of thing, under the pseudonym Walthea Whiteman. The clippings turned up in a cubbyhole in his carrel. *You*," said Gil, "would be interested in his report on recipe plagiarism." He ducked as a pillow came flying at him.

"Thank you, Professor Hewmann," the newscaster said firmly, and fervently assuring her that it had been *his* pleasure, Arthur disappeared from view.

"This week first editions by the likes of Arthur Conan Doyle and Frank Lloyd Wright will be presented as evidence in the courtroom as Midwestern University moves to recover damages. Library officials were dumbfounded when an inventory revealed that books whose value is estimated in the thousands were missing from the open shelves known" (the newscaster hesitated) *"as the stacks.*

"The people in charge of the investigation are saying no comment tonight. However, Channel Three News has learned exclusively that being held in custody are Porter DeMont and Dorothy Drennan."

At the right of the screen appeared a photograph of Porter, seated behind his desk, and Dot, standing next to him.

"DeMont, the alleged thief, is chairman of Midwestern's English department and a highly esteemed professor. It is alleged that DeMont systematically stole books from the library and stored them in the home of Drennan, his secretary and alleged accomplice.

"The FBI raided Drennan's house and found the missing books in the basement, together with a punctilious record, alleged to be in DeMont's writing, of every book stolen from the library. It is too early to say if any indictments. . . ."

Beth stopped listening. She gazed at the photo on the screen. Through some trick of the angle, Dot's hand appeared to be resting on Porter's shoulder. "What will happen to them?" she asked, trying and failing to conceive of the department without Porter and Dot.

"Probably they'll be fined and given a commuted sentence. Fortunately all the books were retrieved and they don't appear to have been permanently damaged. It's not as if his motives were selfish," Gil said, almost to himself. "And they'll have character witnesses," he said, raising his voice. "Someone will testify in their behalf."

"I will." Beth spoke out.

"So will I," said Gil. "If it comes to that, I'll testify for them."

They were silent for some time. Then Beth said, "It's strange. Livy had an inkling about Porter."

Gil stared.

"Not about Porter, exactly — about how he did it. It was at Arthur's party. Livy happened to mention *The Purloined Letter.* Remember," she said, "how the Prefect laughs when Dupin suggests the mystery is a little *too* self-evident?"

Gil looked chagrined. "But that's hindsight," she said hastily. "It wasn't until you told me about the pacemaker that I thought how well it fit. Remember when Dupin says that when the Prefect and his cohort searched for the letter they thought only of how *they* would have hidden it, that they failed," Beth said enthusiastically, "because they considered only their *own* ideas of ingenuity —" She looked at Gil's face. "I didn't mean — it wasn't self-evident." She threw out her hands in frustration. "Good for you for catching on when you did."

"No," Gil said. "I should have caught it earlier. But — I'll show you the list." He reached into his pocket —

". . . *alleged murderer leaving the courtroom today after being arraigned.*"

They looked at the screen and saw Noel walking rapidly down the steps, a man on each side of him, holding him by the arm. He was being chased by television crews, and reporters were firing questions at him. Just before he put up his arms — Beth winced at the handcuffs — she caught a glimpse of a face so tortured that she looked away. Suddenly she thought of Mephistophilis' lines.

> Within the bowels of these elements.
> Where we are tortured and remain for ever.
> Hell hath no limits, nor is circumscribed
> In one self place, but where we are is hell.

"We will be following the drama as it unfolds this week in the courtroom. Still ahead (brightly) — *around the world tonight two hundred people are dead. . . ."*

Beth shuddered and turned off the television.

"Frazier was never at Oxford, was he?" said Gil.

"No — his father was —" She broke off. "Why?"

"Nothing important — just a photograph in his carrel. There was something else — a dish of stones." Gil looked at her closely. "Don't feel sorry for him, Professor. He's as bad as they come. He would have killed you."

"I know. I can't help it. . . . Show me the list."

She looked it over a few minutes and then, pointing to a title, asked, "What's this doing here?"

"The Targ? DeMont came across it when he was looking up Lord Spencer's library. Probably," said Gil, "Lord Spencer was the world's greatest collector of incunabula."

Beth sat up straight and gave him a now or never look. "You can't have learned that at the FBI. And what about the Huxley? That *is* your book?"

Gil hesitated a moment. Then he said in a flat tone, "I wrote it when I was teaching at Yale."

"You taught at Yale? When?"

"During the disagreeable period when structural criticism first reared its head — God help us — and said, 'The text is all.' . . . I remember the day I decided to leave. A student had asked me a question and I answered with a sentence from Huxley."

"What was it?" she asked. But Gil had turned the television on again and seemed not to have heard her.

The late movie was on. For some time they watched as Bette Davis was transformed from dumpy domineered daughter to eyebrow-plucked black-gowned sophisticate. They watched admiringly as Paul Henried put two cigarettes in his mouth, lit them, and gave one to Bette. She took a deep drag and looked out the window at a star-crammed sky. "Oh, Jerry," she said, "why ask for the moon — when we have the stars?"

Gil clicked the television off and gazed at Beth.

She felt her face flush, looked away and said desperately, "Is — is there anything you respect about academia?"

"I admire DeMont," he said, "and you." He got to his feet, picked up their plates and carried them out to the kitchen. Then he came back and sat down close beside her.

After some time Beth leaned her head against Gil's shoulder and said, "What day is today?"

"Tuesday."

"I thought so." She gave a sigh of content.

There was another long silence.

Much later Beth said, "Noel had it exactly — even to the roots."

"What roots?" Gently he ran a finger along her cheek.

"Ancestry, he meant. When he was looking at his palm. 'The hidden roots that can strengthen,' he said, 'just as they can on occasion enfeeble the character.' He had it almost word for word. I looked it up in Sitwell."

Gil sat bolt upright. "You did what?"

"I wonder if some of his expressions were out of *Tom Sawyer.*" She reached past Gil and took a book off the table. Firmly he took the book out of her hand.

Some time later Beth asked, "What was it Huxley said?"

"What he said, my darling, was, 'The great end of life is not knowledge, but action.'"

In the distance the carillons chimed and the last light went out in the library research towers.

ACKNOWLEDGMENTS

The following works have been particularly helpful in providing background information: Mark Twain's *The Autobiography of Mark Twain,* Charles Neider, ed., Harper and Brothers, 1959; *Mark Twain's Notebook,* Albert Bigelow Paine, ed., Harper and Brothers, 1935; Justin Kaplan's *Mr. Clemens and Mark Twain,* Simon and Schuster, 1966; Richard Altick's *The Art of Literary Research,* W.W. Norton & Company, 1981; Julius Fast's *Body Language,* M. Evans, 1970; Stuart Berg Flexner's Preface to *Dictionary of American Slang,* compiled and edited by Harold Wentworth and Stuart Berg Flexner, Thomas Y. Crowell Company, 1967; Joan Friedman's "Fakes, Forgeries, Facsimiles, and Other Oddities," in *Book Collecting,* Jean Peters, ed., R.R. Bowker Company, 1977; David Lampe's "Your Neighbor In the Library May Be a Thief," *Smithsonian,* November, 1979; Alexander Lindey's *Plagiarism and Originality,* Harper, 1952; Roger Shuy's "The North-Midland Dialect Boundary in Illinois," Publication of the American Dialect Society, University of Alabama Press, November 1962.